THE LEGEND OF SNOW WOLF

THE LEGEND OF SNOW WOLF

BOOK 1: REINCARNATION

F. Lit Yu

China Books • South San Francisco

Published in the United States of America by
China Books
360 Swift Ave., Suite 48
South San Francisco, CA 94080

ISBN 978-0-8351-0003-8

Text design: Linda Ronan
Cover design: Nathan Grover
Cover illustration: Chitfu Yu

Library of Congress Cataloging-in-Publication Data
Yu, F. Lit.
The legend of Snow Wolf. Book one, Reincarnation / by F. Lit Yu.
p. cm.
Summary: "A martial arts epic fantasy set in the China/Mongolia
border in legendary times. Wolves and men fight for domination of
the steppes, a young warrior must make a perilous quest to discover
the secret of Snow Wolf in order to save his people"— Provided by
publisher.
ISBN 978-0-8351-0003-8 (pbk.)
[1. Warriors—Fiction. 2. Martial arts—Fiction. 3. Prophecies—Fiction.
4. Wolves—Fiction. 5. Supernatural—Fiction.] I. Title. II. Title:
Reincarnation.

PZ7.Y89593Le 2012
[Fic]—dc23

2011050837

Printed in China

PROPHECY ONE

Amid the barbaric horsemen,
The Jade Dragon surfaced North.
The light of the firefly resembles,
The towering glow of the sun.

"Hold still, grandfather," Suthachai said, lifting his knife.

The old man closed his eyes, released a deep sigh, his soul escaping with every breath. Suthachai leaned forward to constrain him, and waited, waited for the uneven breathing to calm. In a moment, his blade tore into the purple cyst on the old man's back. The old man screamed in pain, squirming against his ragged sheepskin. Suthachai watched dark fluid ooze on the ground.

"Who's Su Ling, grandfather?"

• • •

Outside, the shrieking wind of the Mongolian plains announced the approaching storm. There would be an onslaught of snow and ice that night.

Suthachai sat in his grandfather's yurt, feeding dried horse manure to a campfire that clawed the dangling pot. He was a towering, muscular warrior with piercing eyes and a heavy-set jaw. His tall nose made him stand apart from the flat-faced nomads of Mongolia.

His grandfather's yurt was small, tattered; the thin walls of woolen felt so worn and old that wind entered at will. It was barren, except for a chest no one had ever seen him open, and a sheepskin bed both thin and rigid with age. Most Mongolian tents could be dismantled and packed away in the time of an ordinary meal, yet, the old man hadn't moved his yurt for decades. He had few animals to protect, with no reason to migrate from season to season.

Steam levitated from the boiling water, only to vanish through the round opening on the roof of the yurt. The blackened pot, suspended by a single iron rod over the fire, began to sway with every shriek of the wind.

"Horse meat stew," Suthachai said. It would be half a day's ride back to the main camp, and if the storm arrived that evening, it would be impossible to visit his grandfather in the coming days. But if the Elder's predictions were true, the old man wouldn't make it through the night.

His grandfather shifted with a moan. "Horse meat stew?"

"With salt. I was at the border last week."

There was no response from the old man. A faint smile escaped his lips.

The young warrior's voice lowered. "I can speak to the Elder again. Maybe bring the shaman."

"I don't want the damn shaman!" The old man only managed a croaky whisper. "I don't need anyone!"

Suthachai ignored him. His grandfather managed to lift his finger.

"Is that old rat happy now that I'm about to die? The old rat. I curse them all—their mothers, their children—I curse them all! You watch. They will all meet violent deaths!"

Suthachai drew the ragged sheepskin over the shivering body. "No one's getting killed anymore. Get some sleep."

"And who the hell doesn't get killed on the steppe?"

"That was before the peace agreement."

"Peace agreement. Ha! They named you the greatest warrior on the Mongolian plains. Doesn't that show how little talent there is on the steppe? Bunch of cowards—it won't be long before someone invades your clan. Then they'll all follow me to hell!"

Bubbles emerged in the water again. Suthachai casually tossed another chunk of horse manure into the flames. The steaming pot of horse meat smelled good, but the old man couldn't possibly sit up to eat. Perhaps he could take the food with him to the afterlife.

"Who's Su Ling?" Suthachai asked.

"Who? What are you talking about?"

"You've been saying her name in your sleep."

"Who are you to question me, child?" He lifted a trembling finger and pointed at Suthachai. "How. . . How dare you?"

A cough spasm overwhelmed him. The shriveled body racked with heavy convulsions, and in alarm, Suthachai reached over to restrain his grandfather. But the old man glared back; so intense were his penetrating eyes that the younger warrior withdrew.

Gradually, the anger left him, but the damage was done. The ashen-white face, now streaked with blood, appeared more ghostly than ever.

Suthachai felt a strange sense of relief. Perhaps the Elder was right. His grandfather would leave this world of suffering tonight.

But the old man wouldn't go. Something continued to torture him, to eat his soul, even now so close to death.

Suthachai moved closer. The muscles on the ancient face were twitching, and the fluttering eyelids wouldn't close.

"Grandfather . . . "

The old man lifted a trembling finger and pointed to the wooden chest.

But the chest had been nearly empty for years.

The old man shook, drops of sweat rolling down his crusty face. He opened his mouth but couldn't speak, painfully drawing each breath, his eyes pinned to the chest.

"What's wrong?"

The old man wheezed into another spasm. Dark fluid seeped through the bandages covering his cyst. His entire body heaved in torment, and he lifted a crooked finger to point.

Suthachai sprung the chest open. There was nothing in it except for a knife, a few rags, and a frayed water flask. He looked at his grandfather, staring, and held up each item. But the old man's face didn't change.

"What are you looking for?"

The old man shook with pain, tears in his eyes. He pointed at the chest again.

Suthachai looked, and this time, he noticed. The chest was tall but not deep, with space unaccounted for. There could be additional layers underneath the base. He drew the heavy saber slung across his hip, wedged the sharp edge into the side of the chest, and pried the wood apart. The bottom was loose, and in a moment, it separated.

Suthachai stared. There was a small metal box hidden underneath layers of wood. He lifted it, carefully, like it was a dying rabbit, before showing his grandfather.

Slowly, the old man closed his eyes, settled into the sheepskin, and went to sleep forever.

• • •

The night was dark. Suthachai held the metal box under a dim light, caressing it, his fingers tense, his heart racing. He was in his own yurt, on his own bed. The wind began to rise on the Mongolian Plains, but his clan was well prepared. Every yurt was secured for this storm, the horses tied and blindfolded, and they slept with ease. Normally, when the western wind grew violent, the clan would begin preparing the next stage of migration. They would leave the nearby lakes and search for better grazing grounds. But this year, a great hunt was underway. The predators of the steppe were being eliminated, and over thirty clans united in a hunt that lasted six months. It almost lasted into the winter season.

Despite the daily excitement of the hunt, preparations for the winter had to resume. Winter on the steppe was brutal, and each day, men, women, and children took extensive measures to protect the tents. Heavy layers of animal skin, dried and treated after each slaughter, were lined against the walls of every yurt. Tools for cutting the frozen rivers were sharpened, large sheets of fur were sewn together, and meats were dried and preserved. The Elder said the first storm of winter would arrive in three nights, and it would arrive with rage.

Suthachai, alone, lit his oil lamp, the box clenched in his hands. He ran his fingers across the top, felt its harsh texture, and entertained the idea of burying it. His grandfather had nothing in his lifetime—maybe it should remain that way.

Jocholai was on the other side of the tent, snoring under a thick covering of animal skin. Suthachai smiled. The sleeping warrior couldn't be awakened without a war trumpet.

Jocholai was the only other warrior in the clan who had no family. It was destiny that they grew up together. The new yurt that they shared was built well before Suthachai became known as the greatest warrior on the steppe, and every strip of skin stitched into this massive yurt was awarded to them for their courage and leadership. Suthachai and Jocholai did everything together. From the daily tasks of herding sheep to seasonal hunting and ice cutting, Suthachai always stayed close to his brother.

He turned his gaze back to the box again. It was the one thing his grandfather refused to die without seeing—a hidden possession that no one knew about, yet, the old man clung to it with his last breath. Suthachai leaned back on his sheepskin, carefully opened the box, and looked inside.

A sense of elation riveted him. It was a piece of jade, carved into the shape of a three-headed dragon, dark red yet transparent. The attached silver necklace had already turned black, but the brilliance of the jade carried an enormous, mysterious power. He traced his finger along the contours of the dragon back, a murmur of admiration escaping his lips.

He looked into the box again, and found layer upon layer of cowhide strung together by an iron ring, with dense writing on every surface.

He recognized that language—his grandfather had made sure of it. It was the language of the Chinese. Sutha-chai, as a child, was forced to learn these strange symbols because they enabled the Chinese to communicate without speaking, like using fire to signal the presence of enemies, only more sophisticated. His grandfather told him that, if he could master the Chinese written language, new worlds would appear before him. And every day, the old man would force him to learn.

Suthachai hated it, but learned quickly. The writings

presented him with stories of war, of the rise and fall of dynasties, of warriors who relied on strategy instead of strength. He read about entire empires falling under the hands of a single woman, and warriors who lived and died for a strange set of principles.

Memories, long banished, began to surface, and Suthachai shook his head clear. Something caught his eye. The writings described his grandfather in China, that for years, the old man lived among the Chinese. Suthachai leaned over to read:

The chaos continued. So much looting and killing. The evil that people can do to each other. A few days ago, I saw a young girl slaughtered in the city for a sack of grain.

I've been here for four years, and I want to go home. But I agreed to stay with father so he can train the magistrate's horses. The local government can do nothing to end the violence. They say that only when Snow Wolf returns from the South will the fighting stop and the famine end.

Suthachai moved closer to the light, skimming through the words, a drop of sweat rolling down his forehead.

I was shot by an arrow. By good fortune, I escaped the madness, and after a few days on foot, I found myself in a small village named Pan Tong Village. Most here are farmers, and like all Chinese, they worked on their knees. But here, they are kindhearted.

Especially the girl. Her name is Su Ling. She found me somehow, as I wandered close to death, and oh, I thought I saw a goddess! She was so beautiful, and so concerned about my injury. She brought me into her home, bandaged my wounds, and called a local doctor to treat me.

15

From the moment Su Ling spoke to me, I knew I was in love. I was a mere stranger, a Mongolian, but she cared for me to ensure my wounds were healed. I will never forget her smile, a smile I would sacrifice my life for.

Su Ling . . . I think of the woman who saved me, and I shudder.

Su Ling.

That was the name on the old man's lips before he died. His grandfather was once in love? Impossible . . .

I was still recovering in Su Ling's house that night, and I was awoken by screaming. I scrambled out of bed and into the living room. I saw a man in the main room, covered with blood, and Su Ling weeping and trying to stop the bleeding. The man was her father. I have never seen anyone bleed like that in my life—more blood spilled on the floor than when we slaughter sheep. I moved closer and I saw knife wounds all over his body, as if he had been stabbed thirty times. I didn't know what to do; I only knew that when I saw the pain on Su Ling's face, I too felt pain.

Her father died there on the floor. Su Ling wept for a long time, and all I could do was stand there and watch her. She finally told me to leave her alone. She wanted to burn some candles and incense to her father's spirit, so he could go in peace. It was the Chinese tradition, I learned, and foreigners must not be present. She told me to go to the roof and keep watch. I didn't know what I was watching for, but I obeyed.

Then she handed me something, a piece of magnificent jade from her father. She wanted me to protect it for her. She made me promise that I would never part from the jade, that I would bring it with me to Mongolia, where she would come for it when things settled.

I put the jade in my pocket and went to the roof. There was no one in sight.

Soon after, I heard Su Ling scream. My soul screams with her now. I rushed down the stairs, but moved slowly, like I was in a dream. When I reached her, she was already hunched over in pain. Her skin was blue, her nails were black, and dark blood was jetting out of her mouth in short spasms. I reached for her, held her, but in a second, she stopped moving, and I knew she was gone. I didn't know what to do. I was a foreigner in a strange land . . . I ran out of the house.

Somehow, I stumbled back into the city by dawn.

I never found out what happened to her body. But why should it matter to me? I didn't help her; I left her, and I never cared for her body.

Suthachai exhaled, leaning back. Should he read further?

The wind howled outside, shaking his tent, taunting him to a confrontation.

He folded the book, inserted it into the box, and closed his eyes. Su Ling burned incense to her father's spirit when he died. Perhaps his grandfather would like him to do the same.

Suthachai jumped to his feet, grabbed his saber, and marched out of the yurt.

His tall stallion Arrow Head wheeled in delight when he heard the approach of his master. Suthachai peeled off the blindfolds and stroked the horse's head like he would his own child.

"Let's ride against wind and ride so hard that the neighboring clans think a war is coming."

Arrow Head nodded, as if he understood. Suthachai mounted with a nimble spring and charged into the night. It would be a day's ride by horseback, but Arrow Head, tearing across the plains, was determined to fight the wind. They reached the market by late morning.

. . .

The marketplace was small, cluttered, and misplaced on the edge of a vast desert where sand and dust floated. The small town of filthy stone shacks and unpaved roads were created for travelers, barbarians, patrol officials, and businessmen seeking trade across the border.

Few nomads ever rode south of this town into the heart of the desert. Beyond the desert was China, and they were never welcomed in Chinese society, never regarded as anything more than uncivilized beasts. But here, it was different. In this small town, with its scattered buildings and small cottages, nomads and barbarians from all directions were welcomed.

Suthachai drifted down the main road and passed the Chinese vendors with small booths and tables. Tea, salt, herbs, tools, weapons, all were sold on the street. But he didn't need provisions, or salt, or tea. He came for one particular vendor.

It was a small shop, unusually simple and almost hidden. The front of the shop was merely a window with a rigid man seated inside. Suthachai dismounted. He had seen this shop before, attracted by the smell of burning incense, though this time, only the scent of dried earth filled the air.

The man eyed him, still motionless.

Suthachai walked up to the window. "You will trade for candles and incense here?" He could barely speak the Chinese tongue anymore.

The man leaned forward a little, still eyeing him. "What do you have?"

Suthachai opened his bag and showed the sheepskin. The man nodded, his expression cold. He glanced at the jade dragon around Suthachai's neck, and then nodded again. "Candles?"

"For my dead grandfather."

"A Chinese tradition," the man said with a smile. "Burning candles and incense for the dead."

He pulled out a pack of incense from small shelves next to him. He glanced at the jade again, and then smiled again. "He must have been a great man."

"He was not."

"Regardless. You should light special candles for him, out of respect. I'll give you a pair as a gift."

"Thank you."

The vendor disappeared into the back of the store, and in a moment, reemerged with a pair of red candles. Wrapped around the candles was the print of a fierce, three-headed dragon.

Suthachai stared. "These are beautiful."

"I'll take one skin for the incense. These candles are yours. Thank you for spreading our tradition up North."

"Thank you." Suthachai handed over the skin and tucked the candles deep inside his robes. He took Arrow Head's reins and walked away.

The ride back was much slower, but Suthachai barely paid attention, often permitting Arrow Head to wander across the plains. He carried enough water and food, both for himself and the animal, and the storm was not due for another day. There was no reason to hurry. He closed his eyes and casually leaned against his horse's mane.

How did she die? Her skin turned blue. Perhaps she was poisoned . . .

He shook his head. Who could've poisoned her? No

one else was there—surely his grandfather would've seen it. Suthachai ran his finger along the contours of the jade. It was fifty years ago. Why bother thinking about it now?

Two men had been following him for some time. He turned, finally, tapped his heavy saber with a smile, and they slowed their pace. Horse thieves and desert robbers infested the steppe every summer and winter season, a time when travelers often succumbed to heat or cold and were at their most vulnerable. But Suthachai was clearly a warrior of the steppe, and for bandits to trail him, hoping that he would become lost, was a sign of desperation.

The sun was on its descent by the time he reached familiar grasslands. The atmosphere was peaceful, the wind calm. In the distance, Suthachai noticed scattered clouds of dust. The hunt! He grabbed the reins and charged forward.

The incredible scale and duration of this hunt was something no one on the steppe had ever seen before. Thousands participated, and after six months, the hunt continued. Half a year ago, the wolves and leopards, already too numerous, began to attack their sheep and cattle at an unprecedented rate. The major clans of the steppe joined to exterminate them. The hunters and warriors of the steppe divided into four groups, assembled their families, their herds, and traveled in four separate directions. Then, on the designated day, those participating in the hunt fanned out into lines so incredible in length that an entire day on horseback was required to travel from end to end. Slowly, over the span of six months, the four lines closed in and chased every animal toward a central point, where the carnivores would be slaughtered and the deer and wild horses led back into the open plains.

Suthachai, often revered as the leader of the hunt, had

been absent for days and morale had been low. But that moment, in the final stages of the hunt, where the circle of warriors became so dense that the gap between each man was a mere ten strides in length, he suddenly appeared. The men bellowed with excitement.

They were chasing two packs of wolves. When two wolf packs ran together, the end of the hunt was near.

Suthachai watched Jocholai barging across the smooth grass on a black horse, pursuing two gray wolves at the rear of the pack. Two other hunters followed closely behind, with arrows fitted against their bows.

Jocholai released an arrow that barely grazed his target. His companions also fired in unison, but the wolves were moving too quickly.

Jocholai shouted: "Suthachai! You haven't killed a wolf in days!"

Arrow Head stormed toward the fleeing wolves, crashing in with such a burst of energy the wolves were forced to change direction. Suthachai reached for his bow, realized that he was too close to them, and flung it aside. With a roar, he leaped off his horse and onto a wolf's back. The wolf stumbled under the weight, long enough for Suthachai to wrap his arms around the furry neck. With a violent jerk, he twisted its head to the side. There was a yelp, Suthachai twisted its head the other way, and dropped the carcass to the ground.

The rest of the pack was slain by a shower of arrows. Suthachai climbed onto his horse without a word and returned to his yurt. He left his friends to continue the chase. At dusk, campfires would be built around the perimeter of the hunt, and half the men would sleep along the encirclement to ensure that no predator escaped.

. . .

The world seemed exceptionally quiet in his yurt. Shadows heaving from the Chinese candles seemed to caress his face. The first drops of wax fell like tears. He closed his eyes to the smell of incense, and wondered if his grandfather could sense the burning candles and rest in peace.

The hunt was almost over, and outside, the clan welcomed the winter. But the sounds of laughter and celebration softly floating in the distance couldn't penetrate his tent. Deep thoughts drowned the music of the winter festival.

The flap of the yurt was thrown open and Jocholai stuck his head in.

"The wrestling match started! Where were you?"

Suthachai opened his eyes. His face softened. Jocholai slapped him once on the back before rushing out again. "Come on! Everyone's expecting you!"

Suthachai emerged into the open. The soft winds of the Mongolian steppe rode with the music. Women danced in a circle, people played stone-tossing games, and colorful chatter roamed through the air.

Jocholai stood beside him. "What's wrong?"

"Nothing."

"Did your . . . "

"He died last night."

The girls stopped dancing. A group of men began pounding their drums while young girls clapped to the rhythm. The first pair of wrestlers stepped into the circle and squared with one another. They charged, the audience cheered, and the beating drums overwhelmed the night.

Moments later, the larger of the two wrestlers stood victorious over his opponent. The audience cheered, then began to shout in unison. "Fight the number one warrior! Fight the number one warrior!" They were calling for Suthachai to enter the circle.

Suthachai stepped in. Then, at the first beat of the drum, the smaller warrior charged. Without a glance, Suthachai sidestepped, grabbed his opponent, and threw him to the ground. Second beat of the drum.

• • •

Her cries were an echo. Dark blood spilled from her mouth. Her screams were hollow, desperate; her face twisted. Her skin turned pale blue, her nails turned black . . .

With a roar, Suthachai sprang to his feet, the vivid dream barely faded. Fresh blood flew from his mouth. A sudden surge of pain and searing heat expanded in his chest. He grabbed his ribcage and crumbled to his knees.

He was in his yurt, on his bed. The camp was completely silent.

He dragged his hand across his mouth and stared at his fingers. His eyes widened. His nails were black, his skin pale blue, and the warm blood from his lips was dark—so dark that he thought his liver had burst.

In the distance, he heard a faint rumbling, as if thousands of horses were charging toward him. Suthachai sat back, waiting to awaken from the dream. The rumbling grew louder.

Just like Su Ling.

His grandfather. The selfish old man who saw his loved one poisoned, who abandoned the woman he loved. She died bleeding from her mouth, her skin pale blue . . .

War horns from the perimeter of the camp screamed into the night. "A raid! A raid!"

Suthachai awakened from his spell, scrambled to his feet, grabbed his saber, and dashed out the tent.

Outside, the entire camp was lit by hundreds of torches. Every warrior was charging east while the women and children retreated to the center.

Jocholai, saber in hand, came up to him on horseback. "What took you so long? I thought you'd never wake up!"

"Who's attacking us?" Suthachai shouted. "What happened to the peace pact?"

"I don't know. But there are hundreds of them—all on horseback."

Suthachai bolted east with a roar, sensed Arrow Head appearing next to him, and flew onto his saddle. The enemy was approaching the camp at high speed, none of them emitting a single war cry.

Strange, Suthachai thought. Which clan would come this close and still remain silent?

The Mongolian warriors gathered around him, eager for his signal to charge, eager to watch him kill. Suthachai took a deep breath and quickly assessed the battlefield. The terrain was completely flat, with no trees, no hills. There could be no ambush from the side.

There was nothing left to do but ride out and butcher the enemy. Suthachai drew his saber and screamed at the top of his lungs.

"Kill!"

The warriors behind him charged.

Clad in the light armor of the steppe, the invaders also drew their sabers.

The wind whipped across the plains. The charging horses sounded like never-ending thunder. The two tribes rushed at each other, brought to frenzy by the smell of blood, the

24

delight of slaughter, the fierce eyes of each warrior gleaming as they approached the enemy.

Suthachai shivered, the hollow pain in his chest expanding. No! He was too close to the enemy, too deep in the battlefield.

The pain surged. He couldn't control the dark blood streaming from his mouth. The world darkened, blurred. He rolled off his horse, slamming into the ground with a hoarse choke. The other warriors soared past him, crashing into the oncoming enemy.

He heard the collision of bare steel, the screams, the cries of pain . . . It seemed unnaturally slow, like blood seeping through soft soil. He supported himself on one elbow and stared. The invaders had cut a path through their defending forces and were racing toward their camp. They were after the women and children.

Suthachai forced himself to one knee, a glare of murder in his eyes. A quiver of arrows and a long bow lay beside him—both from a fallen warrior. He slung the quiver over his shoulders, fitted an arrow, quickly drew it, and fired. It sounded like a bullwhip slicing thin air. The arrow pierced the leg of an enemy horse, causing the animal to rear in pain, to stumble and collide into a nearby mount. Three men collapsed at once.

Suthachai fired again into another horse, then another. Nearly ten horses had fallen by the time the enemy turned to confront him. The pain in his chest was forgotten. He leaped off his feet and charged the cavalry. With two sabers in hand, he slashed left and right, dodging the enemy and attacking only their mounts. The animals turned wild in panic, bucking and tossing their riders, crushing one another and beginning to fall. Over thirty horses fell, and chaos ensued.

Jocholai lifted his blade high above his head. With an earth-shattering scream, he brought his warriors blaring down on the enemy again. Suthachai began to slay his dismounted enemies, springing on them like a beast, cutting them down like he was slaughtering sheep.

Soon, clouds of dust circled the air, hovering over the ground now littered with bodies. Suthachai looked on. Everyone seemed to be moving much too slowly. His pale blue skin had become deeper in color, and the nauseous feeling in his chest reemerged. At that moment, he noticed something in his hand, something that he had been holding the entire time. He must have ripped it from an enemy. It was a small necklace with a beautiful dragon carved into a wooden leaf. It was a fierce looking dragon, three-headed, one that seemed to stare at him, laugh at him.

Suthachai reached for the jade around his own neck. He placed the two dragon emblems next to each other, and his hands began to tremble. The carvings were identical.

He stood in the middle of the field, lost in thought. The image of Su Ling resurfaced in his mind, the blue skin, the black nails, the jade dragon.

Two identical carvings . . .

Suthachai climbed onto his horse, blood flowing from his forehead in a steady stream. He gazed into the distance, his eyes out of focus, his mind repeatedly envisioning the moment before Su Ling's death.

Dark clouds hovered over him.

• • •

Much later, Suthachai found himself in a warm bed, the wooden leaf torn from his enemy still gripped in his hand. A thin, bony finger touched his forehead.

The Elder was next to him. "Strange poison," the old man said, shaking his head. "I've never seen it before."

"Poison?"

"Not poison from the steppe. Never seen anything like it in Mongolia."

"How? How could I be poisoned?"

"I don't know. I don't know what medicine to use."

A long silence. Suthachai tried to sit, but felt weak. He stared at the dragon carving. "Am I going to die?"

"The greatest warrior of the steppe cannot be afraid of death," the Elder said.

Suthachai gritted his teeth. "How much longer will I live?"

"Maybe three months. You are strong. You should have three months."

. . .

His grandfather once told him that to live is to struggle. Every day, the animals of the steppe must outrun the fastest predator. And every day, the predators must outrun the slowest prey.

Suthachai opened his heavy eyes. The Elder was still beside him, gently smearing crushed leaves on his forehead. The younger Mongolian breathed a sigh of relief. The Elder was the most respected man in the tribe. He understood the will of the gods, the fears of mankind, the profound medicines of the Earth. The smell of bitter herbs meant that he was still alive.

"Elder?"

"You need rest."

"How many men did we lose?"

"Forty-six."

The young warrior trembled. "And our women and children?"

"They're safe. All of them."

"And the enemy?"

"Don't you remember? You killed most of them. The rest ran away."

Suthachai shook his head. "It's my fault."

"Why?"

Suthachai reached for the jade around his neck. "My grandfather left this behind—this three-headed dragon. The wooden leaf—also a three-headed dragon. The symbols are identical. Somehow, I brought this upon us."

The Elder took the jade and for a long time couldn't tear his eyes from it. "Maybe the jade brought this upon us. Maybe it belongs to someone, and they want it back."

"Elder, I've heard of this poison before."

"Where?"

"My grandfather saw it in China about fifty years ago. A woman, this woman was poisoned. Like I am now. But she died instantly. I even dreamed about her. I dreamed about her last night. Her face turned blue and her nails turned black . . . Like mine. Fifty years ago, and now, it's happening to me."

The Elder held his hand and tried to calm him. Suthachai pushed himself into a sitting position. "She gave my grandfather this jade, right before she died, in Pan Tong Village."

"Pan Tong Village?"

"In China. I have a map. It's on the last page of my grandfather's diary. I can find this village. I can find other people wearing this dragon emblem. Maybe there are answers out there."

• • •

By the following night, Suthachai recovered his energy, though every time he looked down, his bluish hands reminded him of the poison in his veins. Three months left to live. The Elder said so.

"I need to go to China."

The Elder sighed. "You'll die in a foreign land. Are you sure?"

A forced smile. "When can anyone be sure of life or death?"

The flapping door of the Mongolian yurt seemed to beckon him, luring him into the dark, limitless grasslands. He seemed to hear the Elder suggesting that a group of warriors accompany him, but the old man's words faded into the rising wind.

"Not even Jocholai," Suthachai whispered. "If the invaders return, every man counts. I brought this upon my people. I can't put them in any more danger."

Suthachai felt the chill of the earth creep into his spine, numbing his skull, freezing his tongue. He sensed the Elder standing at the door of the yurt behind him, watching, and he was afraid to turn, to bid farewell.

Arrow Head trotted up to him. Almost reluctantly, Suthachai climbed onto his horse. He uttered a short laugh. "Survival. Is that my final destiny?"

He disappeared into the darkness. The dense clouds foreboding the first storm of winter began to gather. Then he seemed to hear the Elder, alone in the darkness, saying, "Suthachai, my boy. Survival, is hardly a worthy quest."

PROPHECY TWO

A blind guide seeks direction
The dormant engravings foretold
The dreamer's potion discovered
Converging thunderheads opposed

"We have no time, Arrow Head," Suthachai murmured, squeezing the belly of his dying horse. "Please . . . we have no time . . ."

He had crossed the dreaded desert in five days, and for the past week, struggled through an endless chain of mountains. The winds were unusually harsh, and the treacherous terrain became impossible with blankets of icy snow blowing at him. Yet, according to his grandfather's map, the destination was within reach; he needed to cross one more peak.

For days, they battled the elements. The barren mountains offered little refuge from the freezing wind, and neither man nor horse had food left.

"No, Arrow Head. Just a little further."

Arrow Head crumbled with a weak whine, his eyes half-closed, thick foam dripping from his mouth.

"We're almost there. No, Arrow Head! No."

The stallion couldn't respond. A film of ice had long settled on his mane, and it was over—without doubt. Suthachai began to draw his saber. A horse too weak to walk must be used as meat. It was inevitable.

Snow began to fall again. Arrow Head would freeze to death, regardless, and slaying him would also mean enough food for a week.

His horse lifted itself and stared. Perhaps it would plea for a quick, painless death. Suthachai waited. He hoped Arrow Head would somehow ask him to end the misery, and tell him that a quick stroke of the heavy saber would help him rest in peace. But his horse only stared.

Suthachai closed his eyes. "Who am I to decide whether you live or die?" He severed the saddle and reins, tossed them aside, and sheathed his weapon. "Fight for your life, Arrow Head, while I fight for mine."

Much later, from a high elevation, he turned around for a final look at the horse he left behind. He thought he saw Arrow Head climbing to his feet.

• • •

According to the map, the terrain would become friendlier after he crossed this last peak. He peered down, and this time, he noticed a trail at the foot of the mountain. It was too dark for him to see where the trail led to, but any man-made road was a sign of civilization. Pan Tong Village should not be far off. He tucked the diary into his inner pockets and began to descend.

The events recorded in his grandfather's diary occurred fifty years ago. It could have been just a legend in a distant land—like the myths the Elder used to tell around the camp fires, about heroes who rode on flaming wheels and fought sea dragons to prove their courage, or great hunters who shot down flying horses that breathed fire.

Pan Tong Village. He thought of Su Ling, of the same poison that he somehow inherited fifty years later. He thought of the three-headed dragons. Those who raided his camp wore carvings identical to the jade. Suthachai shook his head—it felt like it was going to explode. None of this made sense to him. His life was simple, peaceful. He was a great hunter, a champion wrestler who was guaranteed leadership on the Mongolian plains. Never had he thought of riding farther south than the border, of meeting any Chinese outside the marketplace. Why was this happening to him?

By the time he reached the trail at the foot of the mountain, the early rays of the morning sun peered over the hilly terrain in front of him. The wind was calmer then, the cold air less brutal.

A town appeared out of nowhere, built in a strange place hardly noticeable to the common traveler. A tall wooden wall surrounded the town, and there were only four gates, one facing each direction, that permitted entrance. Sentry posts were erected outside each gate but no one manned them, and the few guards seated outside weren't in uniform. Armed men casually passed through the gates with only a light nod to the guards.

After crossing the desert, in one night's time, Suthachai had ventured deep into the land of the Chinese. He hadn't seen a living soul throughout the night, and suddenly, there were Chinese everywhere. He gripped his saber, ready to draw if a Chinese noticed him, then checked himself. He came here to ask questions, not to instigate wars.

From the top of a hill, he was able to see a bustling market inside. He needed a town, a populated one, if he was to learn anything.

Suthachai shifted down the hill, into the main road, before approaching the northern gate. He tried to walk among the others, his head down, his eyes on the ground. The gate was wide open, and those around him simply entered.

A guard called to him. Suthachai's hand flew to his saber, but the guard didn't notice.

"Where are you from, traveler?"

Others continued to pass through the gate. "The North," Suthachai responded, pronouncing slowly to cover his accent.

"Have you seen Li Kung?"

Suthachai shook his head without turning.

"He's wandering around Northern Pass with a girl. If you see him, Master Dong wants him captured. There's a reward."

Suthachai nodded, eager to go.

"He's getting his skull cracked open. He should've known better than to offend the Red Dragons, don't you agree?"

Suthachai nodded again. "I agree." He continued onward. No one followed to question him further. No one was interested.

The town was crowded. There were vendors selling hot tea and buns on the side of the road, and stores selling food, cloth, and dry goods. Every structure was firmly built; so solid they could last forever. Some of them were higher than trees! For the first time, Suthachai saw stairs and balconies, translucent windows made of waxed paper, and the written language of the Chinese in front of every shop. What a strange world. It didn't resemble the makeshift marketplace at the border.

The pungent smell of food was everywhere, and it finally dawned on him that he hadn't eaten in days. He went first to a small shop and traded a sheepskin for a few coins, then found his way into a crowded inn.

Other customers were simply seating themselves. He walked in, found a table in the corner, and sat down with his back to the wall.

The innkeeper came forward, a dirty cloth draped over his shoulder, a greasy smile frozen on his face. "What would you like, sir?"

Suthachai kept his head lowered. He pushed the coins across the table. "Food and wine."

The innkeeper scooped the coins from the table. "Certainly. What would you like?"

"Meat."

"What kind of meat, sir?"

"Horse meat."

The innkeeper stalled. "We . . . we don't have horse meat here, sir."

"Wild boar, then."

The innkeeper paused, before politely turning to leave. "Roast pork loin coming right up!"

In a moment, he returned with more food than Suthachai ever thought possible for a few dusty coins to buy. Evidently, the sheepskins that he traded at the border were worth much less.

He stuffed the dry buns into his pockets, saving them for later, and began to devour the meat and the noodles. He never knew food could be this good.

"Have you heard? Red Dragons are looking for Li Kung."

Suthachai turned to the table beside him and noticed two men, one tall, another chubby, seated face-to-face and drinking rice wine. The tall one replied to his friend, "I heard only Dong wants him. There's a reward."

The fat one asked, "Dong? The Red Dragon master's son? What in the world did Li Kung do to deserve that?"

"Oh, he really asked for it. He couldn't treat the Old Grandmother."

"No one can."

"But he suggested killing her with poison."

"What!"

The tall man shook his head. "He said there's no cure, and the family should just kill her so she wouldn't suffer anymore."

The fat man clapped his hand to his mouth.

The tall one said, "Li Kung could've been cut down, right there on the spot. But they probably didn't want to spill blood in front of the Old Grandmother."

"How long has she been suffering? She's been sick for a long time."

"Ten years, I think."

The fat one frowned. "That's a long time."

Suthachai turned back to his meal, trying hard to follow their conversation without appearing to eavesdrop. He certainly recognized none of the names that they spoke of, except for the name Li Kung, mentioned by the guard at the gate.

"I feel bad for him," Suthachai couldn't help hearing the fat man say. "He did save forty children from that strange fever last month."

The tall one shook his head. "There's no doubt Li Kung is talented. But he's just foolish to say something like that."

The fat one scratched his head. "I wonder why they kicked him out of Redwood Cliff, just to search for him again."

"I told you. Master Dong wants him dead. But it's Cricket who sent him away."

"But Cricket is just a boy. Dong's the older brother."

"I know."

"I guess Li Kung's as good as dead."

"Well, maybe he'll get lucky, and he'll walk away just maimed and crippled."

Suthachai chewed on his last strip of meat. His chest felt hot again, and he noticed the bluish tint on his skin fading. What was he looking for? Who was he looking for? Maybe the jade had something to do with the Red Dragon House. The answers were in Pan Tong Village. He had little time to lose.

. . .

Much later, with his belly full and his inner pockets weighed down by Chinese coins, Suthachai headed for Pan Tong Village. He had shown the map in his grandfather's diary to the fat man in the inn, who pointed him east, along a road called Middle Pass. Before he left town, he traded the rest of his rabbit skins for Chinese coins and purchased a straw hat to keep his face in shadow. Pan Tong was not far, the tall one said. Only another half a day away.

By early afternoon, he spotted his destination. He couldn't believe his eyes. He was there, despite the sandstorms of the Gobi, despite the icy winds of the Chinese mountains. He was there.

Pan Tong Village was entrenched in a valley, surrounded by rugged hills and completely protected from the whipping wind. Yet, it was clearly vulnerable to heavy snow and seclusion.

Suthachai took a deep breath, almost blinded by the afternoon sun. He was eager to find someone in the village—anyone that he could release his onslaught of questions upon.

Pan Tong Village was quiet, motionless except for drifting snowflakes.

Suthachai approached the nearest house, his hand clenched on the handle of his saber. He banged the door, but no one answered. He waited. Could they still be asleep? He pushed against the door with his heavy mass, slowly at first, then shoved the door open with his left hand, his saber half-drawn in his right. They were only common villagers. But anyone could be an enemy. His grandfather had told him so.

He stepped into the house and noticed a cat sleeping in the corner. A deaf cat perhaps. The house was clean, with the floor swept and fine cloth covering the table. It seemed warm, comfortable. With his hand off the saber, Suthachai slipped into the back rooms.

A child was asleep on a bed, his tiny hands folded, his covers tucked. Suthachai gazed at the chubby cheeks, the pale skin. The covers didn't even move with his breathing.

The breathing! Suthachai placed a hand on the boy's face and found it cold as ice. He backed away. The boy was clearly dead. Did no one know this child died in his sleep?

Suthachai dashed into the next room, found an old woman stiffly in bed, and realized that she, too, was dead. He ran further into the house, to a master bedroom, and found both husband and wife, in perfect sleeping posture, dead together in bed.

Outside, the air was colder than ever. Despite the pain in his chest, Suthachai ran down the road from which he came. There were no horses, no livestock, no signs of life. He forced his way into another house, only to find more cold bodies in bed. He felt the covers, which were thick and heavy; he realized the village couldn't have frozen to death.

The snowfall finally subsided. Suthachai stood alone, in the middle of the road, and felt the poison rushing back into his chest. Pan Tong Village, a place that he could only dream about until today. He could finally see the place his grandfather so vividly described, could finally ask the villagers a thousand questions about the poison in his body . . .

But they were dead, all of them, from the infants to the elderly—no one alive. Some of the cooking stoves were still warm from the night before. There was no sign of struggle, no blood, no wounds, no bruises. It was like they had been poisoned.

Poisoned! His eyes widened. Who could have poisoned so many people at once? What killed them in their sleep? If the well water was poisoned, or if the food was poisoned, at least some of them would die on the floor. But every single villager lay quietly in bed, covers drawn, eyes closed.

Unless . . . the poison was emitted through the air.

Suthachai froze at the thought. Prior to the raid at his camp, there was one other place where he had seen the three-headed dragon. It was on the candles that he bought at the border from the Chinese vendor.

He never thought of the candles. When he noticed the dragons molded in wax, he assumed they were common emblems of the Chinese. The candles! Su Ling also burned candles for the dead, and she died shortly afterwards. But when he burned the candles for his grandfather, Jocholai pulled him into the wrestling match. Perhaps he wasn't fully exposed to the smoke, and that's why he didn't die.

The symbol of the three-headed dragon on the jade, on the candles, on the men who raided his camp . . . It all began to make sense.

Just then, he heard flute music in the distance. It was beautiful, haunting, the lonely notes of a tormented soul. He heard a voice that couldn't scream, trapped in a wounded body and unable to break free.

Suthachai took a step forward, then another. The music danced around him, beckoning him, daring him not to listen while drawing him across the land. He glided out of the village with eyes half closed, his mind spinning.

He was deep in the forest when he encountered her. She was kneeling on the snow, her back toward him, a long, metal flute held to her lips. Her flowing hair glistened against the piercing light, creating a wave of sparkles, while her lean body, completely motionless, glowed with an unearthly radiance.

He shook his head clear. He was to find answers here.

She lowered the flute and slowly turned. Suthachai stared, and his jaw dropped. Never before had he seen a woman so atrocious. A large tumor hung over her eyelid, and the right side of her lip was swollen and twisted. The texture of her face resembled the back of a venomous toad. Suthachai took a step back, away from the monster in front of him.

The woman smiled a strange haunting smile, almost pleasant. Again, she lifted the flute to her lips and began to play.

Suthachai glared at her. "Who are you? What happened here? Why is everyone dead?"

The woman stopped. Her voice was coarse, hellish. "So you speak Chinese. Do all Mongolians fight like you?"

Suthachai hesitated.

She smiled. "I recognize you. You're the great warrior they told me about. Where's the jade?"

"The jade . . . "

"If you hand it over, I'll let you live."

"Why do you want this jade? Why is it important?"

The woman sneered. "I heard Mongolian warriors are strong enough to wrestle a bull. But can they fight a beautiful woman?"

Suthachai flinched. The woman darted forward, her metal flute pointed at his chest. He drew his saber to intercept. Sparks flew when their weapons collided. The weight of his blow sent her reeling. She stumbled back, planted herself, and with a smile, tucked the flute back in her belt.

Suthachai took a step forward, his saber lowered. This woman knew about the jade. He couldn't decide whether to attack her or question her. But the heat already began to swell in his chest, and he knew that time wasn't on his side.

He had come to this strange land to find out about the poison. She was maybe the only one who knew. "I will give you the jade," he said. "Tell me how you killed the people in Pan Tong Village. Did you poison them? What kind of poison?"

She blinked at him. "What a thrill. Too bad we have to fight under unfair circumstances. But then, I'm a woman, and I don't have superior strength."

Suthachai laughed. The sight of her face would give him nightmares for the rest of his life. "You are not a real woman."

She held her head high, a look of admiration on her face, and took a sharp step forward. "I certainly have the endurance to make this a long, lasting fight. Do you?"

Under unfair circumstances. His heart stopped. She knew about the poison, about him. There was a sense of confidence on her face—the calm composure of a true warrior in battle.

"Who are you?" he whispered.

She continued to approach him, ever so slowly, like a drawn-out, painful death.

"You know about the poison in my body? Did you poison me? With the candles?"

"Your accent is interesting," she said. "Few Mongolians

ever learn our tongue. It's too bad I have to kill you today."

Like a gust of wind, she drew her flute and swept at him.

His chest began to swell. He had little time left. He suddenly took four steps back, watched her move in to close the distance, and, taking advantage of her forward momentum, charged at her with a roar.

She pointed her flute at him and he jolted back just in time. A thin blade the length of her forearm, hidden in her flute, shot forward and almost pierced his face. He struck the blade with his saber and she retreated.

The flute was now the length of a sword.

The stress fired up the poison in his body, and dark blood trickled from his mouth. His legs were weak, his eyes half-blind, and he was ready to collapse. He grit his teeth and planted both feet in the snow.

She charged at him then, her blade pointing straight for his eye. He lifted his saber, his eyes wide with pain. For a second, he stared at the strange skin on her face, the tumor, the distorted lips.

She spun the flute around and swiped at his head. He saw it coming; he wanted to parry, but his legs wouldn't move. He wanted to block, but his arms no longer obeyed. The flute blasted into the side of his skull, and he collapsed.

She pressed her blade against the hollow of his throat, and he began to spasm.

In a moment, he calmed.

So this is it. This is the end.

He had always thought the moment before death would be a painful, chaotic struggle, where the world would turn red, where he would hear himself die.

His eyes clouded, and he stared into the distant heavens. His homeland was not really that far. He could have walked north after he left the inn, climbed over the mountains, waited for the winds to clear, crossed the great desert, and reached the steppe. He could have been home in no time at all. But it was so peaceful where he lay. The snow so soft under his body, the air so clean and cool . . .

She watched him carefully.

He stared at nothing, lost in thought. He came here to find answers, not to die in the snow.

He thought of Arrow Head then. The horse he abandoned, the horse he left behind at the edge of the desert. Did Arrow Head survive?

He clenched his jaws, a bitter taste in his mouth. He came here to find life, to find a cure.

Who was she to decide whether he lived or died?

She blinked. He reached over, still on his back, and grabbed the blade. She instinctively stabbed at his throat, but the blade wouldn't budge. His other hand lifted the saber to cut her. With a vicious jerk, she yanked the blade from his grip and stabbed his sword arm.

Light flashed from his eyes. With a cry he lifted the saber, permitting her blade to sink into his flesh, then twisted his body and slashed her across the thigh. She stepped back in shock.

Suthachai grabbed the flute handle and pulled the entire length of the blade out of his arm.

She jumped over him, behind him, and kicked him in the base of the skull.

Everything was dark. He thought he saw her stand over him, the blade once more pressed against his throat. He tightened his muscles, summoned the strength that he didn't have, and lifted the saber again. She watched him, watched his trembling hand close around his weapon. Her blade pressed tighter against his throat, and she hesitated. There was a deep cut in her thigh.

In a second, she kicked away his saber and took a huge, clean swipe across his throat. The blood drained from him. She said something before walking away.

• • •

Much later, Suthachai opened his eyes and stared at the dim heavens. The congestion in his chest disappeared, but he felt weak, paralyzed. How could this be the feeling of death?

Why was he still in his corpse?

He was still bleeding from the deep gash in his arm, and there was a stinging sensation in his hand, cut open when she yanked her blade from his desperate grip.

How could a woman, so hideous and ugly, continue to live? Could anyone bear to look at her?

He moved his fingers, then his wrists.

Maybe he wasn't dead yet.

He reached up, touched his throat, and froze. She didn't slash him.

He touched his throat again, to assure himself there really was no gash from ear to ear.

Something was missing. He took off his gloves and rubbed his neck again. The jade. The jade was missing. She slashed the necklace to take the jade.

"He's still alive." It was a young woman's voice. The voice was light, full of energy. "He lost a lot of blood, but I think only his arm is wounded."

The voice of a young man followed from a short distance. "Is he still bleeding?"

Suthachai opened his eyes and gazed into the face of a girl no older than eighteen. She was small, a playful sparkle in her eyes.

"Hurry," she said.

The young man's footsteps became louder. He was unarmed, dressed in the plain clothes of a scholar with a heavy knapsack slung over his shoulder. His nose was tall, his face thin, his eyes sparkling with energy.

"Pun, hand me the three-seven roots," he said. He tore open the sleeve covering the wound.

The girl was named Pun.

She handed a porcelain bottle to the man, who sifted the contents onto Suthachai's wound.

The Mongolian felt cool sensations run through him.

The young man tore off the sleeve and strapped it around the wound. "He'll recover. No major nerves severed."

"Let me put this in his mouth," Pun said. It was a small pill. "Swallow."

The young man stared, a perplexed look on his face.

"What's the matter?" she asked.

"Strange. It's not the loss of blood that's hurting him. You see the bluish tint of his skin?"

"Poison?"

"Strange." He reached out and placed his thin fingers on Suthachai's pulse, felt it for some time, then pulled open the heavy coat and pressed against his abdomen.

Suthachai's energy revived after swallowing the pill. He reached over and pushed the man away. "There is no cure. But thank you for helping me."

"Mongolian!" Pun exclaimed.

Instinctively, Suthachai reached for his saber. He watched the man grab his wrist to intercept. The saber!

"Let me help you with that," the young scholar said, trying to lift the weapon and almost dropping it. "It's really heavy! Shouldn't be lifting anything so heavy. Your arm's injured."

Suthachai froze. Pun rushed over to help. "You want to stand?" She gripped his elbow with unbelievable strength, but barely pulled him to his knees. "Don't get up yet. You're still weak."

The man reached over. "Let him walk—it'll help him feel better. The pain will fade in a while." He turned to Suthachai. "It's deep in your liver. I need time to think about this. I've never seen this type of poison before."

Suthachai grunted, snatched his weapon from the young man's hands, and, planting it deep in the snow, pulled himself to his feet.

"Maybe you should rest here and wait for us," Pun said. "We need to run off to Redwood Cliff to help someone. Li Kung, can we find a safe place for him to rest?"

Suthachai's eyes widened. "Li Kung?"

"Yes," the young man said. "My name's Li Kung. What's yours?"

"It's . . . My name is Suthachai. Did you say Redwood Cliff?"

"I have a patient up there," Li Kung replied. "She's dying, but I just thought of a way to treat her. I think I can extend her life and stop the pain for another three years! It's simple—"

"We should take him," Pun interrupted. "We don't know our way around these woods. We won't be able to find him again."

They want to kill you, Suthachai meant to say, but he checked himself. The business of the arrogant Chinese was none of his concern. So this was Li Kung, the fool being hunted by the Red Dragon House. But why would this mere boy, no older than Pun, insist on treating an old woman even if it threatened his life?

Li Kung studied the Mongolian with interest. "Your

skin's pale, but your eyes are shining. Interesting. You're still incredibly strong." He grabbed Suthachai's wrist and felt his pulse carefully again. "Good. Good. The poison is still in its early stages. Something can be done. Perhaps Shifu Two will have ideas."

"We need to hurry," Pun said, beginning to walk away. "It'll be dark by the time we get to the top of the cliff. Suthachai can come with us, right?"

Suthachai nodded. There really was nowhere to go, and if this Li Kung was truly a talented doctor, perhaps there was hope. He tucked the saber into his belt and followed.

"How did you get poisoned?" Li Kung asked, his thin figure beside the huge Mongolian's. "I can't imagine a race of nomads creating this. It must've originated in China."

Suthachai hesitated.

Li Kung asked again, "How were you poisoned?"

"I don't really know."

Pun became interested now. "Really? So you just woke up one morning and you were poisoned?"

"Yes."

"Then you must've been poisoned while you were asleep," Li Kung said, almost to himself. "Something this potent, if it was ingested, should've woken you in the middle of the night with pain—not in the morning. You would know it if someone pricked you with a needle while you were sleeping, so it must have come from the air. Yes! I think so. The air was poisoned!"

Suthachai looked at him in disbelief, uncertain of whether to laugh or be amazed.

"Did it happen while you were sleeping in an inn?" Pun asked.

Suthachai shook his head, annoyed by their ceaseless chatter and barrage of questions. He was the one who came here for answers. "I was poisoned in Mongolia," he said in a low voice.

Li Kung halted, his long, bony fingers clasped together. "Really? Is that possible? Mongolian poisons are mainly snake venom. Something this complex *had* to be mostly herbal—"

"Now I will ask you some questions," Suthachai interrupted.

"Certainly!"

They emerged from the forest, picked up their pace despite Suthachai's poor condition, and began to follow a large, open road.

"This road is called Northern Pass," Pun said. "It leads directly through White Clay Village and to the foot of Redwood Cliff."

Suthachai disregarded her. "There is a woman," he began.

"You were poisoned by a woman?" Pun asked.

Suthachai glared at her once, turned to Li Kung and continued, "This woman has a dripping tumor over her eye. Her nose is crooked and her mouth is distorted."

"The Flute Demon," Pun said before Li Kung could reply. "They say she's a demon from hell, but because of something bad she did, she was sent into this world to become a woman. That was her punishment."

Again, Suthachai ignored her. "Li Kung, do you know who I'm talking about?"

"The Flute Demon," Li Kung replied. "As Pun said, she's known as the Flute Demon. She works for the Red Dragon House."

"That's where we're going," Pun said.

"Where can I find her?" the Mongolian said. "She took something from me. I want it back."

．．．

"White Clay Village looks dead tonight." Li Kung stared at a tight cluster of stone houses a short distance in front of him. Beyond the village, past a long empty field split by a single paved road, was the towering face of Redwood Cliff.

"Salt fields," Pun said. She pointed to the foot of Redwood Cliff, where large square structures, no taller than a man's waist, lined the open space. "This is how the Chinese make salt. On those salt fields."

Suthachai acknowledged the fields. The only road to Redwood Cliff separated the village in two, and once they passed the stone houses, they would be standing in front of the salt fields. Each salt field was wide enough to cover the area of a small house. The clay surfaces, elevated by strong supports, were completely covered with snow. The spaces underneath were evidently used as furnaces.

"There's no one here," Li Kung said. "Salt workers live here, but no one makes salt in the winter. Too much snow."

"I don't understand."

"The ocean's close by," Pun said. "The workers carry the water here, one bucket at a time, and dry them on the heated clay. They scrape off the salt and send it to that compactor mill over there." She pointed to a small building in the distance. "They press the salt into bricks."

The Mongolian nodded and walked ahead, stopping in front of a furnace, reaching out with a gloved hand to brush the snow off the side. The image of a fierce, three-headed dragon carved in stone looked back at him. Suthachai's face darkened. He pointed to the carving. "This is the Red Dragon symbol?"

"And the Green Dragon symbol," Li Kung replied. "They used to be one House."

Suthachai swallowed hard. "It is they. They invaded my home. One of their men gave me these red candles at the marketplace, and that is how I was poisoned."

"Candles?"

The Mongolian was shaking then. He glanced down the road, past the salt fields, and he noticed a group of Red Dragon guards approaching them.

"Our escorts are here," Pun said with a laugh. She reached out and tugged on Suthachai's sleeve. "Come on, we need to hurry. There's a dangerous stairway that we need to climb and the patient is really very sick."

Li Kung hastened down the road. "Come on!"

The Red Dragon guards, each dressed in dark red, stepped forward with weapons clutched before fanning out into an arc. Suthachai grunted, sensing hostility, and closed the distance behind his new friends.

"Hold it!" one of the guards shouted. "Who are you?"

"I'm Li Kung, the doctor treating the Old Grandmother. I need to see her as soon as possible."

One of the men broke out laughing. "We know who you are! How dare you come back here?"

Li Kung slowed when he neared the guards. There were seven of them, all heavily armed. They began to form a circle around him. One guard, less menacing than the others, lowered his weapon. "Don't you know that Master Dong wants you dead?"

Pun jumped forward. "What do you mean?"

"Please," Li Kung pleaded. "I've just figured out a way to treat her. It's worth a try. She won't be cured, but she'll live without pain for a few more years."

One guard drew his weapon. "The boy has a death wish. Don't kill him. Master Dong has a reward for us if we get him alive."

He waved his sword, threatening them with a gleeful smirk. Pun leaped at him from the side, so quickly that the guard barely noticed her. She planted a stinging kick into his ribs that sent him reeling. The remaining six guards hesitated, looked at each other once, and then drew their weapons to attack.

"Wait!" Li Kung shouted. "Don't fight! We're here to help the Old Grandmother. There's not much time!"

Pun stomped into another guard's knee, causing him to drop in agony, and in the same momentum, spun around and swept the side of his jaw with her heel.

"This is a misunderstanding!" Li Kung shouted. "We're here to help!"

One guard came at him, out of nowhere, his sword swiping dangerously close. Pun spun around too late, still caught in her own battle, too far away to intercept.

There was a flash of steel, so fast that Li Kung had no time to flinch, and the guard in front of him was decapitated. Suthachai stood next to him then, replacing the heavy saber into its sheathe.

The remaining Red Dragons froze. "Intruders! Intruders at the base!" They turned tail and scampered toward the cliff.

Suthachai eyed his friends. "Should we chase them?"

Neither Pun nor Li Kung responded. Both stared with disbelief at the headless body lying at their feet.

"Shall we?" Suthachai asked again.

"We better leave," Pun said. "The guards will raise an alarm."

"You . . . " Li Kung stammered, barely able to speak. "You killed him! He didn't deserve to die!"

Suthachai's eyes widened. He glanced at the three-headed dragon symbol carved into the side of a furnace. "They all deserve to die!"

He spun around to walk away.

Pun grabbed Li Kung's hand and squeezed it. "We need to go. Hundreds of guards are coming down the cliff."

Li Kung, still trembling, pressed his eyes shut and shook his head. "We've seen people kill each other. But not like that. He was so . . . calm about it."

. . .

The gray of dusk dropped into the horizon. The small party was on a narrow, winding road, using the early moonlight as their guide, hoping to reach the city of He Ku before darkness completely settled. They had not spoken since leaving the foot of Redwood Cliff.

"You are a scholar, Li Kung?" Suthachai asked, finally breaking the silence.

"Yes."

"My grandfather once said, the scholars and artists of China view death differently from the rest of the world."

"How is that?"

"Death comes in two forms. You are either killed, or you die from disease or old age. If you die from disease or age, it is because you are not strong. If you are killed, it is because you are not strong. The scholars can accept death from disease and old age. But they are afraid of being killed. Why?"

Li Kung thought for a second. "How can you compare murder with natural death? Murder is premature death."

"Murder? What is murder? When you slaughter a chicken and eat its flesh, does that make you a murderer?"

"A man is not a chicken!"

"A man is different from a chicken because he cannot be eaten, but he can be killed to guarantee survival of another man. Just like the chicken."

"Then, who decides who lives and who gets killed?"

"The stronger man of course."

Li Kung started, but Pun grabbed his hand, looked into his eyes and shook her head. "Don't argue with him," she warned quietly.

"That's not why we have civilization," Li Kung said, breaking away from Pun's grip. "That's not why we're decent, humane people. We belong to a society. Those in our civilization wouldn't slaughter each other for quick profit, or kill without good reason."

Suthachai let out a strange, mocking laugh. "All in the name of justice! So you kill for a quick profit, and then label it 'good reason.' Perhaps your people only kill to save the world?"

There was silence. Pun tugged on Li Kung's sleeve. "We better get going. Uh, we can discuss this later, when we reach an inn in He Ku."

Suthachai nodded and continued to walk. Li Kung and Pun followed closely behind, glancing at each other, aware that they could be in grave danger traveling with this barbarian.

The sky continued to darken. The twisting road toward He Ku was only ankle deep in snow, yet their journey was slow, almost painful. Suthachai remained in front, his head bowed, his eyes on the ground.

"Say something," Pun whispered to Li Kung. "Who knows what he's thinking? Say something and break the tension."

Li Kung was lost in deep thought.

Pun shook her head and ran forward. "Since you're new here . . . I . . . I can explain our world to you."

Suthachai didn't answer. She turned to Li Kung, who continued to walk with his head down.

"We're also new to this area," she continued. "We're from the South."

Still no answer.

"You don't speak much," Pun said. "Well, let me tell you anyway. We're very far from the capital you know, and the emperor really doesn't care about us. That's why you see so many armed men, because everyone's on their own here."

The Mongolian marched forward in silence, ignoring her. She took a deep breath and continued: "The Martial Society is all over the country of course, but because the imperial courts have so little influence here, the Red and Green Dragons became the big warlords around here. They're the two largest and most powerful Houses in the region. They weren't always called the Red and Green Dragons, but the Red Dragon warriors were always dressed in red and the Green Dragons always dressed in green. That's how they got their names. They hate each other, even though their leaders are brothers. Twins, in fact."

"The Martial Society is made up of separate schools of martial arts," Li Kung added from behind. "They all teach a different lineage of fighting styles. I heard the fighting skills of the two Dragon Houses have never been defeated."

It wasn't working. Pun ebbed back to Li Kung's side, an urgent sense of fear in her eyes. Any minute, the Mongolian could draw the massive saber by his side and slice them in half. They began to walk slower to distance themselves.

"Maybe you are right," Suthachai suddenly said.

"Right about what?" Li Kung asked.

"That humans cannot be compared to chickens. Killing a human cannot guarantee survival. Then again, killing chickens cannot guarantee survival either."

All along, Suthachai was merely lost in his own

thoughts. Li Kung breathed a sigh of relief. He took Pun's hand and walked beside the Mongolian again.

"But killing the man back there was done to guarantee your survival," Suthachai said. "That instance was directly related to the chicken. If you are dying of hunger, and a chicken is slaughtered for food, then you live. If the man wants to kill you, and he is killed first, then you also live. It is the same thing."

Pun broke into a laugh, then quickly covered her mouth and choked herself.

"He wasn't going to kill me," Li Kung said.

"They were looking for you. There is a reward for your head."

"Really?" Pun asked. "How much is he worth?"

Li Kung scowled at her. "I know. I recommended putting the Old Grandmother out of her misery. I think they didn't want to hear that."

"Who is this Old Grandmother?"

"The mother of Wei Bin and Wei Xu. Wei Bin is the leader of the Red Dragons—on Redwood Cliff. Wei Xu is the leader of the Green Dragons. They're brothers; and they're enemies."

"Wei Xu is really vain," Pun said with a mischievous smile. "He calls himself Lord of the Garden of Eternal Light. Now everyone, especially his Green Dragons, have to call him Lord Xu. Meanwhile, his twin is just Master Bin to his men."

Suthachai nodded. "But I heard this Old Grandmother has been sick for ten years."

"How did you hear so many things?" Pun asked. "You're Mongolian and you just came here."

"I don't understand how she's still alive," Li Kung said. "Some inner will, maybe, some strange desire to go on living for something. But she couldn't leave her bed, and she's in constant pain. She can barely speak. Most of the time, a person who's been ill like that would resign to death."

"What about someone as ill as I am?"

Li Kung thought for a second. "Whatever blood left in your body is toxic. How could you still be alive?" He reached into the depths of his coat and pulled out a little sack. "There's not enough moonlight. I better light a torch."

Pun handed him a large stick of wood, and in a moment, a blazing fire was ignited on the end of the stick. Li Kung held the torch closer to the ground, reflecting the light off the snow with a brilliant luminance.

"How did you do that?" Suthachai asked.

"Do what?"

"I saw Pun pick the branch off the ground. The wood is wet. How did you light it on fire?"

Li Kung held a little pouch in front of him. "This green powder, in here, can set anything on fire. I just sprinkled a little on the wood so it'll burn. I can even sprinkle this on ice and set the ice on fire."

"Set ice on fire! Where did you get this powder?"

"I made it myself. One of my mentors taught me. He said my spirit belongs to the fire element and I'm destined to set things on fire all my life. Do you want some?"

Suthachai took the pouch, weighed it in his hand for a second, and then returned it. "I would not know how to use it. But now I see. Your civilization is truly advanced."

Pun giggled, reached out, and pushed his hand back. "It's easy. Just sprinkle it on something and light it on fire."

Suthachai thought for a second, and then pocketed the pouch with a whisper of thanks. Pun and Li Kung smiled back, relieved that he accepted the gift. Perhaps the barbarian was not so dangerous after all.

The Mongolian's eyes suddenly flashed in alarm, and with a quick slap, he struck the torch from Li Kung's hand, extinguishing it. "People coming," he whispered, moving off the road. "This way. They are armed."

"Where?"

Suthachai grabbed them, pulled them to the side of the road and into the woods. They crouched low.

"Coming from where?"

"From both directions."

After a long time, the light plodding of horse hooves could be heard. Li Kung was deep inside the bushes, a good distance away, but he could see them. It was a large group of men, dressed in dark red, apparently unarmed and riding in perfect unison. In front of the group was an old man with long white hair. He lifted his hand to halt his men.

Another group of men came from the other side of the road. Li Kung counted ten, eleven of them on horseback, all of them armed, all of them in light green robes. They were carrying broadswords.

A short, stocky man dressed in green rode forward on a chestnut horse. "Red Dragons! What business do you have here?"

The old man with the long hair brought his horse forward. "So it's Stump. What a coincidence, bumping into you on this little trail."

Stump winced at the old man calling him by his nickname. "So it's the great strategist Tao Hing," he said in a low voice. "Traveling unarmed in my territory."

"We don't carry arms during mourning," Tao Hing replied. "But of course it doesn't concern you, since you're not related to the Old Grandmother. Weren't you informed?"

"Informed of what?'

"The Old Grandmother just passed away."

57

Stump fell back. The men behind him lowered their arms and bowed in silence.

"The Old Grandmother's dead!" Li Kung whispered. He squeezed Pun's hand, his heart pounding. "We're too late."

Tao Hing threw his head back and laughed. "I nearly forgot. You're adopted. Your surname's not even Wei. By the way, Stump, do you know who your real father is, or does your mother not even know?"

"The old man's unarmed," Li Kung whispered. "He's in great danger!"

"The short one is in greater danger," Suthachai replied. "The old man dropped spikes in the snow already, but the short one did not see it."

Stump pressed his horse a few steps forward. "What business do you have here?" he repeated his question. "You didn't come down from Redwood Cliff in the middle of the night to tell me the Old Grandmother passed away. Foot messengers do that."

Tao Hing drew his horse two steps back, yielding the ground with spikes in the snow, and smiled. "An adopted bastard coming forth to make a name for himself. If Wei Xu's son weren't so worthless, Wei Xu wouldn't need to adopt a bastard."

Stump's face turned red, and he reached for his sword. Tao Hing laughed again, and this time, the men behind him also broke into jeering laughter.

Stump charged, sword fully drawn and raised high. His horse took two steps and instantly reared backwards with a cry. The spikes were long, designed to penetrate horse hooves, yet subtle enough to remain invisible in the snow. Stump was thrown off his mount, and he landed with a sick thud before leaping to his feet with a wail. His feet, legs, and side were punctured and bleeding. He screamed again, yanked the spikes out of his side and lifted his sword to charge. Another step, and he froze. Spikes were everywhere.

"How dare you attack me at a time of mourning," Tao Hing said. "The Old Grandmother just passed away, and you Green Dragons are already looking for a fight. Get out of my way! I have an important message for Wei Xu."

"Refer to him as Lord Xu, you insolent old fool!" Stump shouted.

"The message is about the jade dragon."

"Jade dragon!" Stump lowered his sword. "What do you know about the jade dragon?"

"I said before, the message is for Wei Xu only. Let me pass!" The old man's voice was like thunder. Stump's men eyed each other for support, and then began to step out of the way. Tao Hing circled his horse around, moving to the side of the road to avoid the spikes on the ground. His men followed.

"We'll meet again in three days, Stump," Tao Hing said with a laugh. "You're coming to the funeral, aren't you?"

Stump staggered to the edge of the road, pulling the remaining spikes out of his foot and legs while swearing under his breath. His eyes were red, murderous.

In a moment, Tao Hing and his group of mounted warriors were gone. Stump spat on the ground. He screamed at his men while mounting his frightened horse. They formed a single line and trotted past the buried spikes in the snow.

"Jade dragon . . . " Suthachai said. "The old man said something about the jade dragon!" He suddenly stood up.

"What are you doing?" Li Kung whispered. He glanced at Stump, no more than thirty steps away, assured himself that the Green Dragons didn't notice, then turned to say something. But the Mongolian was already gone.

"Where did he go?" Pun asked.

"I don't know. But he's in no condition to run so fast. Let's go. We need to find him. He's after the old man with the long hair."

"He'll never catch them. They're on horses, and he's poisoned and on foot."

The last of the flickering Green Dragon torches disappeared from view, and Li Kung ran out into the open. He pointed down the road in the direction they were traveling just moments ago, and prepared to chase.

"What about the spikes?" he started, changing his mind and turning around.

"The spikes?"

"They're still in the snow. People use this road every day. They'll get hurt."

"But . . . " Pun glanced quickly at the snow. "Make me a torch. I'll find the spikes while you go after the Mongolian. We can meet later at the Blue Lantern Inn."

Li Kung looked at her in amazement. "You want to split up? You're not afraid he'll hurt me?" He smiled and took her hand. "You trust my judgment."

"I trust your medical judgment," she said with a pout. "You said he's in no condition to run, which means he can't hurt you. If you really want to find him, you need to go now."

He reached over, took her hand and drew her to him. She collapsed into his arms. "Be careful," she said.

"I will," Li Kung whispered into her ear. "He's far from home with no one to help him, and he's very sick. We should at least try to help."

She nodded, reached up and squeezed his tall nose. "Make sure he doesn't cut you in half."

Li Kung laughed. He grabbed an old branch from the ground, covered it with green powder and ignited it. The flame roared for a second before calming into a steady ball of light. He handed it to Pun, then turned and hurried down the road.

For a long time, Li Kung trudged through the narrow trail, often stopping to catch his breath. He found Suthachai on his knees, hunched over in the middle of the trail, a small pool of dark blood around him. Li Kung crouched down and peered into his face. The Mongolian was pale, shaking with intense pain and dripping with cold sweat.

"Why did you run?"

"Jade dragon . . ." Suthachai managed to say.

Li Kung pulled out a small porcelain jar and handed it to his new friend. "Take a couple of these pills. They'll give you strength."

Suthachai struggled to lift his body. He planted his saber deep into the snow for leverage, twisted his body, and somehow climbed to his feet. He took the little jar from Li Kung's hand and uncorked it, dropped two pills into his mouth, and returned the jar.

"Keep the bottle," Li Kung said. "Should be at least nine more in there. You're going to need them."

Suthachai nodded and hid the jar in his pockets. "Jade dragon," he said again, his voice weak and lifeless. "The old man said something about the jade dragon. It is mine. My grandfather gave it to me."

"Your grandfather? No, no. You made a mistake. The jade dragon belongs to the Dragon House. It's their ultimate symbol of leadership."

"It is the same jade!" Suthachai leaned forward, stronger now. "The ugly woman with the tumor stole it from me. The carving is like the three-headed dragon symbol—we saw it in the salt fields. It is the same dragon symbol. Identical to the candles that poisoned me. Whoever has my jade also has my antidote!"

"I see," Li Kung said softly. "You had their jade. In Mongolia. From high in the barbaric North . . . "

"We need to find the old man with the long hair. He knows where the antidote is."

"He went to the Garden of Eternal Light."

"Then we go," Suthachai said, tucking the saber inside his coat.

"We can't go there. It's an island in the middle of Lake Eternal, and it's heavily guarded. And Lake Eternal never freezes, which means we'll need to ride one of their boats. It's impossible. Come, I need to show you something. It's about the jade dragon."

• • •

"Stone tablet?" Suthachai asked, much later. "At the floor of this lake?"

"Yes, the lake is almost completely dried. There's a poem on the tablet about the jade dragon, and how it could be found in the barbaric North. They say the gods engraved this poem down there."

"How much longer?"

"Soon. We'll be able to see it when the moon is directly above us. It's right under the ice."

They were seated at the bank of the lake, staring at the moon's reflection against the frozen surface. The pale, silver glitter of the ice accentuated the mysteriousness of the night, appearing ghostly, like a dream.

"The Chinese have a saying about the moon in the lake," Suthachai said. "'The moon in the water, the flowers in the mirror.' My grandfather told me when I was very young, but I did not understand."

"It's an old Buddhist saying. The moon in the water and

the flowers in the mirror. They both symbolize illusions, like all worries in life. Mere illusions of what's real."

"Even if you are about to die? Is that also an illusion?"

Neither of them said anything, then. The moon rose quickly, and the reflection against the frozen lake became smaller. Nothing stirred.

Li Kung shifted his body and turned on his side. "Why did you come here? Just to find out? To find out who did this to you?"

Suthachai's voice was hollow, distant. "I thought there might be a cure."

"There might be. Every element has a counter element. We'll find something."

"I will not have enough time to find it."

"My mentors will help you. We'll be there tomorrow morning."

Li Kung turned to face the lake again and noticed the reflection of the moon had changed. He lifted a long, rotted branch and tapped it on the ice.

"Your home is far away?" Suthachai asked.

"My home's in the South. It's always warm and you can see the ocean within a half-day's walk. Our mansion was large enough to house a hundred guests, so when we held banquets, our dining hall could seat six hundred people. And—" He paused, almost as if a sharp memory had washed over him, covering his eyes, his soul. Suddenly he was lost in thought. "I haven't been home in many years."

"Why?"

"I . . . " Li Kung couldn't go on. "I've been here, in the North, for about a month now," he said, changing the subject. "We came to find a poison."

Suthachai turned to him, sitting up. "A poison?"

"A strange alchemy. We heard that a new type of alchemy appeared in this region, more cruel than anything ever seen."

"How does it kill?"

"It doesn't."

Suthachai laughed. "What good is a poison that does not kill? It is like using a whip as a weapon. A man cannot die from a weapon used to punish cattle."

Li Kung shook his head. "They say it's magical. It's worse than death."

Suthachai was fully alert then. He turned his entire body to face the younger man. "A poison that is worse that death. Similar to what poisoned me?"

Li Kung shook his head. "This one is strange, and it can do strange things to you. I heard that a person is able to fly after they've taken it."

"Really?"

"But they don't really fly, they only feel and think that they're flying. Some people see very strange things. They lie on their own beds, they go far away to a distant land, and they meet the gods in the heavens. But when a man takes it, he can never stop taking it. He becomes dependent, and he wants more, and he will soon become a slave to the man who feeds it to him."

"I have never heard of such a thing," Suthachai whispered. "And the alchemy will never kill the man?"

"I don't know. So far, no one has died from it."

"Who is doing this?"

"It's a secret. My mentors went to the only village it was rumored to be in, but they found nothing."

"What village is this?"

"Pan Tong Village."

Suthachai planted a hand in the snow. "Pan Tong Village? Did you say Pan Tong Village?"

Li Kung stared.

Suthachai leaned back. "The entire village is dead. Everyone died in their sleep—not a chicken or a dog or even a cat was spared."

"They died in their sleep? How could that be?"

Suthachai clenched his fists. "I think they were poisoned."

"How did you? What were you . . . ?"

"I saw it with my own eyes. There was no sign of struggle. They looked so peaceful, like they were sleeping. But it could not be the same type of poison you are looking for, because this one was quick. It's a poison that killed right away, not a magical alchemy."

"What in the world could have killed off an entire village?"

"The woman with the metal flute—she is a monster."

The moon reached the height of the winter sky, but neither of them seemed to notice. The cold air suddenly became much colder. Li Kung leaned back against the snow again, muttering something.

"What did you say?"

Li Kung paused.

"You mentioned a poison-user," Suthachai said.

"Just rumors. I heard of a great poison-user serving under the Red Dragons. People say that if the gods were to become poison-users, they would study under him."

"Really! Then he must have an antidote for my poison!"

Li Kung became excited again. "Yes! Maybe he can . . ." But his expression darkened. "If there is such a person, he's probably the one who poisoned you. There could be no one else."

"Maybe it is! Maybe he is the one who poisoned me. But if he has an antidote, I will beat it out of him! Red Dragons?"

"That's what I heard," Li Kung said. "He serves the Red Dragons."

"The Red Dragon House—who are these people?"

"It's a long story."

"I have time," Suthachai said. "I don't have much time left, but I have time for a story."

Li Kung nodded. "I don't know the whole story, just pieces from local storytellers."

Suthachai was staring at the lake, his eyes half closed, as if he were in a daydream. Li Kung followed his gaze. "We have to wait for the moonlight, I guess. Well, here's what I know. A long time ago, there was only one Dragon House in this land. Back then there was famine everywhere. The government was corrupt, and careless, and every time a flood struck this region, thousands would perish. But the Dragon House was strong and virtuous. They organized the people, raised money, and sent their men across the country to bring back food and supplies. They fought the famine. They helped people rebuild their homes and farms, almost replacing the government here. Heroes from across the country came to join the Dragon House. People prospered under their leadership."

"It is different now," Suthachai said.

"Very different. The Dragon House split thirty years ago when the leader died and the twin brothers fought for the throne. The younger twin, Master Bin, formed the Red Dragons, and he controlled the original *zhuang* on Redwood Cliff. The older brother, Wei Xu, now known as Lord Xu, formed the Green Dragons and built his *zhuang* in an island in the middle of Lake Eternal. It's not far from here. The two Dragon Houses hated each other ever since. Many branches of the original Dragon House broke away. They didn't recognize either of the twins as the true inheritor, since the in-

66

heritor must have the jade dragon, but neither of them had it. I heard that their territories were reduced by half."

"The jade?" Suthachai was alert again. "What about the jade?"

"It's the seal of the House. The one who possessed the jade was the true leader."

"But my grandfather had it. Until the woman with the flute stole it from me."

"Now, one side will rightfully absorb the other, but not without a fight. There will be a new wave of violence in the Martial Society. The jade coming back is bad news. Bad news." Li Kung sighed. "I heard that this lake had been drying up for years. Then came the drought last year, and an old fisherman found the stone tablet. Everyone said it came from the gods. It described exactly where to find the jade. When the old fisherman discovered this stone, it was embedded in the floor of the lake. The stone must have been there forever—underwater plants grew around it and some plants grew right through it."

"Someone must have planted the stone. How could anyone carve words while holding their breath?"

"Some people dived down there to feel the words," Li Kung said. "And the edges were smooth. Any new engraving couldn't be that smooth, only stone eroded by water for many years could be that smooth. They say the stone has been there for two generations."

Suthachai jumped to his feet. "I have to see the poem."

Li Kung observed the position of the moon, then at the reflected light from the icy lake. "I think we can see it now."

"You said this stone told the Dragon Houses to look north for the jade dragon?"

"North to the land of the nomads."

Suthachai stepped onto the ice, tapped it lightly with

his boot, and began gliding toward the center. Li Kung tried to follow but slipped on the first step and landed hard. He struggled to his feet.

"Near the center of the lake? Did you say near the center of the lake?"

Li Kung managed to stand, and took a tiny step forward. "Straight in front of you. Don't worry about me, I'm right behind you."

Suthachai didn't turn his head as the freezing wind slashed through his hair and pierced him—but he moved like he was possessed. Far behind him, Li Kung tiptoed with tiny steps toward the middle of the lake.

"Here? This?"

Suthachai stopped above a mammoth stone slab underneath the thick ice. Suthachai pulled out his saber, and, using the point, pounded the surface, sending thousands of tiny fragments into the sky. Li Kung approached carefully, pieces of ice raining on him while he watched the Mongolian beat the frozen lake to pieces.

With a splash, the ice caved into the water before floating back to the surface. Suthachai backed away from the hole that he punched. More ice collapsed, revealing a large opening of clear water. He tested his footing, dropped to his stomach and stared into the water.

Though raindrops fall like dying flies
Though people fear the moon at night,
The leaders of the greatest House,
By destiny, should long unite.

Flying high in the barbaric North,
The dragon soars without regret.

Acquire the jade and rule henceforth,
We see the dragon in the sky.

The elements of life,
In five directions.
The great leader must arm them,
between Heaven and Earth.

Facing East, the archer points,
Man on Earth points back.
The nine dragons speak to us,
He will answer, as a god.

Tonight, the jade dragon sits waiting,
The true ruler to claim his right.
Across the desert he'll seek destiny,
Though people fear the moon at night.

The lake was not deep but the words were clear. Suthachai lay face down on the ice with his four limbs spread apart. "Flying high in the barbaric North . . ." he muttered to himself, the frost from his breath dissolving into the air. "Acquire the jade and rule henceforth . . . "

Li Kung finally caught up to him. He placed a hand on the Mongolian's shoulder and looked down at the stone tablet. It was huge, magnificent, deeply embedded into the floor of the lake and partially covered with algae and vegetation.

"The gods planted this here," Suthachai said under his breath. "Only the gods knew where the jade was. Only they could have sent this to the bottom of the lake."

PROPHECY THREE

Two soaring dragons know no regrets,
With filial piety as vanguard.
Both deaf dragons were not forewarned,
They ascend the white wolf's lair.

By early morning, every household in the city of He Ku displayed articles of mourning. A grand funeral had been arranged for the Old Grandmother, to be held in three days at the designated burial sites of Redwood Cliff. Word had spread that the recovery of the jade could spark renewed violence in the Martial Society. Fear permeated every household.

Li Kung and Suthachai arrived at the Blue Lantern Inn the night before, as expected, and found Pun already asleep in one of the two rooms she rented. By late morning, all three were well rested and set for travel.

The day was bright and warmer than usual. Suthachai felt strong and walked briskly through the forest, always a few steps in front of his new friends.

"Tell me about your mentors," Suthachai said.

"Three old men, gone completely mad," Pun piped in.

"Don't say that," Li Kung retorted. "They're not mad. In the South, they're known as the Three Saints of Yunnan."

"But in the North," Pun said. "They're known as the Three Lunatics of Yunnan."

"My mentors are hermits," Li Kung said. "And people don't understand them."

"Hermits?"

"They live in seclusion, away from politics and excess. They live simply."

Suthachai stared at the ground. The nomads of the Mongolian steppe also lived simply, and separate from the world. Perhaps Li Kung was describing a deeper form of seclusion, like the kind experienced by his grandfather. Why would anyone choose to live in such hardship and loneliness?

"We're here," Li Kung said. A large house, void of decorations or embellishments, stood before them. "This is where we live."

There was a subtle sound. Out of the corner of his eye, Suthachai saw the snow on the ground fly up in flurries, and he slid back, drawing his saber with lightning speed and slashing out. The figure of a man shimmered past him and stood safely at a distance. It was a wrinkled old man, bald, his filthy beard completely white, his beady little eyes curved with joy. He had a long face like a horse's, the size of his nostrils competing with his gaping mouth, his chin enormous.

"You're good," the old man said. "But how would you know which direction I'm coming from if you're blinded by snow?" He swept the ground and sent a towering wall of snow into Suthachai face. Suthachai closed his eyes, stood completely motionless, listening for movement. In a moment, the snow cleared from the air and Suthachai saw the old man standing far away again.

"Shifu Three," Li Kung said. "Stop! This is my friend."

The old man jumped up and down, opened his mouth

in a burst of wild laughter, and clapped his hands with joy. "Excellent! Just excellent! I haven't seen anyone this good in almost thirty years! He didn't even move! Let's try something new. Now, what if your opponent is always changing his distance? Then what are you going to do?"

Li Kung tried to step between them. "He's been poisoned!"

By then, Pun was giggling so hard she held her stomach and doubled over. "I bet . . I bet you've never seen a lunatic . . ."

"A blue-tinted face!" The voice was powerful, eager. Another old man appeared and took Suthachai's hand. He was even uglier than the first old man, with a short, round face and bulging, bright eyes. His beard was equally filthy, his long hair thinly scattered. "Poison!" he said. He placed three fingers on Suthachai's wrist. "How lucky you are. There's only a minuscule amount in your blood. For such powerful stuff, you should have died fifty times."

The first old man slapped the other's hand. "He's my guest, Old Two. He came all the way from Mongolia to challenge me, so don't you interfere!"

Suthachai turned to Old Two. "What did you say about my poison? Is there a cure?"

Old Two laughed. "You see, Old Three, he's more interested in my medicine. He's not here to fight. Go away!"

"No, that's not true. The Mongolian wants to fight."

Old Two reached out and slapped Old Three, who covered his bony cheek in shock. "How dare you slap me?"

"I'm the older brother! I do what I want! This Mongolian is coming with me!" He turned to Suthachai. "Come. Come this way. I can see you're interested in poison. I have eighty-one different types of poison in the back room. Let me show you."

"His condition is grave," Li Kung said, running up from behind. "The poison's already in his liver."

"Shut up, boy. Of course it can wait. He's only vomiting blood. You can start worrying when the blood is coming out of his nose." He tugged on Suthachai's wrist again. "Come, let me show you my poison collection. I have scorpions, snakes, venomous toads, some very toxic peacock's gall—"

"When I bleed from my nose?" Suthachai asked. "Is that when it is too late?"

"No, when blood gushes out of your ears, it'll be too late. Come."

Li Kung stepped in again. "I've already tried to treat him with—"

"I know what you've tried," the old man retorted. "I taught you."

"You couldn't teach him anything better!" Old Three shouted from behind.

"What do you mean?"

Old Three threw his head back, pointed a crooked finger at his brother, and laughed. "He couldn't defeat a cockroach in battle. He studies your foolish medicine. Now, ask him how he would save himself with *your* skill when an army of five hundred come charging down that hill over there?"

"Don't worry, they're completely insane," Pun whispered into Suthachai's ear.

"Then go teach that boy how to fight!" Old Two shouted. He turned to Suthachai.

Old Three slipped in front of them like lightning, crossed his arms, lifted his massive chin, and said, "You don't expect my weakling brother to walk past me like I don't exist."

"Listen, you old fool," Old Two said, increasingly impatient. "How can I pretend you don't exist? You're louder than the rooster outside my window every morning."

"I'm not old! You say that one more time and I'll pound your head like a clove of garlic."

Old Two broke into laughter. "Talk! All talk! You don't dare hit me! Old One will have your neck if you touch me! I'm your older brother. You don't dare hit me!"

Li Kung pulled on Suthachai's sleeve. "Shifu Two is a great doctor," he whispered. "I'm sure he'll be able to cure you. Let's wait for him inside."

"You know, Old Two. You're almost ninety years old. How much longer do you think you'll live? What good is this medicine going to do for you then?"

"You're going to be ninety soon yourself. You still think you can fight like a young man? Even if you beat every warrior in the world, how much longer do you think *you'll* live?"

Pun scrambled after Li Kung and Suthachai, each backing into the house. They closed the door behind them, but the voices of the two old men could still be heard. "They'll stop in a little while, and they'll be brothers again," Pun said.

The back room was bright, with cloth sacks stacked to the ceiling, porcelain jars and wooden boxes scattered everywhere—on old shelves, on the floor.

"These are my mentor's herbs. He gathered most of them himself."

"None of the jars are labeled," Suthachai said. "How does he know which one is which?"

"Somehow he does," Li Kung said. "I even remember most of them. And once the jar is opened, he recognizes them."

The door swung open and Old Two hopped in, a grin on his face. "Old Three backed off and apologized," he whispered. He held a finger to his lips to indicate silence. "Don't tell him I told you he apologized or he'll start shouting again." He winked mischievously to a giggling Pun, then ran over and took Suthachai's hand. "Come. Let me examine your pulse again."

Suthachai looked back at Li Kung, glanced at Pun's concerned face and hesitated. This was it. He traveled all the way from the other side of the desert in search of an answer with little time left. Old Two's warm fingers pressed against his pulse, and he closed his eyes.

The silence was unbearable. To Suthachai, each breath felt like a subdued scream, an exaggerated moment of torment. Old Two's fingers remained on Suthachai's wrist, for what seemed like forever.

"This is not going to work," he finally said with a smile. "Nothing is going to work. You're going to die."

"Is there nothing you can do?" Li Kung asked.

"I can. I can ask Old Three to kill him, and that'll end the pain early. Death is not that bad if it's painless, you know."

The Mongolian's eyes flashed fire, and he stared, speechless. Li Kung placed a shaking hand on his shoulder. "We'll try something, Suthachai. There has to be another way."

Old Two opened his box of herbs, pulled out a large needle, and reached for Suthachai's hand. "You don't need this blood, right? It's full of poison anyway. Might as well give me some."

Suthachai broke from his trance. "What was that?"

"I'm saying, you're going to die anyway. Why not give me some of your blood. I can use it to poison a couple of rabbits, and I can try some new prescriptions on them. You don't need so much blood."

Suthachai looked at the old man, at the red face, the white hair, the wide grin. "Blood?" he whispered. "You want blood?"

"That's right. I've tested with bear's blood and chicken

blood. But nothing like yours. Yours is toxic. I really should try with yours."

Suthachai trembled, shook until his clenched fist rocked against the table. "Blood," he said in a cold, quiet whisper. "Warriors have traveled hundreds of miles and fought armies to seek my blood. But none of them were good enough. And you want it so easily?" His voice tightened, the heat swelling in his chest. He continued to shake, his voice barely audible. "You want my blood? Call your brother to come and fight for it!"

"You need to rest," Li Kung said, trying to lift him. "Here, take one of the pills I gave you."

Suthachai spun around and smashed Li Kung across the face, sending him flying back and crashing into the floor. Pun leaped across the room to Li Kung's side.

"What are you doing?" she shouted.

Suthachai shook for a brief second, his eyes distant, the poison suddenly overwhelming his sense of judgment. He toppled over, unconscious. Li Kung scrambled to his feet, backing away from the fallen Mongolian. His mentor hurried over with a porcelain bowl. "What's happening?" Li Kung asked, shaking.

"Come. Let's get the blood."

"Don't go near him," Pun shouted. "He's dangerous!"

"What did you do to him?" Li Kung asked.

Old Two seemed annoyed. "Haven't you learned anything yet? When you want to find out anything about anyone, you read his pulse."

Li Kung reached over cautiously and placed three fingers on the Mongolian's wrist. "Did you just poison him?"

"No, I'm only helping him get some sleep," the old man chuckled. He looked at Li Kung, at his frightened eyes, and laughed harder. "Come and help me. We can't allow such valuable blood to go to waste. Look at him. He wanted to fight, just like Old Three. And he didn't want to give me any blood, even though he doesn't need it anymore. How selfish."

The old man pierced Suthachai's arm once, then raised the elbow to flow his blood into the bowl. Li Kung watched in amazement.

"Come and help!" Old Two barked.

. . .

Old One's thin, bony hand placed a Wei Chi chess piece on the board in front of him. He was ancient, his luxuriant silver hair tied neatly behind him.

Sitting on the other side of the chessboard was a man almost as old as him with shabby white hair and bushy eyebrows. He wore a dirty coat that had never been washed. "I'm going to win this time," he said with a light chuckle. "Just wait and see."

Old One lifted another white piece. "Is it my turn, Old Huang?"

"It certainly is."

They were in a small round pavilion, on the top of a steep hill with narrow steps extending to the very bottom. Only four red columns formed the pavilion, with an arched roof of broken tiles and a little stone table in the middle. Nothing shielded the two men from the wind.

Dangling from a steel frame in the pavilion was an old metal pot, a glowing fire pit underneath it. Steam was spewing from the mouth of the pot. The hot water was ready. Huang reached down to a pile of logs next to him and began feeding the fire while Old One carefully opened his pouch of tea leaves. He chuckled. "My little student is just in time for tea."

Li Kung slowly, painfully reached the top of the hill. He paused to catch his breath and wipe the sweat from his brow before stepping forward to bow. "Shifu One. Mr. Huang."

"Your mentor is losing the game and I'm in a great mood," Old Huang said.

Old One laughed. "You know, Old Huang, I should've moved here sooner. We could've been playing together for the past sixty years."

"And Lady Wu was alive then—the three of us would play all night."

Hot water was poured into a clay pot. Li Kung sat by the stone table and placed a cup in front of each person, then opened the basket he brought with him and lifted two bowls of rice. Plates of vegetable and bean curd followed.

"Excellent!" Old Huang said. "We have good tea, hot food."

"Can't play chess without a full stomach," Old One said. Li Kung placed chopsticks in front of them while they rubbed their hands in delight.

"The tea should be ready," Huang said. He stuffed his face with food.

"Eat," Old One said to Li Kung.

"I already ate before I came."

"Pun cooked this?"

"Yes."

"Pun's a good girl. You should marry her when you have time."

"I . . . I'll try," Li Kung stuttered.

Huang laughed. "Only young girls are shy when faced with the topic of marriage."

In a short time, every scrap of food was gone. Li Kung packed the dishes into the basket.

Old One chewed on the last piece of bean curd, looking

at Li Kung with interest. "From the frown on your face, I would think you didn't have anything to eat yet."

Old Huang stood up. "I need to relieve myself." He walked briskly down the hill.

Old One turned to Li Kung. "You were gone for a few days."

"I went to see a patient with liver disease. It didn't go well. The patient died."

Old One poured himself a cup of tea.

"I met a Mongolian yesterday," Li Kung said. "He's been poisoned and I don't think he'll live more than a couple more months. Even Shifu Two thinks there's no hope. There may be one more chance, but . . . " Li Kung paused. "But I don't know if I should help him anymore. He's a violent man. I don't know if saving him would be a good thing."

"Have I ever told you the three great philosophies in life?" Old One asked.

"I don't believe so."

"Well, let me tell you now. One: you must eat well. Two: you must sleep well. Three: you must shit regularly."

There was a long silence. Old One sipped his tea.

"I . . . I don't understand."

Old One chuckled. "If you try too hard to figure this out, you'll lose sleep. If you're too busy helping people who didn't ask for help, you won't have time to fill your belly. And I know for sure, people who try to save the world will die of constipation."

• • •

Li Kung gazed into the horizon. Far away, in the dreary distance, at the same elevation of the mountain he was standing on, was Redwood Cliff.

At the foot of Redwood Cliff was the small cluster of houses, White Clay Village, where he had visited the Red Dragon salt fields just a day ago. Millions depended on the few salt suppliers in China. The Red Dragons had the capacity to distribute anything they wanted, and they could reach the far corners of the world.

He settled his eyes on the top of the distant cliff again. The buildings on Redwood Cliff were large and encompassing, with scores of structures built to house the members of the Red Dragons. It was a city unto itself, almost half the size of He Ku, a self-contained society of warriors that formed the most powerful House in the land.

Li Kung thought of Shifu Two's face that morning, at the anxious and disappointed glint in the old eyes.

"It's not the same," Old Two had said. "Not even close."

"You're sure?"

"The Mongolian's blood is toxic. But this new alchemy is far more destructive." Old Two wiped his tense face. "It can spread!"

"Like disease?"

"I don't really know." For once, Old Two appeared solemn. "We need to find out."

Li Kung had never seen Shifu Two so serious before. The moment he took Suthachai's blood, the old man disappeared into a back room that only he used. When he finally re-emerged, his face covered in filth and sweat, the old man was different.

"We need to find out," Old Two repeated, but this time, his face relaxed. A casual smile returned to his face. "And besides," he continued in a saucy tone, "I've run out of things to do, but I have some more years to live. Where am I going to find my next pastime? Since I'm going to have fun, I might as well do a good deed on the side."

Much later, Li Kung stood by himself on a nearby mountain and stared at Redwood Cliff in the distance. It was bustling with activity, radiating with arrogance while reaching high into the clouds. Those on its surface looked down upon the world.

Shifu Two needed a small sample of the alchemy—something for him to work with. Then, perhaps the old man could find a counteragent. It must be on Redwood Cliff, hidden with the legendary poison-user. No other poison-user in the world could create something so powerful, so deadly, so evil. He would go home to fetch Pun, and maybe Suthachai, and they would find their way to the surface of Redwood Cliff.

With a deep sigh, Li Kung turned away to descend the mountain, and maybe to find an antidote for Suthachai.

. . .

By the time Li Kung returned, Suthachai was already awake and armed, standing tall in front of the main door. His skin was ghastly pale, his face occasionally twitching, perhaps in pain, and the layer of cold perspiration on his forehead made him appear feverish. Li Kung approached with caution, the bruise on his left cheekbone still stinging.

Suthachai's eyes widened. "How did you bruise your face? Did someone hit you?"

Li Kung paused. "What do you mean?"

Suthachai lifted the heavy saber in his hand and pointed the butt of the handle to the side of Li Kung's face. "The bruise," he said, his eyes suddenly sparking with rage. "Who did that to you? I will kill him."

"No one," Li Kung replied, looking away. Suthachai didn't remember what he did. Perhaps the poison is destroying his mind as well. "No one hurt me," Li Kung said again. He pointed toward the door. "Come inside. I have something to discuss with you."

Suthachai shook his head. "I am about to leave. I was waiting for you, to bid farewell."

"Farewell?"

"I will never repay you for helping me. I am going to die soon. But I want to say thank you before I leave."

Li Kung took a step forward. "Where are you going?"

"Your mentor could not cure me. My only chance is to find an antidote myself. I will go after the poison-user on Redwood Cliff."

"Good," Li Kung said. "I'll go with you—let's discuss how we'll disguise ourselves. Come inside."

• • •

"The Old Grandmother died," Li Kung said, once inside. "I heard she'll be buried next to her husband the day after tomorrow. So many people from the Martial Society will be there. And Lord Xu will be there."

"Green Dragons?"

"Thousands of them. But we can infiltrate. We'll disguise ourselves as Taoist holy men. There must be hundreds of them hired to pray and chant at the funeral."

A glimpse of a smile briefly appeared on Suthachai's tortured face.

"We'll leave at dawn," Li Kung said. He handed another small porcelain bottle to the Mongolian. "Some more pills, for the journey. You'll need them."

The door creaked open. Pun peeked in, glanced at Li Kung, then at Suthachai, and stepped in with a smile. They seemed to be on good terms. She jumped onto Li Kung, and threw her arms around him with a cry of joy. "I know! I heard. We're going on a trip!"

"You heard? You were outside all along?"

She gave him a sly look and a wink, then turned to Suthachai. "I need to discuss something with you."

The Mongolian nodded.

"Is it true?" Pun began, holding her nose. "Is it true that you Mongolians only bathe three times per . . . lifetime?"

Suthachai nodded again.

"What?" Li Kung grabbed for Pun's wrist, but she slipped away.

"Three times," Pun said again. "Once when you're born, once before your wedding night, and the last time after you're dead."

Suthachai nodded again. Pun covered her mouth and couldn't contain her giggles.

"Are you married?" she asked.

Suthachai shook his head.

"So it means you don't know what it's like to bathe?"

"You Chinese are strange," the Mongolian finally said. "How many people could drink the water you waste cleaning yourselves?" He turned and said as he walked out, "I will be ready first thing in the morning."

Pun ran to the door and then turned to Li Kung with a big smile. "I bet you I can get him to take a bath before we leave." She ran off and left him shaking his head.

. . .

The journey to Redwood Cliff could have been long, tedious, and plagued with silence. Dressed in silk Taoist robes and armed only with religious articles, Li Kung and Pun walked slightly behind their barbarian friend at all times.

Yet, Pun chattered endlessly along the way about how difficult it was to borrow the Taoist robes from Old Three, who refused to loan his old clothes because he was not invited to join. When they approached He Ku, Pun tugged on Li Kung's sleeves. "Do you smell something different?"

"Smell?'

Pun giggled. "He took a bath this morning."

She laughed and danced around the Mongolian for a second. By late morning, the three entered the gates of He Ku.

The streets of He Ku were full and alive like the day before. Articles of mourning still hung on every storefront, but no one seemed to be mourning. Children laughed and played, running about while their parents shopped at the busy marketplace. Vendors yelled at the top of their lungs to attract attention to their products, and carriages bustled about the streets, carrying the wealthy citizens around the city.

At noon, they decided to stop by an inn to eat, with plans to reach Redwood Cliff by early evening. Seeing the Taoist garbs and anticipating a vegetarian fast for a ceremony, the innkeeper came by to offer the vegetarian dishes of the house.

"A gourd of wine, two goat's legs, and a baked chicken," Suthachai said without hesitating.

The innkeeper looked at him for a second, unsure of what to say, then muttering to himself, returned to the kitchen.

"Will someone find me an empty seat?"

All eyes turned to a blind man standing by the door, his long walking staff extending into the inn. The waiter quickly ran to his side.

"This way please, Mr. Fan. We have an empty seat right here."

85

A fat woman clapped her hands in delight. "Oh, Mr. Fan is here! What story are you going to tell today, Mr. Fan?"

The blind man ignored her and seated himself. "The usual," he said to the waiter. Another waiter had already brought his food and wine to him. He smiled.

"Ah, the smell of sorghum wine!" He lifted the cup to his lips and breathed in the aroma. "Such good wine on a fine day."

Out of nowhere, the inn became very crowded. People trickled in from the street and seated themselves to hear Mr. Fan's story. Those who couldn't find seats stood in the back against the wall. They waited patiently for Mr. Fan to finish his wine; crowds of children sat on the floor in front of the blind man, while the waiters hustled to serve everyone at once.

"A story!" Pun said. "I haven't heard a good story in a long time."

"I've told this story many times before," the blind man began, his arms waving dramatically in front of him. "But today is such a fine day, and I should tell it again. I will tell a story about Snow Wolf."

Li Kung stopped eating. The entire room was cheering and applauding. Snow Wolf's name was well known in the North. He had seen paintings of her, sculptures carved in her image. He had heard that she saved the lives of thousands, and for many years, she had protected the region from invasion, from bandits, from corruption and rebellion. He had seen people worship her, speak of her teachings, pray to her for blessings.

The blind man held up his hand to quiet the audience. "All of you have heard of the great Snow Wolf," he continued, his voice exaggerated. "But not many of you know about the time she single-handedly fought off the pirates from the

East. Known as Lady Wu when she was young—but few people now know her as Lady Wu—Snow Wolf was barely forty then. The pirates who came from the Eastern oceans were short; they set their hair like a wet towel and wore sandals on their feet instead of shoes. Their language was strange. Every word sounded like they were barking at someone. Nevertheless, they were feared—yes, they were feared. When their ships were seen on the horizon, fishermen rushed through as many villages as they could, screaming at the top of their lungs: "The pirates are here! The pirates are here!"

Mr. Fan's voice raised in volume. The children's eyes widened. "And the pirates would come into the villages, and rape and plunder everything they could, and by the time any government troops could arrive, they were safely back at sea. No one could stop them. No one, except Snow Wolf.

"When Snow Wolf first arrived at the coastal towns, the pirates had just left. Villages were burned, women were raped and beaten, men who tried to resist were slaughtered. The pirates stole all the grain they could find, and this time, they killed twenty government officers and promised to be back in seven days to collect a sum of gold—or else more people would die.

"The provincial government sent hundreds of troops to the border in response. The young commander of this little army was proud and over-confident, but inexperienced. He deployed his men on a hill facing the ocean and waited for the pirates. He thought that when the pirates charged up the beach, his troops would blare down on them and be victorious because of their sheer numbers. The hill they camped on was full of dense foliage, with tall trees at the top. Scouts were placed high in these trees to watch for the pirates."

Mr. Fan's voice became more intense. "The troops scattered themselves in the thick bushes of the hill and waited and waited. Soon they were running around playing shooting games, because day after day the pirates, numbering no more than a hundred, did not come. But Snow Wolf warned the commander that the pirates were near, and they were watching, waiting for them to relax. Snow Wolf told the soldiers that they must change their positions at once, because even though they had the advantage of numbers, they were in plain view. They didn't have the advantage of surprise. But the commander would not listen to such great wisdom! He was foolish! And that brought about his destruction.

"Snow Wolf knew then that defeat was imminent, and she returned to the bordering villages and began organizing the people. She found fifty men, strong and willing to stand up and fight the enemy. She organized thirty women, and she asked them to lace several carriages and chests with silk. In the following week, the entire village made thousands of sand bags, and together with Snow Wolf, dammed the Chang Shu River.

"Meanwhile, the pirates left their ships far from view and approached at night by rowboat. They quietly circled to the back of the hill and gathered behind the government troops. The men were sound asleep, with the exception of the few scouts looking out at the ocean—but little did they know the pirates were already behind them! Then the slaughter began. The pirates climbed up the back of the hill and silently came down the front. They killed every single government troop on the hill. No one was spared. After the massacre, they anchored their boats offshore and marched toward the villages. It was right before dawn."

A look of horror gripped every face in the audience. Mr. Fan's gestures became even more dramatic. "And they marched. They saw a group of women and a few old men pushing carriages into a small road by the forest. The boxes on the carriages were laced with fine silk, a sure sign of wealth. Seeing the women and what they thought was their gold, they pursued. The women quickly disappeared into the forest, and the old villagers ran the opposite direction. The pirates chased, but the foliage was thick; they heard the sounds of the women again and again but could not see them. They pursued and ran deeper and deeper into the forest.

"Meanwhile, Snow Wolf brought ten men and rowed into the hazy waters. They quietly boarded the pirate ship, killed the few pirates left on board, and burned everything before rushing back into the forest.

"The pirates on land eventually came upon the wooden chests, abandoned deep in the forest. But the women were nowhere to be seen. Thinking the villagers were scared away, the pirates pried open the boxes—only to find them completely empty. Now they knew they fell into a trap! The leader gathered all his men and rushed back to the beach. And what did they find at the beach? Their ships burning, of course! They could not believe it! They thought they killed all the government troops. Didn't their scouts report that there were no more? Who could have done this?

"At the gray of dusk, they saw torches everywhere, surrounding them. There were thousands of them dancing on a hill. Light from the torches swarmed the land like flies on a dead deer, and war drums were beating. Seeing an opening on the left side of the hill, the pirates ran for their lives. And the torches? Not troops, my children, but villagers, led by Snow Wolf. All the villagers were there: the women, the children, all of them. They each held two torches to create the effect of massive numbers. The pirates could do nothing but flee—but everywhere they ran, war drums sounded in front of them, and the torches followed. They were finally chased to a river, a wide river almost completely dry. Or so they thought! They tested the waters and assumed it was shallow enough for them to wade across. In the panic of the moment, they scrambled into the river and tried to cross. That was when they heard three loud beats of the drum, in perfect rhythm, followed by three more. There was a shout at the top of the river, and the fifty men pulled the sandbags. Every one of the pirates drowned."

The blind man paused, and his voice became slower and deeper against the deafening silence. "So that was how Snow Wolf destroyed the pirates that harassed the Eastern coast for so many years. She used villagers—civilians consisting of women and children—instead of trained warriors. She killed the fearsome pirates without the loss of a single innocent life. She heard about the suffering and pain of the common people, and she answered."

The audience stood up to applause. Mr. Fan produced a tin bowl from his coat and placed it on the table. One by one, the people in the inn stepped forward and placed a coin in his bowl. Fan bowed and thanked them.

Pun also came forward to pitch her coin. "Mr. Fan," she said, "so where's Snow Wolf now?"

Everyone stared. The blind man smiled. "Young lady, you're not from around here, are you?"

"No, sir."

"Well, fifty years ago, Snow Wolf ascended the heavens and became a goddess. She's watching over us now, much like how she watched over us before. She's up there, and if you pray to her, she will answer."

• • •

The road to Redwood Cliff was unusually busy. Thousands of people traveled across the land to pay their respects, effectively cluttering the only road to the Red Dragon *zhuang*. Men and women walked with heads bowed, afraid to speak, each careful not to display anything but sorrow. Their carriages and mounts, with men in the forefront and servants in the rear, resembled an endless wave of refugees. Li Kung and Suthachai maintained a low profile in their Taoist disguises—even Pun was silent.

The burning rays of the afternoon sun illuminated the side of Redwood Cliff. The frontal surface of the cliff was vertical, barren, with neither a single branch nor a protruding rock that could be used as a foothold. The peak of Redwood Cliff reached far into the clouds, with the only path to the top guarded by an army of warriors impossible to penetrate.

Near the foot of the cliff, Li Kung noticed armed guards, each dressed in dark red, watching every person. He stood on tiptoes, peered over the shoulders of men in front, and breathed a sigh of relief. They were not the same guards from two days ago.

In a moment, they approached the main entrance. Li Kung lowered his head in deep lament and steadily followed.

"Taoist priests?" one guard asked.

"Yes."

"Taoist priests from where?"

Li Kung stalled. Pun stepped forward, her lips pouting. "We're from the Realm of Immortal Senses on Mount Hua."

"Mount Hua?'

"I can't believe it!" Pun exclaimed. "A guard of the famous Red Dragons doesn't know the Taoists on Mount Hua?"

"Of course I do! But Mount Hua is so far from here. How did you . . . ?"

"Our master summoned the White Phoenix of the Western Paradise to carry us here. He was a childhood friend of the Old Grandmother, and he conjured up such magic that it left him seriously ill, all so we could arrive here on time!"

The guard gulped and without another word waved them on. Li Kung thought he heard someone behind him announce, "Master Liang of the White Tiger school." He glanced back to assure that Pun and Suthachai were closely behind. "Welcome to Redwood Cliff, Master Liang." No one paid attention to them anymore.

Beyond the main entrance was an endless spiral of steps, chiseled into the stone that wrapped the front and side of the cliff. The stairs were so steep that those ascending had to lift their knees above their waists in order to reach the next foothold. There were no railings or barriers along the outer edge, and the vertical drop from the side seemed to reach down forever.

"Are you tired?" Pun asked, watching the sweat flow from Li Kung's brow.

"I can make it."

Suthachai showed no signs of fatigue. He took large, bold steps, pausing only to wait for Li Kung to rest. In front of them, the marching caravan of warriors maintained a constant speed.

Redwood Cliff was like a peninsula, not surrounded by water but by a sea of clouds covering the world below. The summit was cold—colder than the darkest of winter nights at the base of the cliff.

The sun began its descent when the three reached the top of the cliff. Stretched in front of them was a stone-paved road that led to numerous building clusters. These buildings were not tall, though large and solid, each emitting its own sense of grandeur. The mansions built by the side of the cliff were so enormous they seemed capable of housing hundreds. Armed guards were everywhere. Many stood beside the main road, personally greeting each guest before leading them to their lodgings for the night.

Li Kung bowed to the warrior that approached them.

The warrior returned the bow. "Taoist priests? This way, please."

He walked toward one of the mansions. Li Kung stole a glance at Pun, then at Suthachai. Both of them seemed to be thinking the same thing. What an incredible display of wealth and power!

• • •

The burial ceremony was to take place the following morning. After a brief rest, the guests were called to pay their final respects to the Old Grandmother. The sun had lowered itself below the horizon, leaving behind a glow of golden twilight on the surface of Redwood Cliff. Li Kung, Pun, and Suthachai followed the crowd to the main hall, behind a long line of mourners already outside the doors.

The main hall, located on a hill, was immense. Its tremendous doors were like gaping mouths that faced the clouds beneath. From the road outside, behind a long line of people, Suthachai could vaguely see a coffin at the far end of the hall.

Each guest was ushered into the room, followed by a gong signal to bow to the closed coffin. Senior warriors of both Dragon Houses stood inside the hall, all of them in mourning attire. They respectfully bowed back.

A bearded man stood in line behind Li Kung.

"Taoist priests?" he asked, his eyes on Suthachai.

"Yes," Li Kung responded.

"You must've come from far away."

"From a distant province."

The man broke into laughter. "Just a word of advice for the young and inexperienced. Don't look directly at the Red Dragon princess, or you'll be in deep trouble."

"Why?"

A thin man, standing behind the bearded one, stepped forward to join the conversation. "You're sure you don't know? Don't lie. You must've heard. Master Bin wants no one staring at his daughter. Otherwise . . . " He laughed. "Otherwise it'll be dawn before we pay our respects to the Old Grandmother!"

"Why would I be staring at Master Bin's daughter?" Li Kung asked.

Suthachai leaned closer to listen.

"Stop pretending," the bearded man said. "Half the people here are hoping for a glimpse of her."

"Master Bin's daughter Fei Fei," the skinny one pitched in. "They say she's so beautiful, he had to pluck out the eyes of his servants—or they would be staring at her day and night!"

"Really?"

"You're just a boy," the bearded man said with a sneer. "You wouldn't understand!"

They laughed. Li Kung grumbled and resumed his position in line.

The bearded man was still snickering when his smaller companion elbowed him in the rib and flashed a glance to the side. The bearded man froze and eased into a solemn expression of lament with his eyes lowered and hands folded.

Suthachai noticed that every person around him had fallen silent, with heads lowered, looking away as if afraid of something.

A tall warrior dressed in short robes, carrying two

swords, one on each side of his belt, walked past them. There was absolute quiet until he was gone.

"The Butcher," someone whispered in the background. Li Kung turned to the bearded man. "Who was that?"

"The Butcher," the bearded man said, no longer coarse and taunting. "He's Master Bin's famous assassin, even more dangerous than the Flute Demon."

"Someone tall and skinny called the Butcher?"

"He doesn't butcher animals."

Night fell. Each followed the procession with head down, lost in deep thought. Much later, Suthachai, Li Kung, and Pun finally found themselves in the main hall.

The coffin was dark chestnut, buried in layers of white flowers. Standing closest to the coffin were two middle-aged men, both of them striking in appearance, each commanding an imposing presence.

Suthachai kept his head bowed, eager to finish the formalities without bringing attention to himself. Out of the corner of his eye, he caught a glimpse of a woman beside the coffin. His eyes traveled involuntarily to her, her long black hair, petite nose, pouting lips. He noticed her lean figure wrapped under the garments of mourning, her large, almond eyes staring blankly into the distance, as if thinking of a loved one, lost in a world that she could not share.

Suthachai's heart pounded out of control. Her eyes reminded him of the soothing wind on the Mongolian plains, of the endless grasslands and the morning dew while he galloped toward the first rays of dawn. In her eyes, he saw a lonely soul standing against freezing rain, a woman troubled but strong, lost but unyielding. He could almost touch her cheeks, her full lips, her breath warming the frozen air. Never in his life had he seen anything so beautiful.

Her eyes turned to him, and his heart stopped. "Beauty

that could destroy entire kingdoms . . . " he seemed to hear his grandfather say. In a moment, she looked away.

The guests were given the signal to bow. Both Houses returned the bow in unison, and the guests were ushered out of the hall. Suthachai wanted to look back—just to catch another glimpse of her would have made his life worthwhile. But there were too many people, too many guards. They were hurried out the side door.

• • •

Back in the guest lodgings, Pun folded all three Taoist garbs and placed them in small bamboo baskets by the bed. She replenished the oil lamps, closed the windows, and returned to her own room.

Suthachai was already in bed, huddled against thick covers. "Did you see the girl they were talking about?"

Li Kung looked up. "You mean Master Bin's daughter, the Red Dragon princess? I didn't notice. Did you see her?"

"I did."

"As beautiful as they say?"

Suthachai sighed. "More. Much more."

Li Kung shook his head with a smile. He moved to the window, pushed it slightly open and peered into the heavens. The sky was clear, the moon was high. He tucked a large canvas bag into his robes and turned toward the door.

The Mongolian lay quietly on the bed, expressionless. Under the dim light, Li Kung watched Suthachai's eyes slowly close, as if his soul had left him for a faraway land, a better land. Then, faintly, a smile appeared on his bluish face, like ice rising to the surface of a pond.

Li Kung frowned. He may not be able to save this man. The poison-user was the only chance he had.

Li Kung slipped into Pun's room and found her curled up in bed, fast asleep. He lowered the canvas sack he was carrying, tiptoed to the candle in the middle of the room, and extinguished it. He knelt before her bedside and stroked her long hair, her full cheeks.

"Pun," he whispered. "I'm going to look for the poison."

She moaned in her sleep and turned away from him. He brushed her lips with his long fingers, and leaned forward to kiss her earlobe. "I'll be back before you wake up."

He retreated from the bed as quietly as he could, picked up his canvas sack and inched out of the room. She was tired, and he wanted her to rest well. He breathed a deep sigh. He needed to rest too. But there was no time for that. Once outside, he slowly closed her door, threw a coat over his shoulders, covered most of his face with a cloth shawl, and began walking.

His movements were swift but cautious, staying in the shadows, veering away from the guards in the distance. When he was alone in the dark, Li Kung reached into his overcoat for the canvas bag and held it for a moment like a child before pulling apart the drawstring. The head of a little brown monkey appeared.

Li Kung's monkey was named Peppercorn. Long hours were spent training her to search for the unique scent of arsenic, which every poison-user would keep in abundance. The poison-user of Redwood Cliff could be nothing other than a great alchemist. A simple stash of arsenic should not be hard to find.

Peppercorn climbed out of the bag and peered left and right for a moment before dropping to the ground. She leaped across the icy snow.

Li Kung followed on light tiptoes. The monkey pranced through the darkness on all fours, pausing here and there to smell her surroundings, often stopping to wait for Li Kung. She climbed to every window, peeking inside like a child looking for candy, then reluctantly loped to other buildings, other windows.

For a long time, Peppercorn scrambled about. Sometimes, guards with bright lanterns patrolled the main roads, and they huddled in the shadows until they passed. Often, the slightest sound inside a window would send Peppercorn scurrying into Li Kung's arms, and they would hide together, in darkness, until the world was silent once more.

But the monkey found nothing. Much later, Li Kung placed Peppercorn back in the canvas bag. All buildings on Redwood Cliff were concentrated by the edge of the cliff, and they had covered most of it. Why couldn't they find the walnut smell of arsenic? He observed the cluster of concentrated buildings, the dense pine trees lining the side of the cliff, the dark, eerie forest by the Grand Stairway.

Then it came to him. A great poison-user would practice in solitude, would never store his unique creations where hundreds of people passed each day. He must practice somewhere hidden, quiet, unnoticeable.

The northern side of the cliff, densely engulfed by pine trees, lacked roads. All activities on Redwood Cliff seemed to point away from the north. Li Kung cradled his monkey, took a deep breath of icy air, and slowly headed north.

The pine trees were unnaturally tall. Their hovering arms formed a canopy, completely covering the sky, leaving him no light from the moon. Li Kung closed his eyes, his arms outstretched, and stumbled across the icy earth. Soon. He'll find the poison-user soon. Then what? What would he do then, against the greatest poison-user across the land?

A pavilion appeared out of the darkness. It seemed abandoned for decades, with the red paint on its four main columns cracked and faded. It was slightly elevated by five marble steps; grayish, almost ghostly in appearance. Li Kung absently opened the canvas bag.

Peppercorn tested the frozen ground, shook her small brown head, then scampered away. She was on to something.

Li Kung ran on tiptoes, breathing in short, quick gasps, straining to keep up. Peppercorn didn't stop to wait for him this time.

Moments later, a bare pine tree loomed before them. The monkey paused, sat on her hind legs and gawked at the tree. The branches had already fallen, and pine needles darkened with decay littered the ground. It was clear that the tree died recently, perhaps no less than a year ago. It rested against a small hill of hard earth and stacked boulders, the trunk so massive that four men couldn't wrap their arms around it.

The monkey inched toward the tree, stopping every two steps to wait for her companion. Li Kung stepped past her, reached into his pockets, produced a silver stake, wiped it on his coat and stabbed it into the tree.

The dead bark gave way, and the rotted wood underneath yielded with a soft crumbling sound. Li Kung yanked the spike and stared. The silver had turned black. The tree was toxic.

Li Kung circled behind the trunk and noticed fallen pines accumulated behind it. He hid Peppercorn in his coat again, peered around the trunk, and discovered an opening in the rock barely large enough for one man to squeeze into, but unmistakably an entrance to a tunnel. He drew his pouch of green powder, bundled together some dry twigs, which he sifted the powder onto, and in a moment, held a blazing torch in his hand.

The descent into the tunnel was slippery, the rocks covered by moss and slime. It led into a damp room.

Steel urns and ovens occupied most of the room, with newly built shelves lining all four walls. There was a familiar smell of herbal debris in one of the urns. He trembled with excitement. This was it. This place was too well hidden for the production of ordinary medicine.

He couldn't believe his luck. Redwood Cliff was a known fortress, impossible to penetrate, and the few who actually visited never found their way without a guide. Now, with only the help of a tiny monkey, he was able to locate a room so well hidden, and so secretive.

Li Kung directed the shimmering light to reveal row after row of porcelain jars, all in different colors and sizes. He stabilized the torch in a crack between two urns, pulled many tiny pouches from his pocket and reached for the closest jar. There was no way he could take a sample from every jar in the room, and he didn't know what the elixir looked or smelled like. There was no choice but to grab a small handful from as many jars as he could.

At the other end of the room was a sub-den too low for a child to walk into. Li Kung dropped to all fours, waved his torch inside, and noticed wooden boxes, stacked neatly with cloth seals around them. He crawled in, picked up a box while lying on his back, and began unwinding the seal.

"Why are we here, Master Bin?" The voice came from the tunnel. Li Kung froze. Someone was coming. He dashed the torch into the ground and extinguished it, then curled himself into a ball and waited. Peppercorn scratched his coat, and he silenced her with a firm pat.

"It's private here. Too many people on Redwood Cliff tonight." It was a younger but overpowering voice.

Li Kung could see the light of a bright lantern coming through the tunnel. Soon, two men emerged and stepped into the room, one leading the other.

Li Kung felt himself growing weak. He recognized them both. The middle-aged man was Master Bin, leader of the Red Dragons and commander of Redwood Cliff. Li Kung had spotted him in the main hall just after sunset. There was a silk fan in his left hand, despite the cold winter, which he rocked in front of his chest as a matter of habit. The spines on the fan were made of metal. Behind him was Tao Hing, the old man with long white hair and a general's splendor, who, two days ago, dropped spikes into the snow to ambush Stump.

"Who can be out at this time of night?" Tao Hing asked.

"Maybe a Green Dragon is snooping around," Master Bin said, seating himself on a long bench and extending his hand for Tao Hing to do the same. "Maybe Black Shadow."

Tao Hing chuckled. "And what chance do we have of stopping Black Shadow if he's here on Redwood Cliff? No one's ever lived to describe how fast he is. Although, the last I heard, Wei Xu couldn't find him. Maybe he's not here."

"Black Shadow only appears when my brother's in grave danger, and there should be no reason to suspect danger at my mother's funeral. Everything will go as planned. Now, what exactly did you say to my brother?"

"I told him exactly what he dreamed of hearing," Tao Hing said. "He could hardly believe his ears."

Master Bin laughed a cold, eerie laugh. He closed his fan with a snap of the wrist and clapped it against his palm. "That brother of mine. How could anyone in the Wei family be so stupid?"

"I told him we found the jade dragon, and the Old Grandmother wanted us to share this leadership, and we must unite as one family and keep the wealth and power within the family. I told him it was your wish that he keep the jade—because he's the older brother—and we wish to live in peace. I told him you didn't want new shifts in power."

"And what did my brother say?"

"He was too pleased. He agreed to complete peace during the funeral, and he'll call a banquet afterward to discuss a truce."

Master Bin broke into a short laugh. "Excellent. Very well done. Although my brother's words can't be accepted at face value, of course. He's certainly here with a battle plan."

"Any battle tomorrow would lead to massive loss of life," Tao Hing said. "This'll be the first time in many years our two Houses will stand together in one place. It won't be easy."

"And what if the Green Dragons pick a fight?"

"I've instructed Old Snake to prepare a poison fog," the old man said. "It'll weaken, but not kill."

Old Snake! That must be the name of the poison-user. Li Kung craned his neck forward.

"Excellent!" Master Bin said again. "We can't risk a battle tomorrow, for the sake of our long-term strategy."

"Long-term strategy?"

"I see my old strategist is not aware of the long-term strategy. Well, this is it. The medicine we create in this room."

"I don't understand," Tao Hing said. "We already dominate the salt business—and salt is always in high demand—but that didn't make us supreme leaders of the Martial Society. What can we accomplish by selling an herbal tea?"

"You'll see soon enough. Everyone will buy our tea, even the Green Dragons—even my dimwit brother. You'll see. Tao Hing, would you notify our men? Any hostility from our side means execution. We'll shorten the ceremony, host the lunch in separate banquet halls, and they'll leave peacefully by mid-afternoon."

"Sure," Tao Hing said with a bow. Master Bin stood up to leave.

"Rest well tonight," Li Kung heard him say. In a moment, they were deep inside the tunnel. Master Bin's voice echoed with a low tremor. "We all need to be wide awake tomorrow."

The silence broke in so abruptly Li Kung felt like he was in a dream. The room was pitch dark, and for a second, he thought he was blind and deaf. Somehow, he found his pouch of green powder, ignited the bundle of branches, and, shying away from the stinging light in his hand, clambered out of his hiding place. The porcelain jars seemed to stare at him, and he looked away with a shudder. These were the ingredients to the tea Master Bin spoke of. Could it be the elixir that he came to find?

He needed a sample from every jar on the shelves. His cloth pouches, lined with multiple pockets, were already pregnant with ingredients from the room. He barely collected half of what he found.

Time seemed to freeze when there was so much to find and so much to know. Li Kung struggled to relax his hands so his cold fingers could peel off the sheets of waxed parchment that he had prepared. Perhaps the residual compounds would give Old Two a hint of the actual specimen. He began to smear portions of the herbal mixture from each urn, his eyes turning often, waiting for another light to emerge from the tunnel. Would Master Bin unexpectedly return?

Time was not on his side. It never was. He gathered his pouches, secured them inside his coat, and ran for the tunnel exit. Near the narrow opening, he threw down his torch and extinguished it before emerging into cold air.

The ground was heavily frozen. It yielded no footprints and made it difficult to retrace his steps. But once he found the strange pavilion again, he would recognize the pine forest to the south.

The air was even colder than before. The wind lifted out

of nowhere and tore through the pine trees; his ears were so numb he could hardly hear the screams of agitated wind. Metallic silver reflected from the millions of silver needles around him, waiting to pierce him, waiting to draw his blood. He began to move slower, his head down, his back hunched over, fighting the powerful gusts that struck him again and again.

Out of the corner of his eye, Li Kung saw a weak, yellow light emerging from the woods. His heart stopped. Guests were not allowed outside the mansions. Being caught would mean the end.

He spun around, gasping for air, searching for a place to hide, when suddenly, he realized that the old pavilion was behind him all along. He had found his way, but that didn't matter now. He recognized the yellow lantern—the Red Dragon night patrols carried them, and with the stolen herbs bulging from his pockets, he wouldn't survive one stroke of a Red Dragon sword.

Li Kung scrambled for the pavilion. Behind it was a small ledge of dirt and cobblestone, with a drop no taller than the height of two men. It was a hiding place. Li Kung saw his chance and jumped. The whistle of a gust of wind muted the sound of his landing. He crouched low, and prayed.

Li Kung watched the lantern brighten, began to hear the large, bold footsteps of an approaching man. The ledge was too shallow, even if he lay flat on his stomach. He could be exposed.

Then he saw it—a tiny opening between the rocks, almost completely hidden underneath the ledge. It must be another tunnel, like the one behind the massive pine tree. He crawled toward the opening, climbed in feet first, and lowered himself downward. But he couldn't feel the ground underneath. He kicked and couldn't find footing. Perhaps there was a slight drop into the tunnel, he told himself. He dangled from his arms, stretching to reach the ground, and slowly felt himself weaken.

Li Kung closed his eyes and allowed his hands to slip.

He thought he heard himself gasp and he felt his heart skip a beat when he realized that he was still falling—the pit was very, very deep. With a dull slap, he felt himself land on soft sand, felt something jolt into his throat, felt his bones rattle against the impact, and saw the yellow light somewhere above him become very, very dark.

. . .

"Peppercorn!"

Li Kung reached into his coat for the canvas bag. The drawstring was open. She was nowhere to be seen. "No!"

He groped the sand around him, tears in his eyes. She must have fallen out of the bag during the drop. He blindly combed the sand for her body.

There was not enough light to see anything, not even the soft soil underneath him. He stopped, exhausted, and sat back, wiping the sweat from his brow. The opening he fell from appeared tiny and distant, and for the first time Li Kung realized how deep the drop really was. Peppercorn could not have fallen so far from where he landed—perhaps she saw the ground earlier and landed safely.

He was convinced his monkey was still alive, and he felt relief from the thought. He pulled out a small knife and severed the left sleeve from his coat, twisted the thick wool, shaped it into a torch, and lit it on fire. The flame roared, then tapered into a comfortable size.

He suddenly noticed the face of an old woman in front of him. He gasped, nearly dropped the torch, and stumbled back in panic. Her eyes were closed, her pale face shriveled and dried, her white hair caked with dirt hanging over her face.

The old woman flicked her wrist and he felt a sharp pain in his knee. A pebble rolled onto the soil. He collapsed.

"Stop looking," she said, her ancient voice hollow. "There's no way out of hell."

Li Kung held his knee with one hand, lifted the torch higher with the other, and stared. "Who . . . who are you? What did you just do to me?"

"I threw a stone at your kneecap. Massage it for a minute and you'll walk again."

Li Kung gripped his knee and climbed to his feet. He took a step toward her and she lifted her hand, another stone held between her fingers. He froze. Her legs were amputated from the knees down. Her eyes remain closed.

"So, young man," she said. "After a hundred years, you are the first to visit me here. I've been speaking to the rats to practice my human voice, but they never respond. It's destiny that you came to be my companion."

"Who are you? Where's my monkey?"

"Oh, so it was a monkey. I thought it was a massive rat. Enough food to last me for days. I hit it with a stone. Softly. It should be awake soon."

Li Kung lowered the torch, saw Peppercorn on the ground not far from him, and crawled over to scoop her into his arms. The little monkey opened her eyes, frightened for a moment, before snuggling against his chest.

"Where am I?"

The old woman chuckled—it was a strange chuckle that sounded like she was clearing her throat. "You wouldn't know my name. As for where you are? I lost my eyesight in the darkness long ago. How could I tell you?"

"But you're so accurate when you shoot the stones . . . "

"Snow Wolf taught me that. I can hear exactly where you are. Now, tell me young man, how many years have I been down here?"

"Snow Wolf taught you?" Li Kung leaned forward. He checked himself, aware of the stone in her hand. "I don't know how long you've been here."

"You don't know? But you can see daylight! How can you not know?"

"I don't know when you came down here."

"I didn't come down here, I was kicked down here!"

Li Kung shrank back.

"Now tell me!" she said, her voice cold. "How long have I been down here?"

She lifted her hand, a much larger stone between her fingers this time. "Snow Wolf," Li Kung said quickly. "They say that Snow Wolf died fifty years ago."

"Fifty years?" The old woman was lost in thought. "At least a hundred years. I was thrown into this pit the same night she was murdered."

"Murdered?"

"Tell me young man, who's ruling the Dragon House right now?"

"The Dragon House? The Red Dragons are ruled by Master Bin, and the Green Dragons by Lord Xu—"

The old woman slammed her fist into the soil. "I knew it! The two idiot twins couldn't live with each other so they've split the empire in two. What about their mother? I hope she's at least dead by now."

"She just died," Li Kung said. "She was ill for many years. Can you tell me how I can climb out of this cavern?"

"Ill for many years . . . " A strange look of glee filled her face. "Tell me, young man. Did she suffer? Did she at least suffer all those years?"

"Her liver was almost useless for some time," he said. "But for years, she wouldn't die. She couldn't move, she could hardly speak, and she couldn't eat."

"She couldn't move," the old woman repeated slowly. "At least I can still move, even though I lost my legs. And I can still eat, even if there's only one way—to feast on gigantic cave rats—but I can still eat." She chuckled the strange, hollow chuckle again.

"Can you tell me how to leave this cavern?" Li Kung asked again. The torch he made out of his sleeve was almost used up.

"There's no way out of hell!" she shouted. "If there is, I would've gone out already! And screaming won't help—the noise will only irritate me. The gods can't even hear you down here."

Li Kung felt a chill run down his spine. He wrung his hands and swallowed to avoid making noise.

"You're shaking," she said with a smile. "Fear is good. Without fear, humans would all be reckless."

Li Kung tore off his right sleeve and began to twist it. "Is there no tunnel from this cavern, or any way I can climb up the walls?"

"So tell me," she continued, leaning forward with interest. "The two brats Wei Bin and Wei Xu now rule the Dragon House. Who claimed the jade from Fei Long?"

"Fei Long?"

"Ah, you don't know Fei Long either, of course. He was the leader. His wife, Lady Wu, was known as Snow Wolf. Understand?"

Li Kung touched the dying flame of his first torch into the new one, and the cavern was bright again.

"And Su Ling? Where's Su Ling now?"

"Who's Su Ling? And who are you?"

She laughed. "I'm a servant girl in the household. Lady Wu called me Little Butterfly. So, young man, and who are you?"

"My name is Li Kung—"

"Do I look like I care what your name is? What I asked you was, how did you fall in here? This is a banned area! You're not a member of the Dragon House. You're weak and pathetic, and yet, you've come through this forbidden pine forest. Tell me, it's still a pine forest out there, isn't it?"

"It is." Li Kung could not summon energy into his voice. He looked to his left, to his right, then behind him—and found only walls of smooth stone. There really was no way out. "I'm here for the Old Grandmother's funeral, and I got lost in the pine forest. I was trying to find my way out, and . . ."

"And someone saw you. You were trying to steal something and you were afraid of being caught, so you ran and fell in here. What were you stealing, young man?"

Li Kung hesitated. The old woman was unstable. She may destroy his samples if he revealed them to her. But there was no way out of this cavern anyway. The stone walls were cold and slippery, with no footholds. A sense of gloom hovered over him, and for the first time, it dawned upon him that he may be in here for the rest of his life. But the samples! He had to get the samples to Shifu Two. He climbed to his feet and a sharp pain flashed across the side of his head. He dropped to his knees.

"There's no way out of hell, young man. Don't pretend to be deaf!"

"I'm sorry."

"You were thinking about how to leave this cavern. Didn't I tell you there's no way out?"

"I . . . I was looking for some of the gold that they say

Master Bin stashed away," he said, trying to think quickly through the blaring pain. "I heard that he collected gemstones and . . . "

"Pathetic! How do you survive in the Martial Society if you don't even know how to lie? You smell of herbs from head to toe. You were sent to steal some medicine weren't you? Tell me, young man, what do you plan to do with this medicine? Who sent you?"

Li Kung's jaw dropped. A lie, he needed a lie. No one had ever taught him what a good lie should sound like. The pain pulsed through him. He gripped the side of his head. There had to be a way out of this cavern. He thought of dying in there, of eating rats that he would learn to catch with flying stones, of watching the tiny sliver of daylight above him each day until the darkness made him as blind as the old woman. He thought of the hundreds of thousands of families across the land that would suffer from Master Bin's poison—all because he couldn't get out of this cavern. A sensation of stinging heat trickled through him. Li Kung turned to face the old woman. "Snow Wolf sent me!"

The old woman froze, the faint color on her face rapidly fading to a stiff gray. Li Kung squeezed Peppercorn against his chest and bolted for the nearest wall. The old woman paid no attention to him.

Li Kung tossed the monkey to the ground and urged her forward.

Then, he sensed the old woman turn her head, and with a short scream, Li Kung leaped in front of his monkey. A small stone ripped across the air and struck him on his side. He shrieked in pain.

"Run!" he shouted. Peppercorn raced for the wall. Li Kung scrambled to his feet and charged the old woman, screaming as loud as he could. She cocked her head to hear the monkey, but Li Kung's screams overwhelmed every sound in the cavern. In a burst of fury, the old woman fired a handful of stones. Li Kung absorbed the pain, collapsed to one knee, and doubled over to vomit.

His monkey should have been at least halfway up the wall by now.

A new volley of stones slashed through the air and pummeled Li Kung at close range. His head swooned, his vision became foggy, and slowly, he sank into the soil. Far above him came a soft chirp from Peppercorn, and he smiled through the pool of blood in his mouth. He couldn't find a way out—but Peppercorn should.

The waiting seemed like eternity. The old woman was quiet, listening to his breathing. Yes, she could take his life now. But the most she would gain from killing him would be additional meat. He pushed himself up on one elbow. The fire that he created earlier had completely died, and the cavern was pitch black. He thought he saw stars through the tiny opening above.

The old woman moved closer to him, pushing herself forward with her hands. Li Kung lay still and waited. Maybe she decided she could use the extra meat after all.

The old woman moved beside him and leaned forward with a bony finger to touch his forehead, tracing the contours of his eyes and nose.

"A very young man," she said. "So much courage for someone so young." A stiff smile emerged through the maze of wrinkles on her face. "You think your monkey can find help?"

She touched his head again. He shut his eyes, waiting for her to kill him, for her to crush his skull under her bony fingers.

"Silly boy. I didn't strike hard. The pain will go away."

But she did strike hard. Hard enough to kill Peppercorn. He lifted his body and edged away from her.

"You're a brave boy. When help comes, I'll let you leave. Don't be afraid."

Li Kung didn't believe her. He checked his pockets, certain that all his samples were safe, and touched his body for broken bones. There were none.

"While you're waiting for help, let me tell you a story," the old woman said.

A story . . . What did she want from him? He needed to vomit, but couldn't find the strength to lift his body. With a painful sigh, he curled himself into a ball.

"It was so long ago . . . " he thought he heard her say. "Snow Wolf called me Little Butterfly then."

Li Kung closed his eyes under the weight of the darkness.

"I was her maid, but you know, I was also her good friend. She treated me like a daughter. I used to wash her clothing at the foot of the cliff, and Su Ling always came with me. Do you know Su Ling? Of course you don't. She rarely left the area. Snow Wolf was so happy her daughter and I were good friends. Little Su Ling was only eighteen then. She wasn't there that night . . . No, she wasn't there . . . But I always thought I was the luckiest person in the world, until that night." Little Butterfly's voice died out, and then with a painful shudder, resumed.

"Those in the Dragon House called her Lady Wu. Her husband Fei Long was the leader of the Dragon House, but everyone really looked up to Lady Wu. That year was a long, ugly winter. Redwood Cliff was frozen for months, and the whole province was starving. The imperial court couldn't care less about the people. The fat magistrate ate like an emperor, that disgusting pig. He hid in his palace with his ten concubines for the winter while everyone starved. I bet you he's in hell right now, and you know there's no way out of hell. Good thing Snow Wolf took all the food reserves from Redwood Cliff to give to the people. She was gone for months. I heard from these travelers, how she evacuated several villages at a time, and she moved people together so it would be easier to survive. She organized people to collect and dry firewood. She gathered the old and sick into large houses so they could keep warm together. I heard that people dropped to their knees to worship her when she arrived."

Little Butterfly smiled a strange smile of admiration. "At night, I gathered the bones and morsels left over from our dining halls, and I went to the edge of the pine forest to feed her wolves. She trained a beautiful pack of wolves. Each wolf could tear a man apart with one word from her. But even that didn't stop the monsters. She instructed me to take care of them before she left. And I did, and I waited for her to come back, because you know, Redwood Cliff is full of monsters. My only other friend Su Ling was never around. She took some of her mother's burden and she was out there trying to rebuild Pan Tong Village.

"The monsters . . . didn't I just tell you? There are monsters on Redwood Cliff. One of them was named Lin Cha. You know her as the Old Grandmother, but the witch's name is Lin Cha. Wei Bin and Wei Xu, her bastard twins, were already seven years old then. That witch Lin Cha had been eyeing the wealth and power of the Dragon House for some time. Her husband was Fei Long's younger brother—named Fei Xing, a fat, lazy slob who was always happy, the idiot. Of course, the witch Lin Cha wanted more. She knew she would never get anywhere if she stayed with him. So the witch drowned the only child she had with him, then seduced the great leader Fei Long and bore him two sons—the bastard twins Wei Bin and Wei Xu. No one knew about this.

By having Fei Long's children, she thought she could gain control of the Dragon House. But of course, there was still Fei Long and Snow Wolf."

"She planned to kill Fei Long and Snow Wolf?" Li Kung asked.

"I just told you, you bumbling idiot! There are monsters on Redwood Cliff. And when gongs were sounded in the middle of the night, I was the first to run to the center of the cliff. News was spreading everywhere: Fei Long fought the Scholar."

"The Scholar?"

"That's what I just said!" Little Butterfly said. "Don't waste my time if you're too stupid to understand. The Scholar was an imperial knight before he went insane. Legend has it that a fox spirit with nine tails possessed him, and he became an invincible fighter. He came to this region and founded the Sun Cult, and no one in his cult had ever been defeated. The Scholar and his followers hid out and were never found. They appeared when they wanted to appear, and they killed when they wanted to kill. That night, the rumors spread on Redwood Cliff. Fei Long fought the Scholar and was badly injured. No one saw him, and no one was allowed to visit him. His fat brother was by his side, and the witch Lin Cha, of course, was dispatching messengers to summon Snow Wolf. They said that the Scholar and his Sun Cult would attack any moment.

"I waited for Snow Wolf by the Grand Staircase. When I saw the men mobilized for this defensive, I was ready to cry. How many of our men were really working for Lin Cha? Why are they taking orders from the witch?

"Snow Wolf arrived out of nowhere. She showed up with her loyal men, and she gave them instructions. And then she took my hands, and she told me I was one of the few she trusted. She had a special task for me. She asked me to follow her men to the pine forest, and they would tell me what to do. Then she walked off to see her husband.

"So I followed her men, and I asked them what her plans were. They told me that when they approached the cliff, Snow Wolf noticed the same number of guards watching the Grand Stairway, and she prepared for the worst."

"Why?" Li Kung asked.

"Are you really that stupid?" Little Butterfly barked. "If there was an actual threat from such a strong enemy, Fei Long would either decrease the number of guards every hour, and show that his men were deserting, and make the enemy suspect a trap, or increase the number of men to show a robust front, and make the enemy hesitate. Snow Wolf knew her husband. If he were in charge, the defense would look very different. Something was very wrong."

The old woman exhaled, pausing to catch her breath. "I wish I could've stayed by her side," she continued, less excited. "The two men, they gave me Snow Wolf's instructions. It made me sick. My lady was in danger, but I was told to hide in the pine forest and help activate some traps she planted years ago. I should be by her side when she's in danger. I didn't really know what was happening.

"Let me tell you this, my boy, in case you don't have the intelligence to understand: Lin Cha is the most evil monster in the Dragon House, and her two bastard sons are no better. I had a strange feeling then. Everything was a trap for Snow Wolf. I left my post and ran off. Fei Long's quarters were in the middle of the pine forest, near the pavilion—I could still remember it.

"I ran to find my lady because I knew she needed help. But it was too late. Oh, it was too late. Snow Wolf never found Fei Long. Lin Cha had already murdered him in his sleep, and when Snow Wolf arrived, Lin Cha poisoned her, then stabbed her."

"The Old Grandmother murdered Snow Wolf?" Li Kung asked, his eyes opened in shock.

"Yes! I ran as quickly as I could, but when I reached the pine forest, the entire world was in chaos. The silver needles in the pine trees were raining down on Lin Cha's men. These men had gathered by the pavilion, you see. They ran and screamed in fear and pain because the pine needles shot out of the trees and pierced them.

"The earth was raining with silver needles. It was a magnificent sight. The silver was hurting my eyes. Of course . . . Of course! Snow Wolf planned this many years ago. She knew that one day, she would be betrayed by her own people! She knew, and she hid dart projectiles in this pine forest. And I saw her then. She was holding an open wound on her body. She was in pain, but she walked upright, and she was proud, calm, like an emperor. She made her way through the raining needles. The men sent to detain her huddled around the pavilion. Those fools wanted to avoid the poison darts. And they watched her walk away. I searched the area for Lin Cha, because I wanted so badly to see the look on her face while Snow Wolf escaped with her head held high. There was nothing she could do about it.

"After the attack, the witch's men didn't dare follow. Ha! What did they hear? What did they hear? Screams of course! The mansions on Redwood Cliff were on fire—all of them were burning down! Lin Cha's men were frantic. They were worried about their belongings, and they weren't listening to Lin Cha. I bet you she lost her voice that night ordering her men to go after Snow Wolf. The men tried to stop the fire, but not a chance! Snow Wolf's followers burned everything to the ground.

"And Snow Wolf quietly walked down Redwood Cliff; no one saw her in the thick smoke, and no one was capable of stopping her. But she was dying. The poison that Lin Cha used was the most powerful and cruel poison she could ever get her hands on. Snow Wolf was dying.

"As soon as the fire was extinguished, Lin Cha declared her husband the new leader of the Dragon House. Her two bastard sons were sole heirs. Fei Long and Snow Wolf were gone. The few who demanded to know what happened to Snow Wolf were executed, and very soon, no one said a word."

Little Butterfly stopped. Li Kung released a short breath, and then, in a resounding voice that seemed to echo against the cavern walls, she said, "The witch knew I was like a daughter to Snow Wolf. She tried to kill me, but only managed to cut off my legs. I fell into this cavern, and I've been here ever since."

Li Kung stared at the old woman in the dark. A faint glimpse of light seemed to flow gently into the cavern from the hole above. Dawn was upon them.

"If Snow Wolf were alive today, she would want the two twins killed like pigs. They're pure evil! Pure evil!"

Li Kung flinched, felt his back bathed in cold sweat. "What evil deeds are they going to commit?"

The old woman threw her head back and laughed a dry, tortured laugh. "Evil deeds, my boy. You see, Lin Cha molded her sons in her own image. They would betray anyone who ever trusted them for their own ambitions. They would even kill each other—yes, they would definitely kill each other. Snow Wolf knew this while she was alive, she even told me so. The twins will start wars to kill each other, and hundreds will die. And why? Why?"

Li Kung took a deep breath, his eyes still closed.

Little Butterfly laughed. "I can hear you breathing, you idiot! Now listen to me very carefully. Now that you know, you bear the responsibility of stopping them. You can't possibly let them kill thousands. You need to go out there and stop them!"

"Then what about you?"

"Me?" the old woman laughed. "You can't carry an old woman out of hell."

. . .

"Li Kung?"

It was Pun's voice. Li Kung scrambled to his feet, ran toward the cavern opening, where, high above him, the haze of early dawn brought vertical rays of velvet light, bathing him in warmth and hope. "Pun! I'm here!"

A thick rope dropped in next to him. "Li Kung! I can't see you! Just grab the rope and I'll pull you up."

Li Kung clutched the rope with both hands. He felt a sting from the bruises on his body, reminding him of the stones he was pelted with. He turned toward the middle of the cavern and stared into the darkness. Little Butterfly had already disappeared.

Eventually, he was pulled to the surface. Pun leaped into his embrace, tears in her eyes. Peppercorn climbed onto his shoulders and wrapped her little arms around his neck.

Li Kung peered into the cavern below him. The old woman was still down there, somewhere, without the use of her eyes or her legs. Should he bring her to the surface? But where could he take her? She could not survive on Redwood Cliff, and he would not be able to carry her down, especially now.

"Are you hurt? How did you fall in there?"

Deep in the distance, the hollow sound of funeral gongs reverberated across Redwood Cliff.

"I'm not hurt," Li Kung lied. At least his face wasn't bruised. "We need to go. I think I found what we came for."

"We can't leave now. We need to wait for the funeral to be over or we'll look suspicious."

Li Kung nodded. He severed the rope dangling into the cavern so no one would discover Little Butterfly in there.

Pun skipped through the pine forest with the monkey on her shoulder, endlessly chatting about how each guest was called into the courtyard before dawn and asked to line up in preparation for the funeral. She told him how Peppercorn came to her just in time, when she was about to leave the mansions, and how she was able to slip away in the confusion of the marching procession.

"What's wrong?" She peered into his face.

Li Kung was staring at the silver pine needles, now even more metallic against the morning sun. "She planted the entire forest because she knew there were enemies in the family. She came prepared. How could she have been poisoned?"

"What are you talking about?"

Li Kung shook his head. "Lin Cha murdered Snow Wolf? How is that possible?"

"Who?"

"Nothing." There was no time to tell her the story now. "When does the funeral begin?"

"Soon, I think." There was a tinge of disappointment in her voice. "There are so many people on Redwood Cliff this morning, I don't think we'll get close enough to see anything. Did you know that people continued to arrive all last night? People are still climbing those stairs this morning. The cliff will be so crowded people will get pushed off!"

Li Kung didn't seem to hear. Wei Bin and Wei Xu are

evil, and they must be destroyed . . . He clenched his teeth together until his jaws hurt. What if Little Butterfly was telling the truth and these two madmen had the inclination to kill thousands of innocent people? The alchemy . . .

"Do you know," Pun continued, "I heard two warriors talking this morning. They both agreed that people didn't come here because they wanted to pay respects to the Old Grandmother. They actually care very little about her. Members of the Martial Society are here because they learned that Master Bin found some jade. I wonder what this jade is all about. Could it be Suthachai's jade? But anyway, they said that because Master Bin has the jade, everyone wants to be his friend again."

The terrain began to slope downward, and swarms of people gathering together could already be seen. Pun raised her hand to shield the sun from her eyes. "Too many people," she said. "I heard the Red Dragons now claim the Green Dragons are their inferiors. They think the Green Dragons should accept orders from them and be driven like dogs. But Lord Xu's men think the Red Dragons are treacherous scum, and that the jade really belongs to the Green Dragons. I think they want to kill each other today."

Pun paused. Li Kung was not listening. She pinched him on the arm. "What are you thinking about?"

"Nothing, just . . . I saw something down there. I'll tell you about it later."

The pine forest was behind them, and far across the rocks, along the main grounds of Redwood Cliff, came ghastly sounds of weeping, of tormented wails and melancholy cries. They were mostly women's voices, and they screamed so passionately that for a moment, Li Kung almost believed that true sorrow filled the air.

A sea of people resembling a colony of ants paraded

through the barren terrain of Redwood Cliff. From the higher vantage point, Li Kung could clearly identify the twins, Master Bin and Lord Xu, walking side by side in front of the coffin. They were dressed in coarse white canvas, a white headband around their heads. Lord Xu was holding a silver bowl with a tall base, the water in the bowl high above his head.

"See that gold dagger in the Green Dragon master's topknot?" Pun asked.

Li Kung squinted and noticed a thin blade horizontally inserted into Lord Xu's hair, in place of a traditional jade pin.

"I heard this morning," Pun continued, "that he always dresses his hair with a gold dagger even though he's never stabbed anyone with it. What a strange man."

A train of people followed behind the coffin; close relatives of the Old Grandmother. Some of them tossed thin shreds of paper into the air, while others carried lanterns, fans, pavilion-shaped floats, or melon-shaped paper ornaments on a pole. They all walked respectfully, side-by-side, hands close to their weapons.

Li Kung's eyes panned across the barren rocks into an area where the soft soil rested under a thin layer of glassy ice. This was the destination. Below them, on an empty strip of elevated land overlooking the cliff, was an area containing multiple tombs. The gravesites were all built the same, with a solid cement dome behind the tombstone, and a wall erected in a semi-arch around the back. The tombs higher on the hill appeared older.

"The Old Grandmother will be buried beside her husband," Pun said quietly, pointing to an unfinished tomb in the middle of the hill. "They kept his grave unfinished so he could wait for her."

"Look," Li Kung said. "They haven't dug the grave yet. I wonder why?"

"I heard it's disrespectful to her late husband if they opened the ground ahead of time. It would be too close to his grave."

"Let's get closer," Li Kung said. He took her hand and hurried around the top of the hill overlooking the main stretch of the cliff. The line of mourners, with white flags high in the air, rapidly approached the designated gravesite. Li Kung pulled harder on Pun's hand. "Let's hide over there. We'll be in front of everyone, but they won't see us because we're high up."

They took a long, winding detour and hid behind a boulder.

"Can you see from here?" he asked.

Pun poked her head out and nodded. "They're right below us."

On the side of the cemetery was a stone furnace, and a blazing flame fed by fresh coal danced from within. A striking old man stood beside the fire, his long robe fluttering, his beard hanging loosely below his chest. The poison user, Li Kung thought to himself. Something about the old man: confident, alert, proud, standing next to a source of heat without a single weapon on him. He had to be the famed poison user.

Thousands of guests, with Master Bin and Lord Xu leading the coffin in front, began to enter the cemetery. Li Kung noted the faces arriving behind the two leaders, recognizing Dong and Cricket, Master Bin's two sons. The younger son, Cricket, though merely a boy, stood out to defend him only a few nights ago after he angered all on Redwood Cliff. He suggested that the Old Grandmother should be allowed to die, to end the pain, and the Red Dragons wanted to kill him on the spot. It was Cricket who persuaded Master Bin to release him. He would never forget.

Behind Lord Xu were also two younger men. Li Kung instantly recognized Stump and wondered whether his foot had recovered from Tao Hing's spikes yet.

The Butcher followed. Flanking the two Dragon House leaders were numerous armed warriors moving in tight clusters, only differentiated by their robes in deep red or light green. They carried broadswords, double-edged swords, spears, and heavy cudgels. The stout men carrying the cudgels wore red headbands.

Horns sounded. The sea of men halted in their tracks. An old Taoist priest stepped to the front, waving a white tassel above his head and shouting to the thousands. "The auspicious hour has arrived! Please open the ground for the final resting place of our Old Grandmother, Wei Lin Cha!"

Twelve muscular men appeared with shovels in their hands and began to dig the designated plot of earth. Soil was hurled high. The twelve men burrowed into the frozen ground.

The old Taoist priest then shouted. "We will prostrate ourselves in final respect and kowtow three times to the dead. Would the oldest son, Wei Xu, kowtow first!"

Lord Xu dropped to his knees and pressed his forehead to the ground.

"We need to get these samples to Shifu Two as soon as possible," Li Kung whispered into Pun's ear.

She shook her head. "There's no way we can get down now."

"Would the second son, Master Bin, please kneel!" The Taoist priest shouted at the top of his voice. Master Bin dropped to his knees.

"What if they find the samples on us?" Li Kung whispered again. "We'll have no chance of leaving Redwood Cliff."

"Would Lord Xu's son, Jian, please kneel! Would Master Bin's sons, Dong and Cricket, please kneel! Would the adopted son, Ho Tin, please kneel!"

There was a brief murmur among the guests at the mention of an adopted son being in a position of such privilege. Stump stepped forward to kneel.

The Taoist priest shouted: "Would the Red Dragon warriors, the Butcher, and the Flute Demon please kneel! Would the Green Dragon warriors, the Chaos Spearmen, please kneel!"

Li Kung peered into the distance, squinting against the sun now high in the sky, and watched a group of men with long spears, dressed in light green, prostrating themselves.

"Would the Red Dragon warriors known as the Gentle Swordsmen please kneel!"

"These are the elite," Pun whispered into Li Kung's ear. "I heard some men talking about them this morning. Any one of these elite warriors could take on twenty ordinary fighters by himself. You can imagine how powerful they are when fighting together."

"Would the Green Dragon warriors known as Thunder Broadswords please kneel! Would the Red Dragon warriors known as Red Headbands please kneel!"

"Where's Suthachai?" Li Kung suddenly asked in a loud voice. Pun clasped a hand over his mouth.

"I don't know," she whispered in response. "He was there this morning, but I slipped away with Peppercorn and didn't have a chance to tell him."

"Would the junior students of the Green Dragon House

and the Red Dragon House please kneel! Would Master Chen of the Tuo Shan House, among the guests, please kneel in respect to the Old Grandmother!"

One after another, each school of the Martial Society was called. Small groups prostrated themselves in response. Li Kung scanned the sea of warriors in front of him, hoping to find Suthachai, but the Mongolian probably hid himself in the rear, among the less significant schools, to avoid being discovered.

"Look!" someone shouted. "What is that?"

The twelve men backed away from the pit they were digging.

"What is that?" one of them shouted again.

Dong and Stump both leaped forward and stood over the opening in the ground. The murmur of thousands instantly swept across the surface of Redwood Cliff.

"You!" Dong shouted, pointing at the men with shovels, his thick eyebrows instantly knit together. "Come and take this out!"

"Yes, sir!" Four men ran back to the pit with their shovels, jumped in, and began to dig again.

By then, every man on Redwood Cliff was on his feet, with hands close to his weapon.

"What is it?" Lord Xu asked.

"A cauldron of some sort," Stump responded. "An old cauldron."

Master Bin stepped forward, the metal fan folded and rhythmically tapping his palm. "What's a cauldron doing in my mother's burial spot? Who's in charge of the cemetery?"

"Master Bin, I maintain this area," one of the men with the shovels said. "The ground was untouched this morning. No one has touched this plot of land for a very long time!"

"Look!" one of the men inside the pit shouted. "There are roots growing through the copper. It must be a hundred years old!"

"Nonsense!" Lord Xu fumed. "Bring it to the surface!"

In a moment, the four men lifted the copper cauldron out of the pit. The surface of the copper was green with decay and already crumbling. Parts of tree roots dangled from crevices on its sides. Both Dong and Stump took a step back and looked to their fathers for help.

"Open it," Master Bin said.

Dong glanced once at Stump before yanking away the rotted lid. Stump peered inside. "There's a porcelain urn in there. It's sealed with wax."

Dong pushed him aside, drew a knife, and sliced the cover off the urn. "A scroll!" he shouted. He pulled away the fragile cover. "There's a scroll in here!"

Another murmur swept across the surface of Redwood Cliff. Dong tossed the lid to the ground, shattering the brittle porcelain, and reached into the urn. "Let me see."

The scroll was made of thick cloth. Both Master Bin and Lord Xu moved forward for a closer look.

"Read it," Master Bin said to his son.

The guests fell silent and held their breaths to listen.

"It's an ancestral decree!" Dong declared.

"Read it!" Master Bin said again.

"At the passing away of my wife Lin Cha," Dong began. "I, Wei Fei Xing, believing that the Dragon House could never be united, and acting to prevent further turmoil within the family, hereby designate Wei Bin to be the new ruler of the Dragon House, and hereby order all possessions, land, and disciples that belong to my elder son, Wei Xu, to be surrendered immediately to Wei Bin. I also mandate my elder son, Wei Xu, to obey and submit to the authority of Wei Bin, and to henceforth fall under his command."

Stump shouted something and swiped the scroll from Dong's hands. "How dare you . . . " Stump's face was red, his eyes on fire. He couldn't finish his sentence. "How dare you!"

Dong took a menacing step; disregarding the thousands of eyes pinned on his every move. He lunged forward to snatch the scroll back. "Read the ancestral decree!"

Stump evaded. Lord Xu's son, Jian, who stood behind his father the entire time, leaped to the forefront with sword in hand. "Only a child would believe these lies. This is Redwood Cliff. A Red Dragon could bury whatever he wants here!"

Every Green Dragon on Redwood Cliff reached for their weapons.

The Red Dragons responded, partially drawing theirs.

Master Bin spun around to face his men. "Hold it! Sheathe your weapons!"

The Red Dragons obeyed.

"Jian, step down!" Lord Xu called.

"You saw the tree roots growing through the cauldron," Dong hollered. "Admit it! This is a legitimate ancestral decree written by our grandfather. How dare you call it a lie!"

"Silence!" Master Bin roared. He leaped to the front with one nimble step and shoved his son aside. "My Red Dragon students! My Green Dragon nephews! My friends in the Martial Society! Please listen to me!" He pulled the jade dragon from his pocket and held it in the air. "The ultimate symbol of power is here!"

Everyone on Redwood Cliff fell silent.

Master Bin clasped the jade with both hands. "But

it's my mother's wish that this symbol be offered to my older brother. I heard her instructions with my own ears. Now, does anyone dare dispute the final words of the Old Grandmother?"

No one responded. Dong stood with head bowed to the side, his thick eyebrows pressed together, his eyes wide with frustration. This sudden change of events brought the thousands on Redwood Cliff to utter disbelief.

Master Bin presented the jade to his older twin brother with both hands, his head bowed low. The older twin eyed his lifelong enemy with distrust. But he had no choice. With a forced smile on his face, he accepted the jade.

"Hypocrites!" Stump screamed. "Admit it if you're afraid of us! Why sneak in this pathetic ancestral decree?"

"Hold it!" Lord Xu shouted. But it was too late.

Stump clenched the opened scroll with both hands and tore it in half with one vicious rip.

Dong screamed, drew his sword, and charged at him. "You dare destroy the decree of my ancestors, you adopted bastard!"

Lord Xu, suddenly fearing for the safety of his adopted son, jumped forward with his hand up. "Hold it, Dong!"

Dong swung his sword, completely missing his uncle, but the damage was done. Every warrior on Redwood Cliff drew his weapon.

"Did you see how much dust came out of the scroll?' Li Kung whispered into Pun's ear. "It looked like powder!"

"What does that mean?"

In front of them, the silence of thousands amplified the unbearable tension.

PROPHECY FOUR

Death and power but a dance,
In a romance of murder and ruin.
Revelations quelled in silence,
As eggs bombarded the stone.

Stump glared at Dong with the eyes of a predator about to pounce on its prey.

The Red Dragons stood on the left side of the cliff, restless, tensely waiting for Master Bin to order the attack. On the right side, the Green Dragons had already drawn their weapons. The world was silent, frozen. Muscles were taut, fists and jaws were clenched, feet were firmly planted and ready to charge. The motionless sea of warriors stood like a fully drawn bow, straining to release a single arrow—a cough could have shattered the silence and brought about such bloodshed as never before seen on Redwood Cliff.

Li Kung saw the Butcher inch closer to Master Bin in anticipation of danger and realized that mayhem was inevitable.

There was something in Lord Xu's eyes, a strange confidence impossible for a man standing on enemy territory, faced with a battle no one could predict. Did he know something that Master Bin didn't? Perhaps the Green Dragons somehow infiltrated Redwood Cliff and planted the cauldron to start a war that would make them seem like victims but for which they were fully prepared.

Master Bin reached for his metal fan again, steadying his gaze on the mass of Green Dragons, all poised with hands on weapons.

Li Kung's eyes followed Master Bin's to the old man beside the furnace. The poison-user was ready. He turned to the thousands below him. Hundreds of guests were completely enclosed by two hostile Houses, and no one was concerned for their safety. There would be little time to reach the only path to the Grand Stairway. The guests belonged to inferior Houses, and Master Bin couldn't possibly bother with their survival. More than half would perish.

Stump suddenly shrieked in agony. His sword fell to the ground. His hands had become charred black, with dark blisters on the back of his palms. He stared at his trembling fingers in horror, tears flowing, screaming again and again.

"Poison! They poisoned me!" His voice choked in a sudden gust of frozen wind. Every last warrior on Redwood Cliff drew their weapons. Master Bin spun around to Old Snake, still standing next to the furnace, who shook his head in disbelief. The old poison-user was not responsible for this.

Master Bin urgently raised both hands and faced the masses in front of him. "Be calm, my brothers!" His voice projected far across the cliff.

Stump's charred hands finally closed around his dagger. He screamed and hurled himself at Dong. With a quick whip of his body, Lord Xu's adopted son slashed Dong across the waist.

Dong staggered back, helpless.

"Stop, Stump!" Lord Xu shouted. But the crowd drowned out his command.

Stump lurched forward, wielding his dagger, screaming. Dong continued to fall back. There was an onrush of men. Immediately, a swarm of Red Dragons lined up between Stump and Dong.

"Gentle Swordsmen!" Stump gasped. He fell back.

The Red Dragon swordsmen, their red robes flowing behind them, their dancing blades ripping the air like arrows in full flight, quickly pressed Stump into a steady retreat.

Without warning, a group of Stump's men stormed into the Red Dragon Swordsmen. The Green Dragons were poised to attack, and now, the opportunity to draw enemy blood drove them to madness. With blades pointing forward and straining for release, the men of the Green Dragon House charged.

Master Bin inserted himself in the midst of the fray with hands held high, planted both feet into the frozen ground like a wall in front of his assailants, and roared, "Stop!"

The power of his voice thundered across the cliff. There was not so much as a pause.

"Kill him!" The Green Dragons responded with a cry of war, bringing their swords down like a storm. Master Bin's face ignited in fury.

There came a second cry of war, more earth shattering than the first. A swarm of Red Dragons tore across the ground to pummel the rear of Master Bin's attackers.

Dong climbed to his feet and barked, "Kill them! How dare they attack Master Bin! Kill them!"

The original onrush of Green Dragons couldn't be stopped. Master Bin waited for his assailants to close in before leaping clear to the side, drawing the metal fan from his belt and striking his enemies in the throat with casual precision.

With a massive surge, Master Bin's men slammed into

the backs of the Green Dragons, raining their weapons upon every man who attacked their master and quickly slaughtering those who couldn't turn around in time. In response, hundreds of Green Dragons charged in from behind. More Red Dragons also swept in, driven by the hate and rage that gripped both Houses for decades. Redwood Cliff flooded with blood.

High up behind the tombs, still a safe distance away, Pun pulled Li Kung into retreat. "Let's go. Go before the battle gets to us."

Li Kung prepared to run, but something caught his eye. The old man beside the stone furnace now lifted two canvas bags over his head and threw them into the flames.

Then, a roar shook the earth. The contents of each bag ignited and spewed golden balls of fire into the heavens. Sheets of flaming wind propelled through the air and scattered into the masses. The fire didn't burn the warriors it landed on, but thick smoke emerged where the flames fell. The warriors in green robes instantly weakened and began to fall back.

"Poison!" some of them shouted. "Be careful of Old Snake's poison!"

The Red Dragons, protected by an antidote, didn't seem affected.

The Green Dragons could do nothing but retreat. Each struggled desperately to move away from the smoke.

Meanwhile, every warrior on Redwood Cliff was fighting for his life. Men from both Dragon Houses attacked anyone they didn't recognize, striking with such fury and hate that many died without knowing who murdered them. Most of the guests managed to fight their way to the Grand Staircase, only to be bottlenecked in a chaotic attempt to descend. The mouth of the stairs swirled into battle.

Li Kung circled in front of Pun, wrapping his arms around her and shielding her body with his. She pushed him away.

"Stay behind me!" she shouted. "I'll break open a path for us."

She leaped forward to kick someone out of the way but was thrown back when a barrage of steel blades crossed in front of her.

Li Kung panicked. "No, Pun!" He charged forward, stumbled over a decapitated head, and with a short yelp, fell sprawling to the ground.

"Where are you going?" Pun shouted. She leaped into the air and pounded a flying kick into someone who came too close, then rushed to his side.

"We'll circle around the battle," Li Kung said, grabbing her by the waist and hauling himself to his feet. His legs were shaking, but he spun her around and pushed her behind him, his frail arms reaching out to form a protective barrier between Pun and the warriors killing each other.

Pun yanked him back. "Let's go!"

They climbed back to the safety of the hill behind the large boulders, and Li Kung turned around to stare. She could pull him no farther. He gazed at the raging battle with tears in his eyes. Warriors with bashing weapons were smashing the skulls of others. Swarms of swordsmen hacked each other. A group of spear users shoved the entire length of their spears into a man, and then continued to pierce the body.

"We have to wait," Pun said. "There's no way out right now."

The Green Dragon master was completely surrounded by the Gentle Swordsmen. They were taking advantage of their numbers, surrounding him with their fluttering red robes and dancing blades, slowly wearing him down with hit-and-run tactics. But Lord Xu fought with patience, the gold dagger in his hair gleaming against the sunlight, his light sword cutting and piercing in quick, accurate movements. So far, neither side could overwhelm the other.

Meanwhile, the Butcher remained close to Master Bin, and together they fought off wave after wave of Green Dragon warriors. The Butcher's tactics were brutal, merciless, his movements a remarkable blur. He seemed to be everywhere at once, his double swords covering so much distance that he resembled a flashing wall of bare steel in front of his enemies. Behind the Butcher's relentless onslaught, Master Bin tucked his metal fan into his belt and comfortably walked away.

The battlefield began to separate. Lord Xu's Green Dragon elite, the Chaos Spearmen, had pushed their enemies to the back of the cliff where the silver pine forest stood in its magnificence.

Another group of Green Dragons forced their assailants into the edge of the cliff. The Red Dragons, whose backs lingered over the vertical drop, began to fight in a deranged frenzy. Those shoved over the edge screamed all the way to the bottom, and they seemed to scream forever.

In the middle of the hill, in front of the ancestral tombs, the worst of the massacre continued to unfold. Weakened by the poison smoke and unable to break free, over a hundred Green Dragon warriors perished. The Red Dragons slaughtered them one by one, effectively surrounding and stabbing them. The pools of blood on the ground caused many to slip and fall.

Then Li Kung saw him, the massive warrior with the blue-tinted skin and heavy saber hanging from his belt. The Mongolian slowly moved through the heart of the bloodshed, tossing and hammering with his bare hands, clearing the warriors in his path like they were hollow figures of clay. His saber remained sheathed, his piercing eyes locked onto the distant figure of the old poison-user, his elegant acts of brutality bringing a new dimension to the battlefield. Li Kung realized that to Suthachai, there were no enemies, no friends, no one he shouldn't kill on Redwood Cliff. The poison-user stood within seconds from him.

Li Kung looked below him and noticed a familiar face. It was Cricket, Master Bin's youngest son, who had escorted him safely from Redwood Cliff a few nights ago. Next to Cricket, moving like lightning, was a figure with a demon's face and a woman's body. She held a strange metal flute in her hand; a long blade extended from one end of the flute, smeared with dark blood and torn flesh.

"That . . . " Li Kung managed to lift a finger and point. "That's the woman with the flute weapon. She stabbed Suthachai through the arm!"

Pun looked down. "That's a woman?"

Li Kung shouted, "Suthachai! Suthachai, we're over here!" The Mongolian didn't respond. Li Kung tried to run forward, but was thrown back when a wounded body was hurled into him. He crumbled to the ground, instinctively wrapping his arms together, protecting the little monkey hidden in his coat.

"What are you doing?" Pun was immediately by his side. She pulled him to his feet. "Suthachai can take care of himself. Let's go!"

• • •

Suthachai exploded into a mad rush, reaching the poison-user in two steps. Old Snake crumbled under the steeled fingers around his neck. Suthachai lifted him by the throat, threw him, then drew his saber and slashed the old man in midair.

Old Snake landed painfully. He gingerly touched his chest and a look of deep fear crept over his face. Only his coat was slashed open, so perfectly that his skin wasn't even grazed.

Suthachai wasted no time. He brought his saber down with such vehemence that Old Snake squeezed his eyes shut and prepared to die. The blade stopped inches from his head. "Antidote!" Suthachai said, his voice empty but firm. "I want the antidote to your candle poison or you will die."

The familiar sound of a metal flute cutting the air came from behind. Suthachai instinctively parried. His eyes flashed fire, the hate in his chest swelling. He spun around and slashed at the monstrous woman. She owed him—owed him for attacking him, for humiliating him. She owed him his grandfather's jade. But most of all, she owed him answers. With a deep roar, he covered an unreal amount of distance with one forward leap and struck at her. The Flute Demon slipped back and barely managed to cover her retreat. Suthachai followed the same momentum, slashed at her from a different angle, forced the flute from her hands, and slammed her with his shoulder. The Flute Demon choked, gasping for air, and flew back from the impact.

Suthachai felt the urge to move in and finish her, but a group of suicidal warriors stood in his way. Behind them, a boy appeared beside the Flute Demon and pulled her to her feet. "Who's that barbarian?"

Suthachai reached into his coat, produced one of Li Kung's pills, popped it into his mouth, and turned toward the poison-user. He will kill the demon later.

"He's going to kill Old Snake, Cricket," the Flute Demon said behind him. She wrenched free, picked up her flute, and rushed forward again.

This time, the Flute Demon barely managed to stand between Suthachai and Old Snake. She used hit-and-run tactics—once proven to work against the poisoned Mongolian—to force a lengthy battle and wear him down. But well before he showed any sign of fatigue, the Flute Demon began to feel strain in her own body. The Mongolian was different this time; he was so much stronger. She stumbled back every time their weapons crossed. Her arms began to numb. She knew that little time was left before she would make a mistake, and his heavy blade would slash her in half. She felt as though a stampede of wild bulls charged her from every direction, each one capable of running her through. But she held on, worn and injured, certain that she would collapse any moment.

Then, a shout boomed from behind her, "Drop!"

She fell flat to the ground. A cloud of white smoke streaked past her and enveloped the Mongolian. Old Snake came forward to help her to her feet.

The Flute Demon grabbed the poison-user by the coat and asked, "Why didn't you run? Why did you come back?"

Suthachai shook the powder off, swallowed another pill, and stormed forward again.

Old Snake's mouth dropped. "He's not affected."

"He's the Mongolian who had the jade. He even survived the Soaring Dragon Candles. Let's go!" She pulled on his sleeve, but she was too late. Suthachai was already upon them. She threw herself forward to shield Old Snake and watched desperately as Suthachai's saber came down like a whirlwind. If she moved, Old Snake would be killed. "Run!" she shouted.

The blade froze in front of her face. She stared at the

Mongolian, at his ashen face twisted with suffering, at his determined, iron features.

Suthachai stared back, at her crooked nose and deformed lips, at the tumor over her left eye. Somehow, there was no sign of fear in her. Then, without hesitating again, he smacked the side of her head with the back of his blade. The Flute Demon toppled.

In two bounds, Suthachai reached the poison-user.

Old Snake looked at him with interest. "The poison must be in your bones by now, but you're still alive."

"The antidote!" Suthachai grabbed the old man's arm and twisted it. Old Snake screamed in pain, choking, before Suthachai loosened his hold.

"Antidote?" Old Snake said between gasps for air. "For the Soaring Dragon Candles? I wish I had some."

"Come with me! You will find an antidote for me!"

Suthachai lifted the old man, threw him over his shoulders, and smashing through a few men in his way, headed for the Grand Stairway.

The familiar whistle of the flute emerged from behind again. Suthachai secretly marveled at how quickly she recovered. Perhaps she really was a demon. He threw the old man onto the ground and spun around to counterattack.

The Flute Demon was in no condition to fight, and after three blows, she collapsed to her knees. Without taking time to breathe, she climbed to her feet and charged him. Again and again, the force of his heavy saber sent her staggering back, but each time, she fervently returned.

Kill her. Kill this woman now. Out of the corner of his eye, Suthachai saw Old Snake stumbling toward the Grand Stairway.

"Run!" The Flute Demon shouted.

The poison-user was escaping. Suthachai pounded his

saber madly against her flute, causing her to topple back against the pressure, and then, without another glance, flew after Old Snake. The heat in his chest intensified, and he knew there was little time left. Even with Li Kung's pills, he could not fight forever.

The Flute Demon scrambled to her feet and followed closely behind.

The Grand Stairway was cluttered with frantic warriors, each bashing the other for space. Suthachai pursued the poison-user down the narrow steps, his eyes burning with desperation. He had used the last of Li Kung's pills, but Old Snake remained far ahead. The thick crowd of fighters, injured and scrambling down for safety, kept him from his target. He couldn't close the distance.

Not far behind, the Flute Demon chased. The multiple injuries on her body slowed her but didn't stop her.

She smashed through a group of Green Dragons with a painful cry and closed in on Suthachai.

"The Flute Demon!" one of them shouted. "The monstrous Flute Demon!" Other Green Dragons on the Grand Stairway answered.

She spun around and pierced the shouting warrior's throat, reducing his shouts to a child's gurgle, then, withdrawing her weapon, charged toward the base of the cliff.

In a short time, the ancestral gravesite became a gravesite for hundreds. The carnage spun into utter chaos.

· · ·

Meanwhile, on the top of Redwood Cliff, Li Kung stood motionless, his mouth gaping open, his eyes blurred with tears. He watched men do unthinkable acts to their victims, even attacking those who were already dead.

Pun grabbed his hand and pulled him toward the Grand Stairway. "There's an opening! Let's go!"

"Where's Suthachai?" Li Kung asked, turning away.

Pun pulled him harder. "There's no way to find him now. Let's go!"

They reached the mouth of the Grand Stairway. Pun stomped a warrior in the chest with a strong thrust kick, sending him into two other men, toppling them. A path was cleared, and she pulled Li Kung down the stairs.

Men rushed from behind them, in front of them, scrambling to leave Redwood Cliff. Once on the stairs, the fighting ceased—each warrior focused on the long, dangerous trip to the bottom.

Not far ahead, Li Kung spotted Lord Xu, accompanied by a group of his students, descending quickly. Lord Xu appeared unhurt, but almost all of his men were injured and on the verge of collapse.

• • •

At the foot of the Cliff, Suthachai was completely locked in a renewed battle with the Flute Demon. The old poison-user was no longer in sight.

They found themselves on Middle Pass. The road was recently filled with peaceful mourners who traveled great distances to pay their respects to the Old Grandmother. But now, the same courteous men were scrambling through the pass, their hair and clothing disheveled, many of them wounded and bleeding. Men from the Green Dragon House poured from the Grand Stairway in scattered disarray, their faces flushed with pain and fatigue and caked with dried blood.

Suthachai reached into his pocket and confirmed that

he had no more pills left. The heat began to swell in his chest. He felt his throat tighten, knew the dark blood about to fly from his mouth would reveal that the battle had turned. There was little time left.

He pressed the Flute Demon off the road and into the barren field, where hard snow crumbled under his heavy footsteps. He became more ferocious than ever, certain that the poison would soon course through him again, and the hideous woman would have a second chance to kill him. He didn't know where he was chasing her to, but the barren land reminded him of home, of the bright winter afternoons where the frozen earth felt brittle under his boots, where he would wrestle his friends in the soft snow of early winter.

There was no time to think of home. With a thunderous roar, Suthachai surged forward like a charging bull, saber outstretched, throwing his body into hers. The force of his body slam sent her flying into the distance. He knew then that the fight was over, not just for her, but also for him.

Streams of dark blood propelled from his trembling lips. He fell on one knee, his body doubling over in pain. The Flute Demon was unconscious on the ground, and all he had to do was find enough strength to sink his saber into her flesh.

The Mongolian forced himself to stand, his body in convulsions. He should kill her now.

"The Flute Demon!" he heard from a distance. He turned his weary eyes to a group of Green Dragon warriors, dressed in light green, their weapons drawn and running toward them. There were over twenty of them, their young faces eager and excited despite the trauma and fatigue of battle.

"The Flute Demon!" someone shouted. "She's wounded!"

"Kill her! Kill the Flute Demon!"

But Suthachai stood in their path, flashing the glare of a suffering soul who could only find pleasure in the slaughter of men.

The Green Dragons froze.

With a deep growl, Suthachai moved away from the unconscious woman. Perhaps, he didn't need to kill her. Her enemies would do it for him.

He trudged toward the main road in icy snow; his back turned but his ears alert. He thought he heard one of them say: "We'll sever the head. Lord Xu will be pleased and we'll receive the biggest reward of our lives if we bring back her head."

Another said, "She's still alive. Should we take her back alive?"

"No, she's too powerful. We can't risk it."

Yet another said, "Look at that face. How could a woman live with a face like that? Her mother should've killed her when she was born."

A short laugh.

"Let me cover her face."

Suthachai slowed, breathing deeply, waiting for the pain in his chest to clear. Why hadn't they killed her yet?

"She actually looks like a woman with her face covered!"

Gleeful laughter.

"I wonder if she really is a woman . . . "

Suthachai stopped altogether and slowly turned his head. One of the men tore open the woman's coat, while another tugged on her trousers.

There was a scream, and Suthachai knew that she had awakened. He forced himself not to look, to continue forward. Her fate didn't matter to him now.

There was another scream from her and this time, it was not in shock, but in pain. Someone had slashed her with his sword. There was laughter. One of the men shouted, "Keep her face covered. I think I can take her if I don't see her face."

Suthachai reluctantly turned and saw four men pinning the Flute Demon to the ground. The rest stood around and watched. She writhed and twisted, her screams muffled by the coat over her face. Soon, her screams subsided. He could hear faint sounds of the Flute Demon choking in her own blood.

Suthachai stood and watched. He envisioned the image of the Flute Demon, of her dripping tumor, of her skin like a venomous toad's and a crooked mouth so twisted that she always seemed to be sneering. He thought of her face when she stabbed him through the arm and when she prevented him from reaching the poison-user on Redwood Cliff. Because of her, he lost this only chance of finding an antidote.

Never in his life had he dreamed of anything so ugly.

With a silent shout, he charged toward the Green Dragons.

But she didn't deserve this . . .

The burning heat in his chest began to return, but his legs felt strong, and he knew he would make it. He closed the distance in three bounds, drew his saber, and killed a man. He kicked away the coat that covered her face, slashed another, then spun around to kill a third.

The heat in his chest roared through him in a wave of excruciating torment. Suthachai dropped to his knees. The remaining men stumbled back, their weapons drawn but shaking, their eyes in shock.

The Flute Demon gradually turned over. She wrapped the torn coat tightly around herself, held her left ribs, trembling, barely able to crawl. She reached for her flute.

The Green Dragons eyed the corpses in front of them, and ever so slightly lifted their weapons and inched toward the fallen Mongolian. The hot blood trickling from his mouth was darker than usual. The poison must have infiltrated most of his liver. Slowly, he eased into the frozen ground, his rigid frame lying face down in a crooked arch.

One warrior, taking small, careful steps, moved forward to slash him. Suthachai couldn't move, stared at his approach, trying to lift the saber that was too heavy for him. He grimaced in anticipation of the blow.

There was a loud clang of colliding steel. The young man stumbled back, and Suthachai relaxed. The Flute Demon was there to save him.

Maybe she wanted to kill him with her own hands.

The remaining warriors inched forward with weapons shaking. The Flute Demon reached down, unsteady, and pulled Suthachai to his feet.

"How many can you handle?" she whispered into his ear.

His glare was more devilish than ever. "All of them."

He broke free, ignoring the burst of pain in his body, and leaped forward to cut down his enemies. The Flute Demon was not far behind him. In the blink of an eye, five Green Dragons had fallen.

The Green Dragons turned tail and fled. Suthachai charged after them with a roar, but only managed a few shaky steps before a new surge of pain coursed through his body. He collapsed.

"He's injured!" one of them shouted.

Suthachai lifted his face and scowled. They stopped running and began to turn around.

"They're both injured! Come on! There are so many of us! We can kill them!"

"Kill the Flute Demon! Kill the Barbarian!"

Their faces dark with hate and smeared with blood, the Green Dragons lifted their swords and charged.

"Run!" The Flute Demon whispered. She pulled him to his feet and pressed him against her damaged left ribs so her right hand could be free. The Green Dragons shouted their vilest insults, taunting them to stop and fight.

On the far end of the field, a barren forest stood in a sad state of decay. The trees were not dense enough to hide them, but it was better than the open grounds they were running from. The Flute Demon dragged the Mongolian forward. In a few steps, she too collapsed onto the uneven earth.

"Run," Suthachai said. "Do not save me, I will kill you when I recover."

Her lips curved into a bitter sneer. She climbed to her feet, held him tightly against her, and continued down the field. There was no need to look back—their pursuers were still a good distance away. They had time.

Suthachai spat a mouthful of thick blood; so dark in color he began to wonder if he was really alive. He thought he heard her say, "Force yourself to run! We can hide in the forest."

The ground seemed to move away from him with every step. But he couldn't fall. The Flute Demon held onto him, crying softly in pain, but never slowing. The forest loomed closer; the insults behind them became farther away. They passed a thick tangle of rotted branches and entered deep into the forest.

The world began to darken. The gray of dusk seeped through the air, enveloping the snow, blending the earth into one shadow.

With a weary sigh, the Mongolian's knees slammed into the ground. The Flute Demon pulled, but his overbearing weight broke her balance and she crumbled next to him.

Then there was silence. Nothing moved in the forest,

except their heaving chests struggling for air. Suthachai's enormous frame wracked and trembled, struggling to endure, to cling onto life just a little longer.

Then gradually, their breathing eased. Even Suthachai calmed.

"They're not behind us," the Flute Demon said. "We lost them in the forest."

Suthachai shifted his weight to the side of his body. "Wolves!" he whispered.

"Wolves?"

He held up a trembling finger, a signal for her to speak softly. "They are approaching." He indicated the drops of blood in front of him. Very quickly, the wolves would find them.

"They should go for the bodies first," she said.

"The men who chased us will collect their dead. There will be nothing left. The wolves will come for us."

The Flute Demon stared at the empty forest, and slowly, her face darkened. She reached for a stick of dry wood on the forest floor, and began to bundle it against smaller leaves and twigs. The Mongolian drew his saber one inch at a time; the dull sound of his blade scraping against its sheathe seemed to last forever, until the weapon was freed and held in front of him.

"We're losing light," she said. "The wolves will attack when the sun sets."

She stacked the wood loosely in front of her and reached into her pocket for the flint stones.

If they couldn't find their way out before dark, then fire would be their only chance of survival. Grimacing, Suthachai listened for the wolf pack.

The Flute Demon struck the flints and watched a shower of sparks cover her bed of leaves. She struck again, then again.

"How much longer?" Suthachai asked.

"It's too cold. I don't know."

Suthachai lifted his face and stared at the heavens. The forest was silent. He drew a deep breath, planted his saber into the snow, and climbed to his feet. He felt nauseous and weak, his legs rubbery and lifeless.

"Wolves are afraid of humans," she said softly. "Even when they're hungry."

"No," Suthachai said. "Wolves are afraid of the strong; they hunt down the weak. They can sense that an animal is weak or injured."

"Like us?"

"Yes."

The Flute Demon struck the flint, but the sparks died when they fell upon the frozen branches. "The wolves. Where are they? I need more time."

Suthachai reached over her shoulder and sprinkled light green powder onto the branches.

"What is that?"

"Something my friend gave me."

The Flute Demon struck the flints again, and with a gentle blast, the branches were engulfed in flames.

"Incredible . . . " she muttered to herself. She grabbed the bundled twigs, made a torch, and handed it to Suthachai. She picked a separate branch from the ground and ignited it for herself.

Suthachai watched with interest. The thought of killing her began to fade as he stood beside her, holding the torch with one hand and the naked blade with the other. They came into this forest together, and somehow, if he wanted to kill her, he would have to do it after they escaped together.

"Do you know the terrain?" he asked.

The Flute Demon shook her head. "There are no roads

in this forest—no one goes in here. I heard that the other side of the forest is the coastline."

They began to move quietly away, their torches strong and held at waist level. The sun continued to set. Soon, they sensed hungry eyes watching them from a distance.

"How much longer before the poison disables you again?"

"Why don't *you* tell me that?" Suthachai said in a harsh whisper. The forest began to slope downward. They trudged in steady steps and moved through the dense foliage of rotted bushes. The cunning wolves were hidden, but they were certainly stalking them, inching closer with every heartbeat.

"How many are there?"

"I cannot tell," Suthachai replied, his voice weaker than before. "They are quiet when they approach their prey."

"The sun is descending . . . "

A gray figure sprang out of nowhere and closed its dripping jaws on the Mongolian's arm. Suthachai uttered a sudden scream, pummeled the torch into the wolf's face, sent it sprawling, then lashed out a vicious side-stroke across the wolf's head.

The smell of fresh blood aroused the rest of the pack. At once, three more wolves leaped forward, charging directly into Suthachai's extinguished torch. He was losing consciousness, and they could sense it.

The Flute Demon stepped in front, shielding him with her own body, the small flame on her torch twirling before the approaching wolves. She slashed at the nearest predator and tore a gash across its face. The rest backed off.

Suthachai began to collapse again. She slid behind him, preventing him from falling, so he could lean on her.

"Do not run," Suthachai whispered. "They can sense fear. They can sense weakness."

His eyes dimmed, and he could barely stand.

She took a deep breath, maintaining control, supporting all his weight and began to pull away. The wolves trailed behind them.

The sun began its final descent. Golden rays flooded in from the heavens and diagonally sliced through the trees.

There was movement from behind, as subtle as a light breeze. They'd been circled. The Flute Demon turned too late; a wolf sprang off the ground in utter silence, jaws opened, front paws stretching out for her eyes. She jerked back to avoid the impact. The wolf struck her across the face and sent her spinning into the hard ground. Then, the remaining predators charged. She scrambled on the forest floor, and for a moment, couldn't position herself against multiple attackers.

Suthachai suddenly came to life. He bolted forward with a howl and sliced a wolf across the neck. He spun around and slashed at the pack, completely missing, but he caused the wolves to withdraw.

The Flute Demon rushed to his side, her torch pointed, keeping the wolves at a distance. She wrapped her arms around him, protecting him.

There was a familiar object on the ground. Suthachai focused his eyes. It was a piece of flesh, a tumor that used to hang from the Flute Demon's eye. His mouth opened. Half of her face was torn open, the skin dangling uselessly in shreds. But what lay underneath was not blood or ruptured tissue, but fair skin. Her large almond eyes, freed from the tumor, glittered against the golden light.

"Wei Fei Fei," Suthachai whispered. She turned to look at him, the same way she looked at him the night before, standing next to her grandmother's coffin in front of hundreds of guests.

His grandfather's words echoed in his mind again. "Beauty that could destroy entire kingdoms . . . "

Every bit of strength left him, and he collapsed into her arms.

. . .

Master Bin's daughter lifted a frozen hand and peeled the crooked upper lip from her face. She stood firm, like a noble warrior, like a princess, her lean, motionless figure a chiseled silhouette against the setting sun. She was badly injured, supporting a dying Mongolian and surrounded by starving wolves, yet, Fei Fei calmly stared down her predators.

The light wind ceased, leaving behind a perfectly still world. The fire on the end of the torch barely moved; instead of dancing with life and vigor, the dull flame glowed in a ball. It was utter serenity, as if the world came to a complete stop. Not a snowflake moved.

Then she heard it—a low sound. At first, it resembled a gentle autumn breeze. She felt the tree branches rocking back and forth in a mellow dance, singing light notes that eased in and out of the air. She thought she was standing on the edge of Redwood Cliff, her childish face glowing against the reddish twilight, the silver pine forest swaying behind her.

Then, Suthachai lifted his eyes. "The ocean," he said. "I never thought I would live to see a real ocean."

The wolves began to inch forward, their thin lips pulled back in a seething snarl, their long teeth fully visible. Fei Fei drew away slowly, calmly, listening for the sound of waves.

"Can you run?" she asked.

"For a short distance."

"I'll attack the wolves while you run for the ocean,

and when they fall back, I'll follow you." She screamed, her thundering cry so ferocious that the wolves leaped back in surprise. She bolted for the nearest animal, her dripping blade whistling in front of her. Suthachai hesitated for one brief second, then spun around and began to run.

Fei Fei moved diagonally across the line of retreating wolves, sweeping her blade against the ground and sending a shower of snow into the howling faces. The predators continued to retreat. Fei Fei pounced upon them, relentlessly cutting and stabbing. The wolves turned tail and fled.

Fei Fei charged after Suthachai. He was falling. She reached him, grabbed him from behind, and pulled.

"Let's go," she said. "Can you walk?"

"Yes," he said, his voice weak.

The wolves began to trail them again. She spun around and slashed the hard ground, sending blankets of frozen snow into the air. She pointed her torch at the predators, her large eyes glaring, a low growl emerging from her throat. "Run," she whispered. "I can't hold much longer."

They took off, never looking back, never hesitating. Rotted branches brushed across their faces and fresh blood dripping from opened wounds lined the snow, arousing the wolves further. Yet, the predators maintained their distance. There was no more fear in their prey, but a deep strength that propelled the two humans to tread the frozen ground together.

Within seconds, Fei Fei and Suthachai broke out of the forest and crossed a barren plain. Ocean waves drowned out the growls of disappointed wolves.

"Jump," Fei Fei said. In front of them was a short drop the height of three men, and below was soft sand. Fei Fei took a deep breath, locked the Mongolian in a tight embrace, and leaped over.

With a sick thud, the two injured bodies crashed onto the beach. Fei Fei uttered a muted scream in pain. She swallowed the agony and scrambled to his side, her eyes never leaving the wolves standing motionless above them. She pointed her torch, her own teeth bared, a deep growl at the base of her throat. The wolves didn't advance.

She dragged Suthachai far onto the beach while he writhed in spasms, his ghastly face trembling in pain. For a brief moment he managed to stand before collapsing and dragging her onto the sand.

"They will not follow . . . " he managed to say. "They would not . . . They would not go where they are not familiar . . . "

She lifted her lean body and tried to sit. He began to lose consciousness, his head softly sinking into her lap. With a deep sigh, Fei Fei dropped the torch and cradled his head against her bosom.

Light rays of twilight grazed the surface of the sand. The distant howl of wolves floated in the background.

The gentle rocking of waves rolled against the setting sun.

• • •

Darkness began to settle, the gray sky slowly deepening. Li Kung lay on the hard snow, his breathing heavy and irregular, his face ashen white and dripping sweat. Next to him, Pun knelt on the ground wheezing for air.

"Are you hurt?"

"Why . . . Why did we run?" he muttered, gasping. "Why did we run so hard? No one was chasing us. No one was trying to kill us."

"What happened up there, Li Kung? Why were so many people killed?"

Then he remembered. The few moments that were to remain forever imprinted in his mind now appeared over and over again. He buried his face in his hands and began to weep. "I don't know. I don't know."

Pun slid her arm around him, pressing her face to his back, and held him tenderly.

The small head of a monkey emerged from Li Kung's robe, meaning to chirp for food. It glanced once at Li Kung, then at Pun, and without a sound, ducked into its warm hiding place again.

Finally, Li Kung calmed, and he reached around to embrace her. She tried to comfort him, but the words couldn't leave her lips.

"I'm so scared," she finally said. "I'm so scared."

They held each other. Night fell upon them. Soon, there wouldn't be enough light to travel under. "We need to find a place to stay," Li Kung said. "Old Gu's house is just over that hill. Let's see if he's still awake."

"We shouldn't disturb him. He's not in good health, even though you stopped his fever last week . . . "

"He wants to see us," Li Kung said, grabbing her hand and pulling her away. "And, there are too many wolves in these mountains at night. Let's go. Maybe I can examine his granddaughter again."

• • •

The rocking waves ebbed closer and closer. Suthachai's gloved hand clawed into the frozen sand, mechanically pulling himself forward. She followed, a tear in her eye, sometimes reaching out to help him.

Without a glance at her, he half-stumbled and half-crawled through the sand. He had no clue where he was headed, but he wanted to stay moving. He was afraid that the moment he stopped, he would succumb to the poison that ate into his bones, and he would never move again. At times, the pain became unbearable—it was not the same type of pain, but it was equally unbearable. He gazed at her then. Why was she the one who had done this to him?

"Why is there no antidote?" he asked, stabbing his saber deep into the sand for balance.

"I'm . . . I'm sorry. There really isn't."

He paused. The twisted expression formed by his chiseled features darkened, and he turned to her with threatening eyes. She instinctively reached for her weapon, then, hastily dropped her arm. The tense expression on her face softened and she leaned over to touch him. He was frozen, his eyes wide and expressionless.

"Can you walk?" she asked, sliding her arm across his shoulder. "It'll be night soon and we won't be able to find shelter."

He turned without a word.

"I'll ask Old Snake," she said. "I'll ask him if he could find a cure."

He paused, nodded, the bitter curve of his lips softer then.

"There's never been a need for it," she continued. "There's never been anyone we poisoned that we didn't want dead." She wrapped her arm around his shoulder and held his weight as he began to weaken again. He felt her warm body pressed tightly against his side, and his frustration subsided. Maybe he would die now, in her arms, and the last face he would see would be an angel's.

"I'll do my best," she said. "I'll do my best."

The beach ended, and across a field of barren ice and snow was a gray structure built in the middle of nowhere.

The light was almost gone, but they could see it clearly: an empty, dark building that somehow remained steadfast in the open, with nothing to shield it from wind or snow.

"A temple," she said. "I think it's an abandoned temple. There may be firewood there." In her excitement, she took a hastened step forward and callously pulled him. He lost his hold with a crash and collapsed to the snow. She quickly turned back.

"I didn't mean to—"

He suddenly grabbed her, the filth of blood and dirt still smeared all over his face. He drew her down and planted his lips against hers. Her body tensed, just for a second, and slowly, she eased her aching body into his embrace, her entire weight leaning into his kiss. His hand gently brushed against her forehead, her cheeks, glided slowly to the side of her neck, their lips burning against each other in heated passion.

• • •

Deep in the mountains, hidden behind a dense cluster of trees, a local woodcutter's house stood alone and out of place. It was well built, maintained by an old man named Gu who lived alone with his granddaughter. Together, they could chop wood faster than the old man could sell it, and thus they made their living.

Gu's granddaughter was named Ying. She was no older than fifteen, and she was lean and strong and known to attack any mountain bandit who ventured too close. She often wore a straw hat to cover her girlish face, and a little brass bell around her waist so her grandfather would know where she was.

It was late in the night by the time Li Kung arrived with Pun.

"The doctor is here!" Old Gu shouted at the top of his voice. He clasped Li Kung's hand, bowing low. Ying smiled with a shy nod from behind her grandfather. The mountainous area they lived in was lush with medicinal plants and insects. Ever since Li Kung came to the North with the Three Saints of Yunnan, he often hunted for herbs in the vicinity and frequently visited.

The woodcutter was only too happy to see a friend at the door. He insisted that Li Kung occupy his bed for the night, while he slept on a pile of straws in the rear wood shack. Ying and Pun slept together in Ying's room, and late in the night, Li Kung was left alone on a hard wooden bed to ponder the recent events.

He didn't sleep that night. Well before dawn, he noticed a light in the main room, and he climbed out of bed.

Ying sat by a small table, wrapped in thick cloth, a tiny oil lamp beside her.

"What are you reading, Ying?"

Ying lifted her book from the table to show Li Kung the cover.

"*Records of the Historian*," Li Kung said with a smile. "My father gave me that one. You weren't supposed to read it yet. It's too difficult for you."

Ying nodded, agreeing. She pointed to the chair across from her, indicating that Li Kung should sit.

"Have you been taking the herbs?" Li Kung asked, seating himself. "The ones I brought last time?"

Ying nodded.

"But still not a sound?"

Ying shook her head. Li Kung sighed, a frown on his face. "Maybe it's been too long. We can keep trying. One day, you'll have your voice back. I promise."

She smiled and reached out to pat his hand, comforting

him. She pointed to a word in her book, and motioned for him to read to her.

"This word is *gong cheng*. It means to siege a city."

She pointed again. Li Kung read: "This one is *zhen*, meaning battle formation. There were many wars in those days, Ying. We're lucky to live at a time of peace and . . . " He swallowed his words, remembering the slaughter on Redwood Cliff.

Ying pointed to another word.

"*Zha*," Li Kung read. "It means deceit. Deceit is for bad, dishonest people."

Ying pointed at him with a mischievous smile.

Li Kung laughed, leaning away from her accusing finger. "Me, deceitful?"

"Ying should be in bed at this time of night." It was a hoarse voice, so gentle but firm. Old Gu waddled over and patted Ying's head. She looked up in surprise.

"I can't sleep, my child. We have guests. It's been so long since we had guests, you see."

Li Kung moved his chair behind the old man so he could sit. "I hope Pun and I are no trouble to you. I didn't mean to wake you."

"You didn't wake me," the old man said, seating himself. "I don't sleep much, you see. The old hip bothers me at night and I don't sleep much. Please, sit down. It's such a privilege to have a great doctor here. Don't be modest. Most in this area are illiterate, you see, and it's an honor to be your friend. And I can never thank you enough for giving Ying all these books. Even the teacher in He Ku doesn't have access to any of these books, you see."

"Don't mention it," Li Kung said, more relaxed now.

Old Gu turned to Ying. "Put the book away. You should get back to bed."

Ying picked up *Records of the Historian*, bowed to Li Kung, and left the table.

"Beautiful child," Li Kung said.

"She's no longer a child," the old man said with a laugh. "She's almost sixteen years old. I hope to find a good home for her, but the silly girl doesn't want to leave me, you see. I guess I consider that a blessing. I'm sure she'll marry into a fine household. Even if she's mute."

Li Kung laughed, somewhat uneasily.

Old Gu shifted comfortably in his chair. "Tell me about the battle on Redwood Cliff. I heard it was huge."

"I . . . I don't really know what happened," Li Kung began. "It was a burial ceremony, and suddenly they started to accuse each other of different things. Then they started killing each other. There was so much blood."

The old man insisted. "Tell me. I'm curious—unless, of course, Master Li would like to catch up on some sleep. I would certainly not cause you any inconvenience."

"No, not at all," Li Kung said. "This is the least I could do."

So he began describing how he climbed to the back of the hill for a better view of the ceremony, and how the copper cauldron was unearthed, along with the ancestral decree. He related the mass slaughter, the death and destruction that seemed to never end, and how he finally escaped Redwood Cliff by running through hundreds of guests and Green Dragon warriors.

"The face of Redwood Cliff will be smeared with fresh blood," the old man whispered to himself. "And the children of the common people will suffer for their crimes."

"What?"

The old man looked up, startled. "Nothing. I'm talking to myself again."

"What did you just say?"

"Nothing, really. I'm so glad you're safe."

Li Kung looked into the old man's eyes, and he felt a deep sadness creep through him. The old man was in despair; filled with unusual desperation. Li Kung didn't ask further. His eyes drifted outside. Far in the distance was the faint outline of a mountain. "What a beautiful mountain. You can see the snow on the peak, even at night."

"That . . . That's Phoenix Eye Peak," Old Gu said.

"Really?" Li Kung turned back to the woodcutter. "Phoenix Eye Peak. A storyteller in He Ku told me that Snow Wolf's spirit is on that mountain. Is that true?"

"I don't believe in spirits."

"Maybe she's still alive."

"Rumors only. Some woodcutters even heard her screaming up there. Just rumors, you see."

Li Kung leaned forward. "Her scream?"

Old Gu shook his head. "People can no longer tell the difference between heroes and bandits anymore. That's why people hope for Snow Wolf to come back. They dream of her being alive, you see, and one day coming down to make the world right again. It's false hope."

There was firmness in the old man's voice, an iron bitterness on his face.

"False hope is better than no hope when the Martial Society is bound for collapse," Li Kung said. "At least unity among the leaders can prevent total chaos from exploding across the land. If the idea that a role model is still alive, that some past hero is still here and watching us, then the principles she represented would still be alive. Don't you agree, Mr. Gu?"

Old Gu's face softened. "You have a good heart, Master Li. I haven't seen your type in many years."

"You're so certain she's dead?" Li Kung asked. "Aren't those stories too? Of her death?"

"They're not stories, Master Li. She's dead."

"How can you be so sure?"

"I was there, you see. I saw it with my own eyes."

• • •

"To make sure no one would?" Suthachai asked in a low voice, his sheathed saber rigidly positioned between his knees.

Fei Fei glanced at him, a troubled look in her eyes, almost afraid that the sudden rise in anger would stir the poison in his blood again. She watched his hand clench the handle of the saber, the knuckles whitened. "Our mission was to retrieve the jade. It meant so much to the Red Dragons . . ."

The tip of the saber slammed against the floor of the boat. "It was important to your Red Dragons? So you waged war against my people?"

Fei Fei fell silent. The boat rocked against the light currents of the lake. It was a tiny fishing boat, normally steered by the fisherman they stole the vessel from, but tonight, Fei Fei was seated at the back, maneuvering the oar. Suthachai sat facing her on the other end of the vessel, his massive frame leaned against the old wood, breathing in the smell of wet oak, his eyes on the flickering shadows in the sky.

"Bats," Fei Fei said, watching him.

Silence again. There was light in the distance, on an island known as the Garden of Eternal Light. They were going to the Green Dragon *zhuang*.

Fei Fei took a deep breath, her chest still aching from the multiple injuries suffered during the day. But she felt alive, energetic. They had rested for hours in the abandoned temple near the beach, and she remembered the Mongolian huddled against her like a child, shaking in uneven convulsions and painfully drawing every breath. She gently wiped the bloodstains on his face, her own injuries tormenting her, and she held him, never uttering a sound while he slept.

How quickly he recovered. By the time she awoke he was already standing outside, staring at the moon high in the heavens, his cold voice firm and under control. But when he turned to gaze at her, his expression instantly softened.

And just as quickly, his jaws clenched together, the ice back in his eyes. "You hurt me, and I hurt you too. We have also saved each other's lives. But we are not even yet. You took something that belongs to me—it belongs to my grandfather. I will not be alive much longer, but I want it back."

"Who was Su Ling?" Suthachai asked. He sat up so abruptly the boat rocked, and freezing water splashed onto them. Fei Fei jolted from her thoughts. She planted the oar deeper into the water to control the boat.

He lowered his head. "I am sorry."

"Don't worry. Not much water splashed in."

"I am sorry I spoke in a harsh tone of voice."

Fei Fei smiled, the cold water dripping from her face suddenly warmer. The trees on the Green Dragon *zhuang* were visible now, though it would be late in the night before the little boat could cross Lake Eternal. Still, having stolen a smaller boat gave them a better chance of approaching the island unnoticed.

How would they penetrate the Green Dragon *zhuang*?

"Su Ling was my second aunt," she began. "My father's cousin. How did you hear about her?"

"My grandfather was with her the night she died."

"Your grandfather knew my aunt?"

"The name of the candles I am poisoned with," Sutha-chai said, his saber lowered against the floor of the boat. "What was the name again?"

"The Soaring Dragon Candles."

Suthachai took a heavy breath. "Su Ling died from the Soaring Dragon Candles."

Fei Fei stopped rowing and stared. "How? She died with her mother, fighting the Sun Cult. Where . . . What makes you think she died from the poison candles?"

Suthachai hesitated.

"Su Ling was in Pan Tong Village the night she was poisoned," he said. "The same village your men destroyed."

Fei Fei started, meaning to interrupt, but Suthachai broke in, "She gave the jade to my grandfather before she died, and he took it with him to Mongolia."

"Gave . . . Gave the jade to your grandfather? The jade is a symbol of the Dragon House. Supreme power in the Dragon House. Why would my aunt ever give that away?"

"I have his diary. It was all he left behind—that and the jade."

Fei Fei leaned forward, her hands lifeless on the oar. "How did the jade end up in Mongolia? I've always wondered."

Suthachai began to tell her, his Mongolian accent slightly thicker than usual. He recounted the story in his grandfather's diary, of the night Su Ling gave away the jade in a desperate moment, how her father was stabbed to death and how she was killed by poison. Fei Fei's eyes were trans-fixed, her mind spinning with disbelief, but she knew he had no reason to lie to her—this barbarian who knew nothing about Chinese civilization—there was no way he could've fabricated the story.

"Fei Long was killed by the Scholar," she interrupted.

"You know that Fei Long was my granduncle. He was the leader of the Dragon House, and he was Su Ling's father. If the Dragon House leader was killed and Redwood Cliff faced a common enemy, why would my aunt give up the leadership to a foreign friend? It's not possible."

"She knew she was going to die," Suthachai said, his voice firmer now. "She knew she was going to be killed by someone close."

"Someone close?"

"Soaring Dragon Candles. She was killed by the Soaring Dragon Candles . . . "

"Only the Dragon House uses that kind of poison," Fei Fei said, her voice trembling. "Old Snake's master invented them by chance, and no one else in the world knows how to make them."

There was silence. Suthachai moved closer to her and took her cold hand, clasping it in his.

"My grandmother lied about something," she finally said, after a long time. She held her breath, the words at the tip of her tongue. She had to believe him; there was no reason for him to contrive a story about something that happened so long ago.

"My grandmother lied about something," she said again. "But I don't know what. She told me that my granduncle and his wife, Snow Wolf, were killed in a battle with the Sun Cult, and that they had a daughter who died with them. She told me that my granduncle's body was recovered, and so was Su Ling's—and they both died of sword wounds. Snow Wolf's body was never found. But, if Snow Wolf and Fei Long were both killed, why did the Sun Cult never invade Redwood Cliff? I never understood why."

"But she did not tell you that Su Ling was poisoned, did she?" Suthachai asked.

"No. But my grandmother was a great leader with a tremendous reputation. Everyone knows the name Lin Cha—my grandmother was famous for her honor and compassion. Why would she lie?"

"Did she tell you why the jade was missing?"

"She . . . " Fei Fei hesitated. "She said it was stolen."

Suthachai laughed a strange laugh. Fei Fei gripped his hand and drew him closer, hoping to plead with him. "I didn't mean to say that your grandfather is a thief," she said quickly.

Suthachai shook his head. "Mongolians take pride in robbing and pillaging the Chinese, and anything stolen or taken from a Chinese is usually shown around like spoils of war. There was no need for my grandfather to make lies. He would have loved to say that he outsmarted the Chinese and stole one of their most valuable possessions, and he would have been so proud of it." His expression darkened. "We are always being taken advantage of. Our land is so scarce in food and resources, and your land so full of wealth—yet when we barter at the border, we are really left with so little choice. We need the salt, we need the tea, and you have so much of both. But you want so many sheepskins in exchange, and we have only so many sheep that we can slaughter each year. Why should my grandfather not take something valuable from you and be a hero in his land? Why should he have to lie in his diary and tell a story of a woman he loved?"

Fei Fei's mouth dropped. "I . . . I didn't suspect that you hated us . . . " She couldn't continue; strange thoughts spun hopelessly in her mind. She was a princess of the Martial Society, and so many men would readily drop to their knees in front of her. Once in disguise, she could order legions of men to their deaths with a wave of her flute. No one ever disputed her actions. But in front of her was a foreigner who would not bow to her, yet stood up for her in the face of danger. He regarded her with suspicion, but she knew from the gentle gaze in his eyes, from the scent of his body and the touch of his arms, that he would die for her if she should ever need it.

It dawned on her then that she couldn't bear to watch him die. He would face death with courage, but she felt that if he were to die, she would hope to go with him.

Slowly, unconsciously, she drew herself closer to him. Laying the oar down in the side of the boat, she reached out and touched his face. He closed his eyes, didn't shrink away from her. The heat of her soft hands brushed across his nose, settling against the firm corner of his lips.

With a deep sigh, Suthachai said, "My grandfather was not a very good man, and no one really liked him. Everything about his past was a secret, and because he did not have any friends, no one ever knew about his jade or what he saw in China. It is a miracle that the jade ever resurfaced at all."

"The stone slab," Fei Fei said, sliding her arm around his neck and drawing him closer. "The pond on the other side of He Ku dried last year, and a stone slab was found . . . "

"I saw it. I read the prophecy."

"You did?"

"I will never forget the words," he said. "'Flying high in the barbaric North?' Another line read, 'Across the desert, he will seek destiny.' Whoever wrote this knew the jade was in Mongolia. How?"

"I don't know," Fei Fei said. "But everyone believes that the gods left that poem to us, to unite the Dragon Houses once again. The stone slab was lodged into the floor of the pond, and the chiseled words were smooth from erosion. It's been there since well before I was born."

"Is that why one of your men had a candle shop at the border? A station point for all of you seeking the jade?"

"We had many men in the North after the poem was found. Grandmother was ill; she had been ill for years, but it was getting worse every day. She wanted so much to see the jade, so we escalated the search. The candle shop was one of many places arranged by the border. That trade market was our main communications point for our spies."

Suthachai moved away from her, staring into her eyes. "You had spies on the steppe?"

"Only to find the jade," she said quickly. "Mongolians were paid well to help us find information."

"Were there any in my clan?"

"I don't believe so."

Suthachai paused, just long enough to study her, before relaxing. "And what did your spies find?"

"They found nothing, until you wore the jade into the market. I know. You're going to ask why no one attacked you by the border, or when you crossed the desert on your way home. The truth is, there were armies of men out there, loyal to my uncle, looking for the same jade. We couldn't risk the Green Dragons finding it first. If we attacked you and failed, my uncle's men would know about you."

"So you poisoned me."

"Suthachai?"

He looked away.

"I'm so sorry it was you."

He said nothing.

"I heard of you through my spies," she said. "They followed you across the desert, you know."

"I know. I thought they were bandits, but most bandits would never confront me."

"I heard," she said. She leaned forward and rested her

head on his shoulder. "I was so intrigued by the stories they brought back. A superhuman warrior who killed wolves with his bare hands, a man who could endure the Soaring Dragon poison and still beat every wrestler in the clan."

Suthachai slid his hand over her shoulder, gently gliding it down her shoulder blade and onto her back. He pulled her closer. She wrapped her arms around his massive frame, breathing in his scent.

"We only wanted to get the jade," she whispered. "We were already in your camp the night you burned the candles, and we were going to wait for you to die. Without any noise or disturbance. We were going to take the jade from you and leave Mongolia. But you scared us, Suthachai. You walked out of your tent as if nothing happened and entered a wrestling match. How were we ever to get the jade from you?"

Fei Fei closed her eyes, the gentle breeze on the lake colder than ever. The boat continued to drift, slower now, and in the darkness, they didn't realize they were approaching the island.

"It was my brother's idea to attack your camp," Fei Fei said. "Dong, my brother, he has such a temper. I opposed it. My spies told me that you alone could kill half the men we brought to Mongolia, so I fought to prevent the raid. But my father had ordered that we secure the jade at all costs."

He held her tighter. "If Jocholai did not pull me into a wrestling match that night, I would be dead. Then none of this would be happening."

"And we wouldn't be together right now," she said softly.

The bats fluttered above them, the boat floating forward, ever so slowly. He brushed a hand across her cheek while she rested in his embrace. "It will be dawn soon," he whispered.

"I know. We don't have much time." Slowly, reluctantly, Fei Fei reached for the oar, her eyes never leaving his. She smiled, but she was obscured in the darkness, and she was glad he never saw the fear and sadness hidden behind her smile. She bravely planted the oar into the water and pushed the boat forward. The wind lifted. Suthachai turned his face to confront the breeze.

"When I rode across the plains in the spring, the wind blew almost as effortlessly as it does now," he said. "And the faster you ride, the harder the wind blew. But when you look in front of you, there is land that never seemed to end. To your left, to your right, behind you, there is only land that stretched on forever. And when the sun is high in the sky and you can no longer see your shadow, you look into the distance again."

Suthachai closed his eyes and inhaled to catch the oncoming breeze. "But the wind," he whispered. "The wind makes you feel like you are floating instead of flying. My horse can fly, so people have told me. But on the Great Plains, where the open land goes on forever, he can only float."

Fei Fei released her right hand from the oar, her eyes on his back. Her lips trembled once, ever so slightly. "Suthachai?"

He didn't turn to her, but she could almost sense his body relaxing to her voice. She took a deep breath, and asked, "If you could make a wish and have anything you want, what would you wish for?"

For a moment, he didn't answer. Her hand moved to her side, silently, with great effort. Her fingers closed around her flute, a burning tear rolling down her cheek, and she squeezed her eyes shut just long enough to imagine the smile emerging on his face.

"I would like to ride on my horse, ride at a comfortable pace across the land, and I will be free from anyone, anything. The wind would blow gently on my face, and I would float across a land that never ends."

Fei Fei's eyes opened, her face knitted in torment. Tears flowed in long streams then, but she didn't wipe them. She slowly drew her flute. "You're there now. You're riding in the wind, free."

She pulled hard on the oar, her fingers crushing the wooden handle. "And the land never ends, and you are floating."

"But if I could have any wish I want," Suthachai said, his voice distant and soft. "I would want to ride across the Great Plains holding you in front of me, with you helping me guide the horse, even though we would not be going anywhere. We would just ride together, so we could smell the morning frost on the grass and feel the warm sun on our faces. We would just ride together."

The flute inched its way back into her belt. She couldn't help but hear the sound of dripping water, large drops of her own tears slamming against the wooden floor before her. Fei Fei didn't have the strength to wipe them. She clenched the oar with both hands, squeezed her eyes shut and rowed as hard as she could.

"I would love to. I would love to ride with you."

Suthachai stared at the Garden of Eternal Light. "I will die soon," he said. "We will never ride together in Mongolia."

The island loomed before them then, and Fei Fei slowed the boat to approach. Large willow trees stood at the bank, with clusters of bare thorn bushes hidden behind them. Far to the left was a small dock, with a few men immersed in drinking games by the wooden planks. Despite tall torches planted into the ground, the island was dark and lifeless. Fei Fei steered the boat away from the guards and turned toward the other side of the island.

"I will die anyway," Suthachai said. "The jade is not that important."

Fei Fei shook her head but Suthachai didn't see her. He lowered his voice to a bare whisper. "We can turn back. I do not want to put your life at risk. Not for a piece of jade."

"I owe you," she said. "And we're not the rightful owners of that jade anymore. My aunt gave it away. Who am I to take it back?"

They could see the wind swaying the willow trees by the shore. Fei Fei noticed the guards by the dock were indeed drunk, and she lifted a hand to indicate that all was well. Suthachai nodded, lifted his saber, clamped it tightly against his body, and waited. The boat gradually closed in on shore.

There were sharp rocks, some hidden and some protruding in the muddy waters around the island. There was only one way to the shore, and Fei Fei knew it by heart. Lord Xu taught her when she was twelve, because she was the only little girl in the family. She was destined to become an elegant, dainty lady, always welcomed on the island, and now, she was the final, remaining link of goodwill in the Wei family. Her uncle never imagined that he personally taught the Flute Demon how to maneuver around his defenses.

Silence. The darkness that overwhelmed the island seemed to squeeze all life from it. There was something strange on the shore of the Garden of Eternal Light. Something dark and mysterious that Fei Fei couldn't explain.

There was a light scratching sound as the boat glided to shore. She cocked her ears to listen and thought she heard breathing, but nothing indicated danger. She placed one foot on dry land, aware that her own clothing rustled with every step.

Then they saw it, though it was a mere shadow. Covered completely in black, the shadow sat in a kneeling position not far away, a long sword vertically planted in front of him. His face was covered, his feet protected by long boots. Suthachai reached for his saber.

Fei Fei stepped forward and froze in her tracks, the sight of the kneeling silhouette striking her like a giant wave. Black Shadow! She wanted to pull Suthachai back to the boat, but her legs felt weak, her breath short. It was too late. There was already nowhere to run, nowhere to hide.

Black Shadow began to move, turning toward them. He was calm, cold, void of the human elements that made him mortal and destructible.

"You have talent, Mongolian." Black Shadow's voice was low and monotonous.

Suthachai tensed, turning his shoulder to expose less of his body to the enemy. Fei Fei thought she saw the shadow smile.

"I would love to duel with you when you're at your best," Black Shadow continued. "But times have changed, and none of us can afford a casual duel anymore."

"Black Shadow," Fei Fei said.

"I know why you're here, Fei Fei," Black Shadow said. "I know that you came for the jade. The Mongolian believes the jade belongs to him, and maybe it does. But if you steal the jade tonight, the Green Dragon House would have another excuse to hate their cousins on Redwood Cliff, and there will be more bloodshed. Now is not the time to cause further chaos."

Fei Fei's heart was pounding. Suthachai took her hand, his eyes never leaving Black Shadow, and began to move toward the boat.

"Times have changed, my princess," Black Shadow said. "Disaster is about to blanket our land, and there's nothing I can do to stop it. We need your help."

"If there's nothing you can do about it," Fei Fei said, "what can I possibly do?"

Black Shadow took a step forward. "Last night, I was in Pan Tong Village. I heard the entire village had died, and I knew your poison-user was responsible for it. But even Old Snake is not so cruel as to kill off an entire village for recreation."

"It was not for recreation," Fei Fei said.

Black Shadow moved forward, and they took another step back.

"He poisoned them. But they were already dying," Black Shadow said. "Something has caused their souls to shrivel from their eyes! Who is developing such evil alchemy? Is it your father?"

"I don't know what you're talking about. If you want to kill us for trying to steal the jade, then draw your sword and attack. Who are you accusing here?"

"It's not about the jade. The jade means nothing. The people in this land are about to face a tragedy far greater than the famines they faced in Snow Wolf's time."

"Are you implying that my father is responsible for this?"

"Strange things are happening in this land, Fei Fei. Strange things that can't be explained. You've seen some of them. Look at the bodies in Pan Tong Village, and you'll understand."

"What about the bodies?" Suthachai's voice was low, suddenly agitated.

"You've seen them, Mongolian, haven't you?"

"I have."

"Then you must know what I'm referring to." Black Shadow threw something at Suthachai, with such power that it fired like an arrow. The Mongolian stepped lightly to the side and caught the object. It was a small porcelain jar.

"The last of the alchemy that destroyed the men in Pan Tong Village," Black Shadow said. "I tried it this morning, and I suggest you try it too." He began to fade into the shadows.

"Help us, my princess," he said, disappearing into the darkness. "Don't let this happen to the people. Don't let this happen to your father."

"Wait!" Fei Fei called. There were so many more questions she needed to ask. She glanced at Suthachai, and froze. The Mongolian's face startled her, haunted her.

"Pan Tong Village," she whispered.

• • •

"It was fifty years ago, you see," Old Gu finally began. "I was only a young man then. I didn't know any better. I followed the older men in the village, you see, and I did what they did, and I believed what I was told. It was a cold winter. No one had anything to eat, and we were bitter, all of us. The crops failed that year, you see, and by midwinter, our grain was gone. There wasn't enough wood to keep a decent fire at home, you see. We weren't hunters—didn't even know how to find rabbit holes—and the only living creatures were wolves. Sometimes, half the village would huddle together in small rooms, with a single fire to keep them warm. I remember those days, when I would feed the fire one small branch at a time. I thought it would help the fire last longer.

"Snow Wolf sometimes sent food to us. But there was too much snow, and too many villages. We waited every day, you see, and Snow Wolf's men would come and distribute a little food before hurrying to the next village. They traveled great distances, you see, all the way down south, to bring back this grain. We heard Snow Wolf stayed in the South to fight for us so we could continue to have food. But we weren't thankful. We were too hungry to be thankful. We demanded more. There was just not enough.

"Then came the night when different men brought food to us, plenty of food. If I had known better, I would've slain them on the spot. But then, who would've known that the lying scum brought all that meat, and wine, and grain? They were from the Dragon House, you see, but they said that they had nothing to do with Snow Wolf. Oh, Master Li, we should've been smarter.

"They passed around the food, and then they gathered everyone together in the main courtyard. They told us that they brought this food from the south, you see, but it took them two months to get it to us. They told us that Snow Wolf's men harassed them every day, to stop them from coming back with the food. Snow Wolf wanted to see us starve, you see, and fed us once in awhile to keep us under her control. They said she wanted us to suffer so we would always submit to her.

"Then they told us that she stole the gold reserve from Redwood Cliff, and they couldn't buy more food unless the gold was recovered. And we believed them. Why not? The food was real, you see, and their kindness seemed real. They stayed with us the whole afternoon and drank with us, and they promised us the future would be better. And we listened, you see. They talked about the power struggles on Redwood Cliff, how Snow Wolf tried to appear noble and heroic while murdering those whom opposed her.

"They spoke of a new leader on Redwood Cliff, you see. Her name was Lin Cha, and she would bring this famine to a halt. They said that she was kind and fair to the common folk, and she had the friendship and trust of the Martial Society. She would stop Snow Wolf's tyranny.

"When they left, they promised to return in two days with more food and supplies. That night, the entire village gathered again. We discussed our concerns and our future. We were angry and frustrated, you see. Snow Wolf betrayed us. There was proof that it was true, and we all believed it. We were such fools, uneducated and simple fools. We decided right there that our new friends would be our real masters because they brought us food and wine. And Snow Wolf, who protected us all these years . . . Snow Wolf was then the immediate traitor, you see. Overnight if you'll have it. Otherwise, how would these men have so much fine meat and wine for the common people? Snow Wolf only brought coarse grain!

"That night, we feasted. We were drunk and happy, and the entire village slept through the next day thinking life will be good again. We all got drunk again the following night— we were so sure the real leaders of the Dragon House would come back to rebuild our lives. And they did as they promised. They returned in two days. This time, we were each given a flask of wine for a special occasion. We were told to stand along the main road, you see, and wait for someone special. This time, Lin Cha came with them.

"The witch was thin and frail. She wore a silk veil that draped from a bamboo hat on her head, and she was elegant, you see, like nobility. She drank the wine with a toast to our future. We emptied our flasks like it was water. The wine was strong and everyone was in a great mood. But every word she said, every move she made was a trap, Master Li. It's just that none of us saw it.

"The witch Lin Cha spoke to us in a clear voice, and told

us that there is hope, and that together, we can survive this winter. She bought a new medicine from the south and said there wouldn't be any more crop failures. We'd be free from locust plagues and beetles and rats.

"Her men brought a pungent pork buttock, you see, a big piece of meat roasted to crisp red. One man opened a cloth bag and dumped a swarm of beetles onto the meat. Then Lin Cha waved her hand, and a shower of white powder dropped on the beetles, and every insect was dead.

"I walked up to the meat to have a look at the beetles. They were truly dead, you see, not a single one twitched. Lin Cha sliced a piece of meat for herself. I could smell the pork, and my mouth was watering. We watched her eat the meat. Then she ordered her men to bring the pork into the village and share with everyone. But of course, we had already drank the antidote, you see, and it was in our wine. This poison that could instantly kill all those beetles could not possibly be used on crops.

"Her short demonstration was very convincing. The poison she used to kill the beetles didn't poison any of us. She even ate the very first bite herself. So we shared the feast, and more wine was passed around, and by the end of the night, we were ready to obey her every word.

"It was cold, you see, bitter cold that night. We huddled around a fire and Lin Cha sat among us like old friends. The witch laughed quietly, ate her food in small morsels and drank her wine in tiny sips, that hypocrite. Her gentle voice was soothing, you see, and we adored her.

"Then someone noticed a deep scar on her neck. The young farmer asked her where she got the scar from, because it looked fresh.

"Lin Cha sighed and started to pace back and forth. We waited in shock. She walked with her head down, you see, as if deep in thought. That old witch, if I had only known better. If I only knew about the lies she told that night!

"Finally, one of her men pretended he could no longer hold back the truth, and he blurted out, 'Please allow me to tell them! We can't lie to these people!' Lin Cha, the evil witch, looked sad and shook her head. Another one of her followers jumped up and cried, 'We should let these people know the truth! There's no reason to hide Snow Wolf's crimes!'

"Oh, Master Li. The entire village flared up in shock and screamed their hatred. They demanded to know what Snow Wolf did to this fine lady. One of her men stepped forward without permission and told us that Lin Cha battled Snow Wolf to defend the gold reserves. The ancestors of the Dragon House stored this gold, you see, and no one was to touch it. Lin Cha suggested using some of it to fight the famine, but Snow Wolf was so afraid of losing control that she attacked the storage with fifty men and hauled away the gold.

"And then Lin Cha collapsed to the ground in the best show of all, and she wept, and she cried about how she failed her people, and how she was worthless. The villagers tried to comfort her. We all supported her for standing up against the traitor. She wouldn't stop blaming herself, and we wept with her. What talent in acting. Finally, one of her men stood up and screamed. He called for vengeance. They said that without the gold, many more villages would suffer this winter. We must work together to recover this gold so that the common people could eat.

"The entire village approved. I shouted the loudest, you see. I screamed at the top of my lungs and I declared my hatred, and I vowed to destroy Snow Wolf. The rest followed. Instantly, the whole village wanted to kill Snow Wolf and retrieve the gold.

"Thinking back, Master Li, it was so funny. Snow Wolf was famous for killing a hundred mountain bandits alone, and she killed them off so quickly none of them had the chance to run. Did we really think we could capture her?

"Villages across the land suddenly came together. Weapons were devised out of farming tools, you see, and torches were made and food passed around. Large search parties were organized and we were taught new slogans: 'Slay the Wolf! Seek justice! Slay the Wolf! Seek justice!'

"The younger children carried hot water to us, and even they started to shout slogans, you see. For two days, our search parties searched the mountains—the mountains that you see outside this window, Master Li. And each day, someone from Redwood Cliff accompanied us, and they always had new information on Snow Wolf's whereabouts. They told us where she was last seen, you see, how she barely escaped the few men who saw her, and how it never would have happened if more people were there to surround her. We believed everything we were told, you see.

"I will never forget that night. For the rest of my life, I will never forget. It wasn't cold, but we were all shivering. We heard Snow Wolf was seen retreating into a hidden cave, near the peak of the mountain, and we had surrounded every trail leading down from the peak. So there was nowhere for her to run to, you see. She would be captured for sure, and we—the villagers with farm tools—we would be the ones to take her down. You can imagine how excited we were that night, Master Li. We fought for a noble cause, you see, and now we're heroes.

"Master Li, I had never been so frightened before. Out of nowhere, we heard the howling of wolves. I knew about the vicious pack of wolves she had trained—wasn't that how she came to be called Snow Wolf? We were doomed, with all the high morale and slogan shouting, no one remembered her wolves. For the first time since Lin Cha's men came to the village with food, I thought about the situation. Snow Wolf spent her life protecting us, you see, guided us through floods and famine, through good times and bad. Now, in a matter of days, almost a thousand men scaled this mountain to murder her. My blood ran cold. Why would she let us leave this mountain alive?

"The two men from Redwood Cliff urged us toward the sounds, because the howling of so many wolves meant that Snow Wolf was close by, and she was weak, they told us. She was weak and afraid, and that's why she made so much noise with her wolves. To scare us away.

"They stirred us with a few more slogans and pushed forward again. Even I felt better once I told myself that this was all in the name of justice. 'Kill the villain!' we all shouted. We thought the gods were on our side, you see, and the villain who robbed us of help and relief would finally be punished.

"What fools we were—and we deserved to be used by the witch Lin Cha. We realized too late that Lin Cha was a coward; she didn't dare to face Snow Wolf, and now, we were alone on a mountain with little pick axes and wheat sickles. But it was already too late. Snow Wolf suddenly stood in front of us. She moved like the wind, and there was nothing sick or dying about her.

"We drew our weapons as soon as we saw her, but she held a finger to her lips and said, 'Quiet! The show is about to start.' She motioned for us to follow.

"Then, we started to hear these horrible screams. Cries of death and agony were everywhere, you see, but we were mesmerized, and we followed. Snow Wolf took us to a small clearing by the side of a cliff.

"In the middle of the open space were five men tied to wooden stakes, two of them being eaten alive by wolves, the other three watching in horror. So many wolves were sitting in the clearing that we couldn't count them. None of them moved, you see, even with the smell of blood and fresh meat, none of them made a sound.

"Only a few of them were active. We watched one wolf tear off an arm and walked away to eat in privacy, while two others attacked the legs of their victim. I will never forget the sound of their white jaws snapping.

"After a long time, they stopped screaming, you see. The two men were dead. Their eyes were wide open, staring at us, as if we caused their horrible deaths. A few of us vomited. Some of us fainted.

"I noticed the banner of the Sun Cult hanging on one of the stakes, you see, and underneath the banner was a younger man struggling with his bonds. The remaining two captives were twisting and screaming.

"The young man was shouting at Snow Wolf. He said, 'Leave my brothers alone!' but she didn't seem to pay attention to him. We recognized him then, even though few people had seen him before. We recognized him. He was known as the Scholar.

"I'm sure you've heard about them, Master Li. Even children were raised to understand. If you meet bandits, you run. If there is foreign invasion, you stand and fight. But if you come across the Sun Cult, you can only hope for a quick death. How did Snow Wolf manage to capture the leader of the Sun Cult with all four of his brothers? But it was real, in front of us! Two of the Scholar's brothers were already dead. His two remaining brothers waited to die. It seemed the Sun Cult would be exterminated that night.

"Then Snow Wolf snapped her fingers and pointed at

one of the brothers. Two wolves moved in so quickly the poor man hardly had time to flinch, and in front of our eyes, another man was eaten alive. I never knew that wolves didn't kill their prey before eating them, but that night, we witnessed three men watching themselves being eaten. It gave me nightmares for the rest of my life. In seconds, the cries stopped."

"I remembered the Scholar shouting over and over again, 'Come and kill me! Leave my brothers alone! Come and kill me!' But Snow Wolf paid no attention to him, you see. She looked at us for a second, and I saw a look of amusement in her eyes. Some of us stumbled back. We knew that there was nowhere to run to, and our lives were in her hands. But she wasn't interested in killing us, you see. Her attention turned to the Scholar's last brother. That was when I noticed he was only a boy, no older than ten, with a puddle of urine already drying under his feet. He pleaded with his eyes, but his lips were pressed together. The boy had spirit.

"We heard Snow Wolf say, 'My daughter is only six years older than you, but she died so courageously. I'd like to see you die slowly, painfully—I will have my wolves eat you alive.'

"The Scholar shouted his insults until his voice was hoarse. 'Let him go! He's just a boy! Let him go!' But Snow Wolf disregarded him and took a step closer to the boy. She spoke softly, and I thought I heard her say, 'Of course, we can't allow the Sun Cult to disappear so easily, can we? Someone must stay around to annoy the Dragon House or Lin Cha would be bored to death. How about if you kill him?' Snow Wolf suddenly pointed to the Scholar.

"The boy shook his head. He was too frightened to respond. Snow Wolf whispered something into the boy's ear, and the boy began to shake, you see. Then she said with a laugh, 'It would be a quick death for him if you do it yourself. But only if you do it yourself. My wolves are too hungry to inflict quick death. They prefer to eat first, and kill later.'

"Snow Wolf drew a small dagger and slashed the ropes that held the boy, then handed him the weapon. The Scholar, by then, had silenced. His little brother took a step toward him, and we watched.

"The Scholar said: 'Run, my brother. Stab me and run . . .'

"The boy took a step forward, the dagger held tightly in his fist, poised and drawn back to strike. I heard the Scholar shout, 'Do it! Do it quickly!'

"The boy dragged forward another step, and I noticed Snow Wolf making a subtle motion with her hand. Two of her wolves took position behind the boy. The Scholar's eye's bulged; his body was shaking. He opened his mouth to shout. The wolves bared their fangs and growled, and two more wolves had already taken their positions next to the Scholar, and they waited with ears flattened and the hair on their necks standing vertically.

"'Quick, my brother! Stab me now!'

"'I can't.'

"The Scholar shouted. 'Kill me! Do it now! It's an order! I give you the order to strike now!'

"The boy shielded his face with one hand, as if that could protect him, and screamed back, 'I can't! I can't!'

"'I'm bored,' we thought we heard Snow Wolf say. She gave a signal and a wolf pounced on the boy. All we heard was the Scholar shouting, 'No!'

"Then, the boy was screaming. The wolf's jaw closed around his arm. With a quick jerk, the arm was gone. The boy screamed again when another wolf charged him.

"We all shouted in shock. We didn't expect this; we thought Snow Wolf only wanted the Scholar dead. In the confusion, with the Scholar shouting and the boy in agony, Snow Wolf lifted her hand and tapped the ground three times with her foot. Every wolf in the forest lifted their faces to howl.

"I felt my blood boiling. Never had I seen anything like this, never had I seen so many wolves howling together. It was truly musical, but very scary. I felt cold tingles on my skin.

"In that split second, the boy took a final step at the Scholar and stabbed him in the midsection. The Scholar uttered a cry of shock. We thought we saw a smile of satisfaction on his face. The boy stumbled back. He was losing too much blood. He crumbled to the ground.

"The howling became louder. Then, three wolves stepped forward and began to eat the Scholar alive. The boy screamed and crawled forward, but he was fainting from the loss of blood. The Scholar gritted his teeth and didn't utter a sound. The boy continued to scream, but we couldn't hear him. Master Li, the sounds of so many wolves nearly drove me mad that night. For many years to come, you see, I shuddered when I heard its howl. Many times, when I have nightmares, even in my old age, I hear the howl in the background.

"The boy could do nothing; he didn't even have the strength to crawl to his brother, you see. He turned his face and stared at the wolves around him, then at us. Then he fainted.

"Snow Wolf signaled for the wolves to quiet before turning to us. Our hearts nearly stopped. It was our turn.

"She held up a hand to quiet us, you see, then spoke in a loud, clear voice.

"She said: 'It's unfortunate that the suffering of famine and disease today can't compare to the misery that your children will face tomorrow. But the time will come for your children and grandchildren to kill each other, where fathers will murder their sons and daughters will murder their mothers. There will be so much slaughter between the leaders of the land that the surface of Redwood Cliff will be smeared with blood, and their children, and yours, will suffer for these crimes.'

"'The time has come,' she said. 'The time has come for me to leave this world. But I am leaving a world of fear and betrayal and jealousy and dishonor. It's not the world that I envisioned my daughter to grow up in. But my child is gone. This is my punishment for my crude ignorance—this is my punishment. With my mistakes, I have brought disaster upon my family and I have disgraced my name. Allow me today to carry out my redemption.'

"'You have all been looking for gold? It's in this mountain, but my ghost will haunt this mountain forever. You're all welcome to come and seek the gold, but none of you will ever escape alive.'

"She turned, and in three massive steps, reached the cliff side of the mountain. Without looking back once, she jumped. None of us moved. This was so unexpected that none of us dared to utter a sound.

"Little by little, the wolves began to pick themselves up and depart. They paid no attention to us, you see. We were afraid to go to the side of the cliff to look, even more afraid to approach the boy who lay bleeding to death. Finally, one of us who knew a little about medicine ran to him and applied a tourniquet. We were afraid, you see—more than ever, we were afraid. What's left of the Sun Cult could target us for revenge. Lin Cha's men could slay us to seal their secret. But worse of all, Snow Wolf vowed to haunt the mountain, and we hadn't descended yet."

. . .

Well before the first streak of dawn, the crowing of the rooster would normally shatter the silence of the night. But this night, in front of Pan Tong Village, while Suthachai and Fei Fei watched the sun streak into full view, not a single chicken made a sound.

They were high on a hilltop, looking down at the placid village embedded in a snow-covered valley.

"They are all dead," Suthachai said. "The dogs, the pigs, the chickens. They are all dead." He gazed at the curved tile roofs below him, the heavy wooden doors and the firmly closed windows, and thought of the little child sleeping in his bed.

It was the first time either of them said a word. The journey back across the lake was long and silent, each deeply involved in their own thoughts, their own worries. They arrived at Pan Tong Village slightly before dawn.

"The sun is out," she said, squinting at the light.

"I know."

"I was thinking of how peculiar this village is. It sits alone, hidden in between two mountains and far away from other wheat growers." She pointed to the small road that led to the other end of the village. "That road is the only way to a higher elevation. In a bad winter, the snow could cave in and bury the whole village. No wonder my aunt came here during the famine."

Suthachai nodded.

"What did you see in this village?" she asked.

He didn't respond. He looked at the concrete house with the red lanterns, the red silk scrolls with gold writing, and his eyes shifted to the wheat fields in the back of the village. He didn't recognize the crop, but they seemed healthy.

"Is it true that only the wealthy can afford silk?"

Fei Fei turned to him. "The wealthy? Not necessarily. Silk harvests have been good. Good for many years in a row, and common people were able to buy it. Why?"

"Are those wheat fields?" He pointed with the butt of his saber. "Used for food?"

"Yes, we make buns and noodles with wheat. The wheat fields are strong, very strong for a winter harvest. Our entire province has been prosperous for many years now. And with healthy crops, the livestock flourished." She placed a hand on his arm. "Why do you ask?"

"I want to know that the people here had plenty to eat."

"Of course," she said.

"Come," he said, standing abruptly. With a quick jerk, he pulled Fei Fei to her feet. "It is bright enough. Let me show you." He took her hand and guided her down the narrow path to the village. A small tombstone stood cleanly swept by the trail—someone's ancestor, apparently—and Fei Fei steered him away.

"I know," Suthachai said with a nod, then suddenly, "What were you doing here four nights ago?"

"My father sent me here to bury the dead," she said.

"Did your father kill off the entire village?"

"I think so . . . "

"Why?"

Fei Fei shook her head, her eyes lowered. "I don't know. My father wanted it done, and he didn't want anyone knowing about it."

"Of course not," Suthachai said, his voice cold. "There are women and children in there."

"And then you interfered, and I wanted to confront you myself." She squeezed his hand playfully, then said, "We were going to come back the following day but grandmother died. She died not long after we gave her the jade."

"My friend Li Kung said that she was supposed to die years ago. Somehow, she stayed alive. Some inner will, he said, some strange desire to go on living for something."

"For the jade?"

"Maybe it is for the jade."

"Li Kung said that?"

"Yes, he is my only friend in China."

"My brother said that Li Kung's a fake doctor with no real learning."

"He really is a doctor," Suthachai said, his voice firm. "Whoever spread the rumors made a mistake." He suddenly froze in his tracks, as if a bolt of lightning struck him. "I thought I saw him on Redwood Cliff yesterday morning. I do not know if he made it down—your men were killing the guests by the stairway!"

Fei Fei squeezed his hand. "Li Kung? At my grandmother's funeral?"

"He . . . " Suthachai paused, quick thoughts flashing through his mind. For a moment, he could not decide whether his friend's secret should be shared with the woman he loved. Was she really an ally?

"Suthachai? If you would dishonor your friend by telling me anything, then don't tell me."

He breathed a sigh of relief. He thought of Li Kung, of whether the young man ever found samples of this complex alchemy that even Black Shadow knew about. "Let us go," he said. "I will show you why."

Suthachai neared the entrance of the village. He walked over to the well and pointed inside.

"No," Fei Fei said. "Not the water. Old Snake would

never poison a well, because the water could travel underground into other villages. He only kills those he targets."

Suthachai turned to the center of the village, lifted his finger and swept it in an arc before him. "They were all targeted for death? Even the children?"

"I don't know. Old Snake never second guesses my father's orders."

"Neither do you."

Suthachai led her down the main road and turned into a narrow courtyard. In the back, the lanterns of a newly married couple swayed from the tiled roofs. "The air?" he asked again. "Like the poison candles?"

"I think so. I don't really know."

"The air," he repeated. "That is how they were killed. Old Snake poisoned the air."

She gave a subtle nod. Suthachai turned away. "Poison fumes," he muttered. "Poisoned air."

With a heavy kick, he burst the wooden door open, forcing a heavy gust of wind into the house. Suthachai glanced at the brick oven at the corner. He walked into the next room with bold steps, stepped in front of the bed. He grabbed the red covers of the newly wed and threw them aside.

Fei Fei ran up behind him. "What are you doing?"

"They were just married. Even I recognize the red lanterns outside."

"Why are you . . . ?"

Suthachai grabbed the groom's body and shredded his clothing with one quick twist. Fei Fei gasped. The body was thin and shriveled, like someone who hadn't eaten in weeks. His ribs protruded from his chest, his elbow and shoulder joints wedged out sharply from his skin. The abdomen was withered, dried; sagging skin formed deep creases across the waist, and the folds that were once his chest cleanly outlined the rib cage.

"The wheat looked strong," Suthachai said. "There is plenty of food here." He picked up a fine silk outfit folded next to the bed—a man's outfit.

"Only people who have money can buy silk," Suthachai said again. He reached across the bed and grabbed the bride's body.

"Wait!" Fei Fei shouted.

It was too late. Suthachai tore open her gown and pointed at her plump body, stout waist, and full breasts. Though dead for almost five days, the consistent cold left the pale skin unscathed.

"Come," he said, without waiting for her to comment. He took her hand and pulled her out of the house, through the courtyard and back to the front of the village. Fei Fei staggered behind him.

"She may have married in from another village," Suthachai said to confirm her suspicions. He stopped by the well again, turned to face the village and waved his hand across their line of sight. "Pick a house," he said.

"What's going on, Suthachai?"

He didn't wait for her to choose. He pulled her harder and ran toward the center of the village and into a shabbier unit. He broke through the battered door and walked up to a body lying snugly in bed. He pointed to two leftover buns on a short wooden table, now stale and frozen. He grabbed the body and yanked open the fine clothing to reveal yet another man completely withered away. The man couldn't have eaten in a month.

Suthachai held the bony torso erect, just long enough for Fei Fei to see, and dropped it back onto the bed. He turned and opened his mouth to say something, then paused. With eyes lowered and lips pressed grimly together, he lifted the bed sheet and pulled it over the man's face.

"I have seen famine before," he finally said. "Their bodies adjust to it gradually, so their skin would never hollow out like this."

Fei Fei backed out of the door, turned stiffly to another cement house across the road. Suthachai followed.

"If you want to look inside," he said. "The house is in good condition."

She sighed. She rubbed her left side again, drew a deep breath and blasted the solid wood. The door gave way, slowly at first, and then toppled with a loud crack. Dust erupted from the ground. Suthachai stared behind her at the dark room completely barren and stripped of all ornaments. The walls were bare and the furniture was missing. Two bodies lay in bed, a man and a woman. An old rag, thin and worn, covered them.

Fei Fei avoided a dead rat by her feet, pulled open the drawers of an old desk and rustled through some papers inside. She hunched over, against the narrow slit of sunlight beaming through the window and read the papers one by one.

Suthachai stood watching by the door, uneasy with the attention she paid to this particular household. They evidently met the same fate; the man had shriveled to a stack of bones despite the abundance in food. But she expected to find something here. He noticed the clues she followed. The house seemed new, none of the bricks on the oven were chipped, the overhead beams on each doorway newly painted with a light floral design. Yet, the furniture was missing, and the urns in the kitchen not safely covered meant that no food was stored away. The cold winter, though not devastating, required thicker covers than what the couple had.

"Here," Fei Fei said. "This is what Black Shadow meant."

She pulled a crumbled piece of paper from the stack. "A loan receipt. This couple borrowed money from a neighboring village."

Suthachai took the note. "Is this a lot of money?"

"Enough to last this family a full year."

He glanced once at the couple on the bed and swallowed hard before proceeding out the door. "That is how word got out," he said, walking to the next house with rapid strides. "These people were slowly dying from a strange alchemy. This is how even Li Kung knew about it." He smashed down another door, then another. Fei Fei followed closely, sifting through any documents she could find in the household, but always remaining one step behind him.

The day was bright, and the cold, wet air from the night before had yielded to the morning sun. Suthachai stood in the middle of the village, his head bowed, his feet firmly planted in the snow. Every door along the main road had been smashed. He felt the small porcelain jar that Black Shadow threw at him, wondering what really happened to this village.

"Suthachai," Fei Fei called him from behind. He didn't turn around. "Suthachai, I found at least twenty loan agreements—two of which . . . "

She stood next to him then, a stack of paper in her hands, the topmost a letter with a red stamp on it. "This is a letter—"

He placed both hands on her shoulders, looked into her eyes.

"It's a letter," she said, her voice barely audible. "It's addressed to . . . He had one last chance to buy his wife back, at twice the money he sold her for, by the end of the week or she would be taken down south to more popular brothels."

Suthachai looked away and said nothing.

"What happened here, Suthachai?"

"I don't know. But your father knows. That's why he killed everyone here."

She lowered her head. The documents dropped from her hands and scattered across the snow. Suthachai brushed his hand across her cheek.

. . .

Slowly, she slid her hand into his coat pocket. He barely noticed until she pulled out the porcelain jar and said, "Black Shadow told us to try this. This is the alchemy he found. Here, in this village."

Suthachai grabbed her hand and twisted the jar from her. "You and your uncle are enemies—I saw the massacre with my own eyes yesterday. How can you take anything this Black Shadow gave you?"

"If he wanted to kill me, he would've done it last night. The two of us can't stop him." She took the jar back from his hand. "Maybe this really is the poison Li Kung is searching for. But Black Shadow tried it last night, and he's still alive."

"How do you know he tried it last night?" Suthachai raised his voice, more agitated now.

She placed a finger on his lips, gently. "He's the greatest warrior alive. He has a reputation for being a man of honor."

"Is there such a thing? Is there such a thing here, in China?"

"There is," she said softly. "There is honor in our world." She looked inside the jar. A black paste, thick with a subtle scent, glowing against the sunlight. She brought it up to her nose, but Suthachai placed a hand over it.

"No. What if it really is poison?"

She smiled, a bright smile that made his heart stop. "Then I die," she said. "Then we both die of poison, in each other's arms, and we can go to the next life together." She took his hand off the jar and lifted it to her nose, breathing it in. "I'm not familiar with the smell."

Suthachai reached for the jar one more time. "But maybe, when you go back today and you ask Old Snake, maybe there is an antidote for me. Then both of us can live, and we can start with being together in *this* life."

She stared at him, her almond eyes troubled but happy. "There is no antidote, Suthachai. There really isn't."

"I know."

"I'll go with you, wherever you go."

"I know." He lifted a finger to wipe the tear from her eye. "But I am not going yet. So do not go first."

Fei Fei reached into her hair, pulled out a silver pin. "Silver will blacken if the paste is toxic."

"Are you sure?"

"I have to know, Suthachai. And I have to know whether my father is behind all this. Please? I'll be strong. I promise."

He nodded. She wrapped her arms around him in a deep embrace. He held her, pressed her slender body into his, and felt then that if the world were to end, if only he could die with her in his arms, then he could ask for nothing more.

They sat down on the snow together, and Suthachai inserted the silver hairpin into the black paste. He drew a water flask from his belt.

"The water is cold," he said, squeezing the soft cowhide.

"I don't mind."

He pulled the silver needle out, wiped it on his coat, and held it up to the sun. The needle was clean silver.

She peeled off a chunk of the black paste from the porcelain jar, brought it to her nose and sniffed.

"Are you sure?"

"I am," she replied. "I have to."

She smeared the paste on her tongue, hunched over, her lips firmly sealed, and swallowed hard. Suthachai shifted to a kneeling position in front of her and placed the flask to her lips. She drank a little, wanted to say something to him, but her eyes became blank, and Suthachai almost dropped the flask in alarm. He quickly slid his body closer to hers, took her in his arms and supported her weakened body against his chest. Her eyes were partially closed, her hands began to shake, and he waited, calmly stroking her hair and cheeks, whispering into her ears.

"Hold still. Hold still."

She cuddled against him and moaned. A strange smile appeared on her face.

• • •

Her face tingled with a cool, wet feeling when she swallowed the paste, but almost immediately, her stomach flared into a powerful ball of heat. She barely recognized Suthachai; but the smell of leather held to her lips brought her back for a second, and she felt normal. Then, when he sat down next to her, she felt the tingle travel up her face, into her hair, and everything began to change shape in front of her eyes. She looked down, but she was no longer sitting on the snow—the ground seemed to be moving farther and farther away from her. She thought she leaned on something, but all around her, the houses and fields of Pan Tong Village were moving, waning back and forth in a mellow rhythm. Then she was underwater—it had to be underwater—the houses around her began to float, rising and falling with light waves, and she saw bubbles. The light began to change around her, or-ange, then yellow, then a crisp gold, and a colorful bubble with the entire spectrum of colors swirling in its core approached her. She smiled. It was beautiful.

She was in the bubble then, the translucent walls rippling softly to the touch. She felt herself rising, being lifted by the bubble into the heavens. The ground moved farther away from her, the streaming sunlight scattered into a multitude of brilliant colors, and she reached out to touch the light. She laughed out loud, giggled into the blurry sky, her arms flapping in pleasure.

She floated endlessly. Sometimes she was underwater, and the scatter of colors faded to a deep blue, but mostly she saw herself twisting and turning on a bed of clouds, the thin bubble almost completely transparent, carrying her farther and farther away. It seemed to last forever.

A deep sigh escaped her lips when her body finally steadied, and the light blue of the heavens dissolved. Slowly, she saw the houses of Pan Tong Village settle, the fragments of concrete floating across the clouds now returning to its original place. The village was exactly as she left it. Suthachai was watching her, and she smiled.

"You were laughing," he said.

"I know . . . " She reached for the porcelain jar and dipped her finger into the paste. "I want to do it again," she said, her voice distant, dreamy.

He took her hand, wiped the paste from her fingers and drew the jar away. "We agreed," he said. "You have to be strong."

She seemed disappointed, but only for a second. She sat up firmly. "I'm sorry."

"What happened?"

It came back to her then, every image, the sensation of floating clouds, of flying. Her head dropped into her hands, and she held her face. "The pleasure! This is why the villagers couldn't stop using it!"

"Tell me," he said, his arm tightly wrapped around her. "Tell me . . . "

. . .

The Grand Stairway stood in front of her like a winding snake, its treacherous surface inviting, beckoning her to ascend. The guards at the gate, staring at her with gaping jaws, quickly lowered their heads when she turned to them. She did not have her disguise on.

Fei Fei sighed, the pressure of so much suddenly on her back. The world was so simple before yesterday. Under disguise, she was the feared Flute Demon, leader of great warriors, her fighting ability and keen wit undisputed across the land. As Fei Fei, she was the daughter of Master Bin, admired and desired by all who laid eyes on her. People respected her House wherever she went, her family always the true hero in everyone's heart—in her heart.

She touched the porcelain jar in her coat, felt the cold surface, and thought of the shriveled corpses still unburied in Pan Tong Village. Tears welled into her eyes. Was it Old Snake, or was it her own father responsible for something so cruel? The people in Pan Tong Village were executed, most likely to conceal this secret alchemy. What could be gained by hurting these people?

The Grand Stairway stretched forever in front of her. Fei Fei had climbed these stairs almost every day of her life, but this day, her own weight hindered her, and she felt old and slow.

The thought of Suthachai brought a smile to her lips,

but just as quickly, the troubled look reemerged. She remembered the last words he said to her.

"*Come to Redwood Cliff with me,*" she had said. "*My father will like you. He likes men like you.*"

"*Why would I be courteous to a coward like him?*"

"*How . . . How could you . . . ?*"

"*There is a child in there whose body shriveled to a rack of bones! What did the child ever do to him? Why did he have to feed him this medicine that eats into his brain! For control? To control common farmers?*"

"*It may not be my father! You can't believe what Black Shadow told you—he's loyal to my uncle! My father is an honorable man!*"

He closed his eyes, breathing deeply over and over again, and she recalled being afraid that his poison would resurface. He calmed, eventually, and told her to go first. He would wait for her news in the Blue Lantern Inn of He Ku. She wrapped her arms around him then, pressed her lips to his and melted into his embrace.

"*Promise me,*" he said. "*Promise me that I will not have to die under the sword of your people. If there is no antidote, let me die peacefully, with you beside me. Let it not come to slaughter between your father's men and me.*"

"*I promise . . .* " *Tears flowed from her eyes.* "*I promise.*"

The surface of Redwood Cliff was more barren than ever. The few nervous guards posted at the top of the stairs bowed when she approached. The bloodstains on the frozen ground were cleaned, and the bitter wind that swept through the surface had cleared away the remnants of yesterday's battle.

There was a small bloodstain on the road, and this time she saw it; despite her father's orders that every sign of battle be cleared from Redwood Cliff. It was a small stain, merely light drops of blood, still red, perhaps from a minor wound.

"I'm sorry, master," said a voice far down the road. One of her father's men hobbled over on crutches, his right leg missing from the thigh down. "I'm sorry!" he shouted again. "I didn't mean to bleed on the road."

Crude bandages covered the stump that was once his leg, soaked with fresh blood, still dripping. She held up her hand and ordered him to halt.

"Why isn't your leg properly bandaged?"

The man lowered his head. "I'm sorry, master. I did it myself, and I'm not good at it. I'll make sure it won't drip on the road again."

He attempted to leave.

"Hold it!"

"Yes, master."

"Why didn't the doctor bandage your leg for you?"

The man's eyes remained lowered. "The doctors have more important things to do. I can take care of this myself."

A short distance away, Fei Fei noticed another man waiting down the road, a blood-soaked bandage over his left eye. Fei Fei looked back at the man with the amputated leg and pointed in the direction of the barracks.

"See to the injuries immediately. Find the doctors, and tell them that under my orders they are to treat all injured men on Redwood Cliff. Anyone who doesn't comply will be executed!"

The man paused. Fei Fei checked herself and realized she wasn't under disguise. "I'll tell my father," she quickly added. "And he'll execute anyone who doesn't obey!"

"Yes, master," the man said, bowing his head lower. Fei Fei walked past him, down the stone road, and swiftly approached the training quarters.

The training hall of the Red Dragons consisted of a loose cluster of buildings and courtyards, surrounded by a stone wall and heavily guarded from uninvited spectators. The Wei family had taken tremendous measures to safeguard the martial arts of the Dragon House. Though students of the Red Dragons numbered into the thousands, few had enough talent to inherit the entire martial arts system.

To Master Bin's dismay, neither of his sons possessed the gift, nor the interest, of becoming a great warrior. Even worse, his only daughter displayed such genius that Master Bin couldn't resist. He had to train her.

Fei Fei climbed the arched trunk of a tree, sprang over the wall like a cat, and slipped into an isolated building in the rear. This was how she routinely entered the training halls since childhood.

She dropped in front of the heavy doors. Someone was following her. She reached for her flute in alarm, but knew it was already too late to strike. The pain in her left ribs flashed, she fought it, and struggled to gain distance from the enemy.

"Hold it!"

Fei Fei breathed in relief. Her father stood in front of her, casually dressed, his metal fan opened and weaving in front of his chest, as if returning from a carefree walk in the woods.

"You're injured," he said, stepping forward. He took her by the arm and led her toward the door. "Who could have hurt you like that?"

"Father, I need to talk to you."

Master Bin turned and pulled open the heavy doors. "Black Shadow was not on the cliff yesterday morning, so I thought there was no one who could hurt you. How did it happen?"

"It was an accident."

"Cricket told me about an enormous warrior who used a Mongolian saber. Is that true?"

"Yes."

They entered a room where, along the walls, all eighteen categories of weaponry were displayed. None of the eighteen categories included a musical instrument also fashioned into a weapon. She touched her flute proudly. Her weapon was unique.

Master Bin led her to a small table where a jug of rice wine waited.

"Was he really Mongolian?" he asked, pouring the wine into small cups. He motioned for her to sit.

"Yes."

Master Bin stared. "How did a Mongolian end up at my mother's funeral? And more importantly, how did you lose to him?"

Fei Fei shied away with a smile. "He's the greatest warrior on the steppe. He's incredibly strong, and his techniques are strange and irregular. I've never seen a warrior like him, ever."

Master Bin pushed a small cup of wine to his daughter, and then lifted his own cup. "Strange and irregular," he repeated, the wine held steady at his lips. "This Mongolian—is he the same one who had the jade and defeated the two hundred men we sent to raid his camp?"

"That's him."

Master Bin eyed her with interest. "Did you kill him?"

Fei Fei shook her head. Master Bin's eyes glowed. "You came home without killing the enemy? It's not like you."

She sipped the wine and stared at the jug, speechless.

"I'm glad to see you home, Fei Fei. Forget the Mongolian. I was told he's been poisoned with the Soaring Dragon Candles. He won't survive."

Fei Fei looked up, took a deep breath and reached into her pocket for the porcelain jar. "Father . . . "

"Stranger things have happened, Fei Fei. Strange and unexpected. We shouldn't dwell on the past—let's focus on the future. We lost some men, but we have plenty more. The Red Dragons endured a minor scrape from yesterday's slaughter. Nothing to be concerned about. As for the turmoil stirred in the Martial Society . . . "

"Father?" Fei Fei held the jar in her pocket, hesitated, no longer confident that confronting her father would do any good.

"You have something to ask me, Fei Fei?"

She nodded, her throat tight.

"I know what's on your mind, my child. You want to know what went wrong yesterday."

Fei Fei thought of the black paste, of Pan Tong Village, of Suthachai. She felt a surge of guilt in her heart, aware that she never really thought about what happened to her family. "What happened yesterday?" she finally asked.

"Yesterday," Master Bin said with a sigh, "I prepared for the worst. My brother's men arrived in hordes and I already knew something was about to go wrong. So many of them came fully armed. They wanted a war. I even had Old Snake prepare airborne poison, just in case the Green Dragons were to attack us."

"The Green Dragons didn't really come to fight, Father," Fei Fei said. "I watched them carefully all night, and they didn't come for war."

"Neither did we. You know that, Fei Fei. So, who could've planted the ancestral decree?"

"I don't think Uncle Xu would do that. And he couldn't have. Tree roots were growing through the cauldron, and the copper was crumbling with rust. It's just not possible, especially without anyone on Redwood Cliff knowing about it."

"It's not likely," Master Bin said. "And because it's not likely, we're in a greater position of danger."

Fei Fei shook her head and didn't say anything.

Master Bin sipped his wine, as if the close brush with death and disaster just a day ago meant nothing to him. "Let me explain a scenario to you, just so you'd understand."

He leaned on the wooden back of his chair. "Imagine your uncle, who grew up the elder of two twins on Redwood Cliff, who should be guaranteed the right to leadership more than anyone. He was the better fighter, he thought he commanded more respect from the common people. Being the older twin, he felt he deserved the empire that our ancestors built. But as you know, Fei Fei, your uncle only received half the wealth and power he thought he was entitled to. Less than half. He was not the favorite son in your grandmother's eyes, and since she preferred to remain on Redwood Cliff, he had to take his half and rebuild elsewhere. Meanwhile, jealousy and hatred kept him up at night. In warriors, he had plenty, and in wealth and land, he really is our equal. But we're on Redwood Cliff, and he's not."

Master Bin paused, poured himself another cup of rice wine and continued, "But your grandmother's death is the opportunity he had been waiting for. With this funeral, he could resurface as an equal, if not the superior brother of the Dragon Houses. That's why he came with hundreds of armed men to show his strength and power.

"So my dear brother plotted early. He planted the decree in the designated gravesite many years ago, before he even left Redwood Cliff to form the Green Dragon House.

At the opportune moment, he would declare himself the victim in front of the world. He knew he would gain nothing from a decree delegating all wealth to himself, because a piece of paper found in a cauldron could easily be false. So he aroused suspicion against us instead. Now, as a victim, as an older brother about to lose everything, he would be free to attack us and still remain on the side of justice.

"We need to be on the alert for surprise attacks," Master Bin continued, after a slight pause. "It could happen any moment now. He hated us for so many years. Now, with a well-prepared excuse, and in the name of self defense, why wouldn't he destroy us?"

Fei Fei's eyes wandered away from her father, drifted into the full porcelain cup in front of her. It was so complicated, so unlikely. Yet, how could she not believe him? He had always been right, always made the right decisions.

"You don't believe this scenario, do you?" Master Bin asked.

"I don't know. But it could also be someone who wants us to kill each other."

Master Bin leaned back, touched the tips of his fingers together, lost in deep thought.

"Why did you take such precautions not to fight?" Fei Fei asked. "Wasn't yesterday the perfect opportunity to kill half their men? They were on our territory. We could've planted so many traps . . . "

Master Bin smiled coolly. "It wouldn't be right to kill him at your grandmother's funeral."

"It wouldn't be right to kill your enemy? What happened?"

"I have many things to tell you, Fei Fei. I was worried you may be too young, but . . . "

"Father, you can always tell me anything."

Master Bin smiled. "Yes, I can. I have a secret to tell you."

"Tell me."

"Better yet, I'll show you." He lifted his palm and indicated for her to stand.

Fei Fei quickly said, "Father, would you forgive this Mongolian for attacking us yesterday? It was all a misunderstanding."

Master Bin stopped, sat back down and leaned on his chair. "And how was it a misunderstanding?"

"We poisoned him. We poisoned him for the jade and he only came here to search for a cure. To save his own life."

"We poison whomever we please!" Master Bin's face flushed red, then just as quickly, he calmed and laughed. "He wants an antidote?"

She nodded.

"Did you tell him there's no such thing, or did you forget to?"

Fei Fei slowly brought the wine to her lips and left it there, her eyes on her father. Master Bin said again, "You didn't kill him, he didn't kill you, and now you're discussing an antidote."

Fei Fei nodded again. Her father smiled and leaned forward. "Why him, my child? He's a barbarian."

Fei Fei looked away.

"But worse," Master Bin continued, "he's going to die."

A tear welled in Fei Fei's eyes, but she held it down. Master Bin patted her hand. "Come. I have a great secret to show you. Forget the Mongolian, we have the power of the world in our hands."

"I have something to tell you, Father."

"Tell me later. I want to show you my secret." He opened a box next to the table and pulled out a strip of canvas, poured wine into his mouth, then spat the alcohol in a loud spray across the cloth. He took his daughter's hand and drew her to a yellow drape at the far end of the room.

Against the wall was a kettle of water. "Bring that," he said, pointing at the kettle.

Master Bin pulled the yellow drape aside with a jerk, revealing a double door made of blackened stone. Above the door was a plaque chiseled in red wood: "Hall Between Heaven and Earth."

Fei Fei stared. "I never knew there was a door behind this curtain."

"Of course you didn't. I've only been in here once—when I was a child—your grand aunt showed this place to me."

"My grand aunt?"

"Snow Wolf," Master Bin said. He reached for the copper rings on the doors. "She told me the ancients of the Dragon House trained in there."

"Hall Between Heaven and Earth," Fei Fei said quietly. "Something about that name sounds familiar."

"It does," Master Bin said, smiling. He drew open the heavy doors. "Every peasant in the world has been wondering what 'Between Heaven and Earth' meant."

"The poem," Fei Fei said, and her mouth opened in awe. "The poem at the bottom of the lake."

A gust of cold air crept through the opened doorway. Fei Fei peered in, her eyes narrowed. "The energy is strange in here," she thought her father said. She stepped carefully, inching into the room, the words of the poem trembling from her lips.

The room was circular in shape, with intricate dragons carved across the walls, each dragon more ferocious than the next. Four lifelike statues of solid stone stood around the room.

Master Bin pointed to the four sides of the circle, symmetrically split by the stone statues. "The ancients crafted this circular training hall so we could train where there's no direction, no beginning point, no end point. Yet, the four statues counteract the circle, creating corners for the room, and establishing the five elements."

"The four statues?"

"The fifth element, earth, is in the center," Master Bin said. "There's no statue, because whoever is in the room assumes that position."

The door she came through had closed and disappeared among the complex dragon carvings along the walls. Above, a narrow circular opening in the ceiling was the only source of light.

"The elements of life, in five directions," Master Bin began to recite. "The great leader must arm them between Heaven and Earth."

"Did the poem under the lake really refer to this training hall? Between Heaven and Earth?"

"You'll see," Master Bin said. "When the great leader arms the five directions, you'll see."

They stood in the middle of the floor. Master Bin pointed to one of the statues. "That is West," he said, walking across the room to the statue of a fierce general in full armor.

"West belongs to Metal in the five elements," Master Bin continued. He drew a double-edge sword from behind the statue, brought it to the general's outstretched fist and mounted it in the statue's hand. "So I armed the West with Metal."

Fei Fei turned. Across the room was a stone archer on one knee. His bow was fully drawn, his head cocked and his eyes narrowed in sharp focus.

"He's missing an arrow in the bow," Fei Fei said. "That must be East, with the element Wood."

"Yes, my child," Master Bin said proudly. "I merely placed an ordinary arrow in his fingers, and it fits perfectly." Master Bin fitted an arrow, left at the foot of the statue, into the archer's bow.

Fei Fei pointed North, to a stone lady in long robes. The lady held a bowl in front of her. "And that must be the position of Water. The water in this kettle is meant for her bowl."

"And Fire," Master Bin said, addressing the statue in the South. It was a stocky, barbaric man holding a torch. "I'll wrap this strip of cloth on the end of his torch, and we'll have fire."

Fei Fei carried the kettle to the statue in the North and poured water into the bowl. Facing South, Master Bin wrapped the barbarian's torch and ignited it.

The fire from the torch emitted a brilliant light. There was nothing in the room to receive the light—nothing except the broadsword held by the statue in the West. Metal belonged to West in the five directions. The broadsword beamed the light across the bowl of water in the North. The water reflected the light, but diffused it, just enough to encompass the drawn bow of the archer in the East.

The wooden arrow on the statue now projected a shadow against the curved wall. Absently, Fei Fei lifted her finger and traced the shadow, a long arrow pointed diagonally upwards. She looked at her father, her mouth dropping in awe.

"Come, my child," Master Bin said. "This is the secret I should have shared with you a long time ago."

"Facing East, the archer points," Fei Fei said in an irregular murmur. "I can recite the poem in my sleep." She walked to the very center of the room, under the opening in the ceiling, so that the incoming sunlight was directly over her. There was no shadow from her body. "The center is the fifth direction. Man on Earth points back," she continued to recite. "The nine dragons speak to us—He will answer, as a god."

Staring east at the stone archer, she drew her flute, leveled it in front of her, and pointed at the archer's arrow. "Man on Earth points back," she repeated.

Another shadow, this one from the flute, rested against the wall. Master Bin traced it with one hand, while drawing an extension of the archer's shadow with the other. The two pointers met on the face of a dragon.

Master Bin pressed his palm onto the dragon's face. "This is where the two arrows meet," he said. "This is where the secret lies."

He pushed harder against the dragon's face, and a portion of the wall began to cave in and reveal a small opening.

Fei Fei peered in. There was nothing in there.

"I already took the treasure," Master Bin said.

"The treasure?"

"That the gods meant for us to have. It's their wish that the Dragon House unite again and become great again. With this gift, we'll dominate all of the Martial Society, and all of civilization as we know it!"

Fei Fei stared at the bright opening above her, at a light streak of clouds casually floating in the sky. "I was on that cloud before," she murmured. She looked squarely at her father then and asked, "How do you dominate the Martial Society with a single treasure? Unless it's an alchemy that can control man's will."

Master Bin stared for a second, caught by surprise, and then recovered with a smile. "You've heard of something, haven't you? Word has gotten out about Pan Tong Village."

There was a look of glee on her father's face, an expression of a child who stole candy from a younger brother but was never discovered. She frowned. "What is the treasure, Father?"

"A sheepskin," Master Bin said, watching her closely. "I didn't tell you earlier because I didn't know what it would mean for us. But it's a sheepskin, with the formula of a great medicine written on it."

Fei Fei unconsciously touched the little jar in her pocket. "Great medicine?"

"Great medicine," Master Bin repeated. "An arrangement so extraordinary that only the gods could have devised it. Come, let me show you."

Fei Fei pulled the jar from her pocket and held it open.

Master Bin took one look at it and snatched it from her. "Where did you get this?"

"From a dead farmer in Pan Tong Village."

Master Bin stared at the paste, unconsciously touched it with his finger. "This is it—in its final form. You haven't buried the dead in Pan Tong Village yet?"

"Not yet . . . " Fei Fei stammered, suddenly more afraid than she had ever been. She always obeyed her father, and never once did she dispute his orders. He had always been fair to her. But that moment, his voice was cold, almost inhuman. She felt her legs weaken. "I . . . I was going to. I found the jade, and I had to pursue it. Then grandmother died and . . . "

"You didn't really find it on a farmer, did you? You weren't sent to look for anything. Who gave it to you?"

Master Bin suddenly took a step forward, and Fei Fei slid back, her heart painfully murmuring against her stomach. She composed herself, biting her lip while preparing her response.

Master Bin quickly softened and took her hand with a smile. "You could tell your father. If anyone threatens us, we can handle it together. There's nothing father and daughter can't discuss together."

Fei Fei trembled, just once, the familiar kindness from father to daughter locking into her soul. The world was about to fall from underneath her. Life as she knew it could be banished forever. But yet, the hypnotic light in her father's eyes beckoned her to trust him, just as she had done all her life.

She was lost in a mist of shrouded memories among fears of the unknown, and a slow tear trickled down her cheek. "Father!" she whispered hoarsely. "I love him. Can't we find an antidote for him?"

• • •

Old Two opened the pouches one by one. He held them close to his face and smelled them, smiling like a child with a new toy. "You silly boy," he said with a chuckle. "How do you know these are the ingredients? None of these herbs are related to each other. No one ever combines them to make medicine."

"I got as much as I could, Shifu," Li Kung said. "I don't really know how many there are."

Old Two nodded, patted Li Kung on the shoulder, and threw Pun a wink before spreading the samples across the table.

"So many people died on Redwood Cliff," Li Kung said. "I watched the slaughter with my own eyes."

"Really? Did you collect some of the blood for me?" He glanced at the herbs, and then held up a hand to interrupt his student. "Never mind, they wouldn't have this stuff in their blood anyway. Only the people in Pan Tong Village—but I already got some of their blood. Leave me alone now. I need some peace and quiet to see how these old dogs up north do alchemy."

"Yes, Shifu." He turned to Pun. "Let's go."

They were about to leave, hand in hand, when Pun broke free and ran back to the old man. "What about the cure for the Mongolian?"

Old Two scratched his beard, his eyes on the ceiling as if contemplating the meaning of life. Then he snapped his fingers with a smile. "Ah, yes. The Mongolian. I believe I have something. Worked with it just last night. Tell him to come here, and we can draw more blood from him."

Li Kung rolled his eyes. "Shifu Two, don't play with him anymore. He doesn't want to give you his blood."

"But he has to," the old man said. "This might work."

Li Kung shook his head. Pun grabbed his hand and pulled him away. "Come on, we need to find Suthachai."

"You don't really believe . . . "

"Come on!" Pun yanked him harder. "He may have a chance now if Shifu Two says there's a cure. What's a little blood? I know where to find him. There's only one inn that silly Mongolian knows how to go to."

. . .

Iron Hand Liu opened a red brocade box, revealing a gold-handled broadsword. A coarse frown wove itself into his brows. They would be here, and his entire family would die.

A young man scurried into the room. "Master, we've completed the preparations. Anything more we can do?"

Iron Hand Liu sighed. "Let me have a look."

Outside the complex, spiked wooden barricades had

been erected to fend off cavalry, and archers lay on top of every roof to await the enemy. Liu stepped into the courtyard, lifted his face to the tall concrete walls surrounding his property, and sighed again. This would not hold them. He turned to a nearby student. "Any word from the Green Dragons?"

"No, master. They're not back with help yet."

"And the carriage for my family?"

"That's ready, sir."

Liu's lips trembled. He said to another student, "See to it my family gets away safely. Bring twenty students, escort them to the Garden of Eternal Light, and ask Lord Xu for help. Beg him to take my family under his protection. He *is* known as Lord Xu the Honorable."

"What about you, Master?"

"I'll stay here until the end."

Iron Hand Liu climbed to the roof where his archers sat waiting for the worst. All arrows were taken out of storage. There could be hundreds of people attacking any moment. His men were instructed to choose their targets carefully, once the enemy slowed by the barricades.

Liu's son Yun stood next to his father, a long spear in his hand.

"I ordered you to go with your mother and sisters," Liu said, biting his lip.

"I'm not afraid of them," Yun said.

"We'll die here today. And the Iron Palm School will end in my hands."

"Don't worry, father. We'll survive this. And then we'll go south and wait for the Red Dragons to forget us. We can restart elsewhere."

"I hope so," Liu said.

"Father?"

"Yes, son."

"Do you think this is because of the black paste I found in Pan Tong Village?"

"I don't know, son."

"Maybe we shouldn't have given it to Black Shadow."

Liu knelt on the tiled roof, next to two of his best archers, and casually picked up an extra bow. He fitted an arrow and aimed into the distance. "We did the right thing, son."

A small carriage emerged from the side door, and Liu breathed in relief. At least his family would be safe. He was thankful for the presence of his son—he was almost afraid of facing the Red Dragons by himself.

The red carriage passed the spiked barricades and proceeded down the road. Iron Hand Liu sat back and waited.

. . .

"If they live," she remembered her father saying, *"the secret would be out before we're ready, and the god-given chance would be wasted."*

The Flute Demon shook her head and focused her eyes on the road. The tumor over her left eye was new, and the crooked nose she carelessly created had not dried yet. But it didn't matter to her now. Nothing really mattered anymore.

The words echoed in her head. "We can't kill the entire Martial Society, father."

"You're right, my child. That's why we must protect our secret until we're ready. That's why no one else can know about the black paste."

A red carriage was approaching her. She noticed the *zhuang* of the Iron Palm School not far ahead. There was no other road. The red carriage must be an escape transport for Liu's family.

"All of them!" her father shouted.

The Flute Demon's eyes flashed fire. She bolted head-on toward the carriage, and in three massive steps, reached the front horse. She slashed the horse across the throat, killing it instantly, passed the second horse, and with a stomp, destroyed the front wheel of the carriage. With a strained cry, she tore open the carriage door to slaughter Liu's family.

She came alone, despite Liu's preparations against hundreds of attackers, and approached the barricades on foot, with neither armor nor projectile weapons. Her face was too far away to distinguish, but the flute announced her presence.

"The Flute Demon!" she heard Liu shouting in the distance.

Arrows rained on her, but she calmly stood behind the barricades, protected by the defensive wall the Iron Palm School had built. She waited while the arrows pelted the wooden stakes.

Fei Fei crouched behind the fence, tearing apart the ropes that held the wooden stakes together. They were prepared for heavy cavalry. She kept together two units of the barricade—each about the length of her arm—lifted the cluster of wood off the ground, and charged. Arrows ripped through the air, but the wooden spikes protected her. Before another volley of arrows could be launched, she was already at the door of the courtyard. She flung the wood into the door, rattling it, then stomped it down the middle. The hinges gave way and collapsed. She stepped to the side and waited for another volley of arrows to pass through the doorway before entering the Iron Palm *zhuang*.

Men swarmed on her with swords drawn.

"I already have an antidote to this Black Paste," Master Bin said to her.

Fei Fei shook her head clear. The black paste didn't matter to her now.

"As soon as the Green Dragons are under our control, I'll administer the antidote. They'll all be cured. This is what our ancestors want—a united Dragon House."

The Iron Palm students came from all sides.

"He will die anyway. What difference would it make, my child?"

A tear rolled from her eye, blurring her vision for a second but she never lost focus. One by one, she cut the men down. Her movements were clean, cold, and so precise that almost all of her victims died with a wound in the throat.

"Don't fail to bring honor to our House, Fei Fei. Our ancestors expect it from you."

Iron Palm Liu appeared out of nowhere, his gold-handled sword flashing, swinging in a wave of circular strikes. Fei Fei eyed the pattern of attack, sent her blade into the center of his circles, and cleanly severed his wrist. Iron Hand Liu screamed in pain. Fei Fei disregarded him, turned to kill another.

"If the Mongolian tells the world about this, we'll never have time to execute our plan. He must be eliminated."

"Father!"

"He'll die anyway, my child. At least help him go quickly and painlessly. And what is one Mongolian in exchange for the Martial Society?"

"But Black Shadow also knows . . . "

"Don't worry my child. Black Shadow wouldn't upset the Martial Society at this time. He would approach this carefully and give us the time we need. Unlike the barbarian, who wouldn't know any better . . . "

A figure quietly approached her from behind, his long spear held high and poised to attack. Fei Fei broke from her trance and turned around to slash him across the waist. He crumbled with a groan.

A violent roar came from behind. Iron Hand Liu! Fei Fei spun around and ran him all the way through. She thought she saw a wild animal. With a quick jerk, she tore the blade out of his body, slipped back to gain distance, and swiped down to decapitate him. The head rolled with a light thump.

She glanced at the spear user. He was dead, his long spear rolling away from him. Only a few others were left.

"Why me, father? Why must you send me?"

"Only you can get near him, at this point. You have to do this, Fei Fei. You have to do this for the future of the Red Dragons."

"Father?"

"Put him to peace, my child. There's no antidote for the Soaring Dragon Candles. Just pretend he died a month ago in Mongolia."

Fei Fei glared at her enemies, at the frightened students of the Iron Palm School. "Fear of death," she whispered.

"You must finish this, Fei Fei! I order you to kill this Mongolian at once!"

Her lips trembled, a tear rolling down her cheek. Her hand shook. She summoned her energy, her face hot, burning with agony, her eyes clouded and stinging with blood. "Is it worse to die? Or is it worse to kill?"

• • •

The Blue Lantern Inn had no blue lanterns. Criticized by many that the cold blue color from a big lantern appeared spooky and spelled inauspiciousness, the owner of the inn burned all lanterns that once hung by the door and replaced them with a larger sign for the name of the inn. Business had boomed ever since.

Suthachai stayed in the same room and ate the same things. He drank his wine, ate huge slabs of meat, and lay back on the bed to rest his body. The poison bothered him, sometimes in waves of heat and cold, often in nagging pains across his chest. But he felt strong, alive, eager for Fei Fei to come. A light smile appeared on his face every time he thought of her.

He bathed that morning, to the surprise of the innkeeper who told him that even the Chinese bathed less frequently in winter. But the Mongolian insisted, and a tub of hot water with a bar of soap was prepared for him.

By late afternoon, he was in good spirits. He drank plenty of warm wine, lit three sticks of incense taken from the innkeeper's ancestral altar, planted them by a half-opened window, and prayed to his grandfather.

The smell of the incense flooded his senses, and he relaxed. He thought of riding across the plains again, his body no longer in pain, his heart free from the treachery and hostilities of the complex Chinese world. She would ride behind him, her arm around his waist, her long hair flowing in the wind . . .

It was the first time he felt happy since the great hunt almost a month ago, when hundreds of warriors cheered him for killing the wolves with his bare hands. He thought of the wolves that he and Fei Fei killed, a night ago, when fate paved the way for them to confront danger together for the first time. It was the will of the gods, and there was hope. The Elder would have told him so.

The door of his room creaked open. She was there, outside the door, staring at him. The tumor was hanging from her eye, the crooked nose more bent than ever. She was hideous, putrid, but he knew it was Fei Fei—his Fei Fei. He leaped to his feet.

Two steps and he froze. She was motionless outside the door; her eyes sparked with a strange expression. She bit her lip, her body rigid, lifeless.

The soft breeze of the Mongolian steppe faded from his mind. He stood in a fixed position halfway across the room, his eyes locked onto hers, a stinging fear in his heart. He understood the expression on her face. It seemed like a storm brewed in her eyes—it was locked deep within her soul and ready to explode in an onslaught of merciless venom. It was beyond her control. The passion, the remorse burning through her only fueled this frenzy.

Slowly, she drew her flute. Suthachai was frozen. His eyes wide with shock, blurred with darkness, he imagined the ceiling of the room shaking, as if on the verge of collapse. The blade sprung out of her flute. She took a step forward.

"You will die anyway," she said, the voice no longer hers. "There's no antidote, Suthachai. I can end it for you now."

He watched her blade, felt his heart bursting in searing heat. He waited for her to attack. A strange thought crossed his mind, summoned by the barest of animal instincts to survive.

He defeated her on Redwood Cliff.

She cannot beat you . . .

"I want to die," he whispered.

• • •

Fei Fei stared into his eyes, a wave of cold washing over her, then heat, then cold again. He said something to her, but she didn't hear him. Her only focus was to aim her weapon at his throat.

"Forgive me," she seemed to say, the point of the blade leveled. She lunged. Suthachai closed his eyes.

Memories pounced on her from behind. She saw him return for her, when she lay unconscious at the mercy of her enemies. She saw him shield her with his body when the wolves charged, she felt the warmth of his embrace when they collapsed on the beach together. She was safe in his arms, she felt loved, not as a warrior, but as a woman . . .

Her eyes squeezed shut and the blade jerked to the side, cleanly piercing through his shoulder. He stood motionless, his eyes blank but fixed on her tormented face. A tear rolled down her cheek. Fresh blood seeped through his clothing and slid down the blade.

Her mouth twitched. She tore the blade from his shoulder. His hands shook, his body convulsed in short spasms, but he stood tall in the middle of the room, his large eyes pinned to hers. She backed away, unable to meet his gaze, uncertain of what she did. She had to kill him, to ensure the well being of the Dragon House, to bring honor to her ancestors . . . He would die anyway—it would be merciful to end it quickly for him—and she had to do it, because her father wanted her to . . .

She could no longer look at his face. She could never look at her own again. With a burst, she bolted out the door.

• • •

He hardly felt the blade enter his body. Was it really his body that she drilled her sword into? He was frozen, his bulging eyes burning, his brain swollen. The dripping wound in his shoulder seemed to spread across his body. Dazed, deserted in the chasm of human suffering and betrayal, the huge Mongolian lifted his face to the heavens and screamed.

He thought the ceiling had indeed begun to fall. Somewhere in the distance, he thought he heard the music of the flute, slow, wailing, but stripped of all human compassion. The music enticed him, reached for his heart and pulled at him. He saw the floor clean of debris—but he was certain the ceiling had collapsed. Above him, there was only an eerie blackness. He had to take a step forward, then another. The heat in his chest escalated, burning through every sinew of every limb. He unleashed a hideous roar, broke through the door, and smashed his way out of the inn.

"Suthachai!"

He thought he heard someone call his name. He didn't recognize the voice, and he didn't stop to look back. He charged through the streets, without any sense of direction, allowing the heat to consume him, screaming in utter madness.

• • •

"Pun!" Li Kung shouted, running forward. "Where are you going?"

Pun turned her face but didn't stop running. "That was Suthachai! He just ran out of the inn! Come on, we can catch him."

Li Kung breathed heavily, his legs still weak from running down Redwood Cliff the day before. He watched Pun take off in rapid chase, and he knew he would never catch her.

"Suthachai," Pun called. "Wait! Old Two may have found the medicine for you! Hey, Suthachai! Wait!"

They had traveled on foot all afternoon, because Pun was certain that Suthachai would wait at the Blue Lantern Inn. They could bring him the good news. There was no other inn that he knew of, she reasoned.

As soon as the inn was in sight, Pun began to run forward.

"Stop running, Suthachai!" Pun took a deep breath and quickened her pace, closing in on him.

"Suthachai!"

He suddenly drew his saber with lightning speed, spun around and slashed her, just as she reached out to touch him. The blade tore a deep gash horizontally across her body, and she crumbled into the snow. Without looking back once, Suthachai continued to run.

Li Kung froze halfway down the road, his eyes wide with horror. A wave of cold struck him. He saw, and he couldn't believe his eyes. He gathered himself, ran to her as hard as he could, dropping to his knees and lifting her limp body.

"Pun!" he shouted. "No!"

The wound was massive; blood flowed uncontrollably— dark blood. He had slashed open her liver. Li Kung fumbled in his pockets, searching for something to slow down the blood loss, frantically pulling every herb he carried.

A cold hand reached up and touched his face. "No, Li Kung . . ."

Her voice was weak. "I . . . I'm dead . . . I don't know why . . . Can you . . . Can you tell me why?"

"No, Pun . . . I can . . . I can close this wound . . ." He pulled out a bottle of powder and dumped it on her wound. The blood washed the herbs into the snow.

"Li Kung, I'm sorry," she said, her voice slowly weakening. "I . . . I really wanted to be your wife and take care of you. I wish . . . I wish I could live longer . . . because you always need someone . . . to care for you. I'm sorry . . ."

Hot tears streamed down his face. He took her hand tenderly. "Pun . . ."

"You . . . you must learn to take care of yourself." Her voice began to wane. He could barely hear her, but he understood.

It could only be a dream. He would wake up soon, she would be there, laughing and playing, and he would run after her to tickle her.

Maybe she was joking. She planned this trick with Suthachai to scare him, and they would all laugh together over dinner that night. He felt the urge to throw her body aside and reveal her prank.

But her body had never been so cold before. He held her closer to him, pressed her small figure against his chest, and listened for her breathing. Slowly, ever so slowly, her breathing ceased.

"No . . . " His voice was hoarse, feeble.

He lowered his face against her cold neck and wept. Long wails racked his thin body, and his trembling arms held her increasingly tighter.

The sun began to set. He squeezed his eyes shut, begging her to wake him from his nightmare, crying for someone to end his suffering. The wind that blew against him stung the cold sweat on his back, and the limp body in his arms began to feel heavy. For the first time, he realized that he was not in a dream, that he had never gone to sleep—and for the first time, he realized that Pun had really gone.

Slowly, he lifted his face, his eyes flaring with hate and vengeance. He screamed from the base of his throat.

"Suthachai!"

PROPHECY FIVE

A hero born from chaos
Courage nurtured by misfortune
Genius fed by desperation
Can ambition spring from fear?

Suthachai stumbled across the snow, the heavy saber clutched in his hand, his coat tightly wrapped around his trembling body. He was too nauseous to notice Li Kung behind him. A dark trail of blood dyed the ground beside his footprints.

Li Kung grabbed a heavy branch from somewhere and charged. He closed in on Suthachai, and without a word, swung for the back of his head.

The Mongolian was in a distant land. The silver rays of dawn brought colorful glitters to the morning dew, and he paused to smell the grass he knew so well. Fei Fei walked beside him, holding his hand, and they were not going anywhere in particular. She caressed his cheeks and smiled, the beauty of her glistening eyes radiating, overwhelming the magnificence of the morning.

Somewhere, in the back of his mind, he heard the sound of something being swung at him. He stepped out of the way, dazed, uncertain of where he really was, driven only by instinct. He turned to face a young man attacking him with a stick of wood.

He took another step back, and Li Kung missed a second time.

Li Kung lifted his meager weapon and swung at him again.

Suthachai frowned—he didn't recognize the young man. He lifted his arm up to the branch and broke it in half.

Li Kung stared at the stub of wood in his hands, then threw it at his enemy and charged. He grabbed Suthachai by the coat, wrapped his arms around him, and lunged forward to sink his teeth into the Mongolian's throat. Suthachai broke his hold with a simple twist and then tossed him away, effortlessly, like he would toss an empty jacket.

He turned and continued on his way. Li Kung landed hard on his back and remained motionless for a long time. Then, he pulled himself to his feet, shoveled an armful of snow, and charged.

Suthachai looked away when the snow was thrown at him, and, drawing his saber, swept back to cut his attacker in half. Somewhere, in the hovering darkness, he thought he had seen this face before. He turned his wrist in mid-motion and smacked the side of his blade into Li Kung's head. He stepped in for a closer look.

Li Kung collapsed with a resounding thud, sprawled across the snow, unconscious.

Suthachai leaned forward, a troubled look on his face. "Li Kung?"

He sheathed his saber with head hung, eyes tearing, and turned to walk away. "Why do you all want to kill me?"

• • •

The wind grew, changing from a distant wail of fatigue to a powerful roar of rage.

Li Kung lifted a broken shovel high above him and pummeled the icy ground. The side of his head throbbed with pain. He stared into the snow that pelted his face, and screamed.

"I may not have much to eat . . . I may not have much to wear . . . "

Someone was singing to him. A woman's voice, maybe Pun's voice.

"But I can tell you this day . . . It is better to be a swindler, than an emperor . . . "

It was her song, without doubt, though sad, distant, ghostly. A mist of cold blanketed his body, and he couldn't see, couldn't feel. But he heard her, and he knew she was there.

The hard ground began to break apart. He had to bury her, because she deserved at least that.

She deserved more . . .

He took a deep breath, fought the pain and fatigue, and shoveled the ground. Sweat and tears all flew at once.

They met at a small river. It was hot in the south, and he had no pants on—most four-year-old boys didn't wear pants. He played in the mud, made a mess of himself, and had to wash his hands by the river. She was washing her little handkerchiefs, and she gave him one.

Li Kung screamed in pain, threw aside the shovel and dived into the pit. Almost lying upside down, he scooped soil with bare hands and flung them into the air. Some of it rained on him, pelted him like hail, and he closed his eyes to endure the onslaught.

It rained like that once, when they were both about ten. They huddled together inside a cave, and it was freezing cold. Li

Kung had one rice cake, small food that his mother left in his pocket in case he was hungry, and they shared the cake together. She secretly split her half when he wasn't looking and gave it to him, telling him it was an extra piece.

And she sang to him, so he wouldn't be afraid.

The mud flew, and he sunk deeper and deeper into the pit.

Snow began to fall. The pit was already deeper than his own height. Above him, the wind howled more powerfully than ever, but he felt safe hiding in the grave. He wished the grave was truly for himself.

He climbed out partially, used a small wedge by the side of the pit as footing, reached across the surface, and hauled Pun's body to him. He slid an arm under the back of her neck, careful not to disturb her sleep, wrapped his other arm across her waist, and with a deep, longing sigh, dropped his footing and plunged into the pit.

For a long time, he lay in her grave. She was face up, on top of him, his arms squeezed around her cold body, and he closed his eyes and tried to sing to her.

"But I can tell you this day . . . It is better to be a swindler, than an emperor . . . "

Hot tears streaked down his cheeks. He choked on his words, could no longer remember the song she sang every morning. He squeezed his eyes together, pressed his face against her cold flesh, and wept.

How long was he unconscious? It was already daylight. The harsh sun beamed into his eyes, and he closed them again. Insects crawled across his body, but he was too weak to brush them away. It was the middle of winter. The bugs should be in hiding. Maybe they came for the dried blood on Pun's wound. If he'd die soon, they could eat him too.

"I'm dead too, Pun," he said. Her body was colder than

ever. He managed to move one of his arms, touched his own face, and realized that he was burning up. Death would come soon.

"Someone as useless as I am," he whispered into her ear. "Someone so worthless really should die a painful death. I'm so fortunate to die with you in my arms . . . "

. . .

The wind howled again. The sun had set, and the thick clouds invading the sky were so dense the world turned red. Why was he here? Is this where everyone goes after death?

He reached around the corpse on top of him, and it came to him then. She was dead, but he was still alive.

This was his punishment. For being too useless to protect her, for getting her killed. Human suffering. To remain alive so he could pay for his mistakes.

Snow began to fall softly into the pit, and little by little they were being covered. He cuddled her, pressing his face into her shoulder, and wept.

"I'm sorry, Pun . . . I'm sorry I can't stay . . . "

He reached for the edge of the pit, gritted his teeth from the throbbing pain in his head, and pulled himself to the surface.

The sky had darkened, but the world became brighter.

He lifted the broken shovel and pushed the dirt into the pit. He burned with fever, his weakened body limp from illness. Cold sweat broke across his skin, steaming against the heat on his forehead. In a moment, he dropped on all fours and vomited into the snow. He didn't bother to analyze his condition. He had to bury her, because she deserved at least that.

Time passed. He finally stopped shoveling when the

earth seemed level in front of him. He brought the shovel vertically into the ground where her tombstone would be, gasping for air, the world spinning faster and faster around him. He forced himself to his feet.

The snow hurled itself from the heavens, battering him in collapsing carpets, and he lifted his face to receive the abuse. He drew a deep breath of icy snow and wind, lifted his arms, and screamed.

The scream couldn't last forever, though he wanted it to. He dropped to his knees beside her grave, beat his forehead into the ground three times, and with one last look, lifted himself and stumbled away.

• • •

"Look, Li Kung! Those rocks look like bunny ears!"

Li Kung lifted his head, drew in his bare knuckles, and pulled himself to a sitting position.

"Where are you, Li Kung?"

He couldn't see. The snow resembled a million arrows fired horizontally across his eyes. Then, the wind changed direction and freezing ice was swept off the ground, pelting him from below and from above. Li Kung closed his eyes; he sat huddled and halfway buried, wondering how long he had been unconscious.

He had tried to climb a mountain. Some woodcutter he passed on the road told him not to attempt it. It's haunted, the old woodcutter said. He invited Li Kung to stay in his home until the storm passed. But Li Kung couldn't resist. There were ghosts everywhere. The woodcutter said so. Maybe the mountain was a gathering place for new ghosts. Perhaps Pun would be up there.

There was a trail, vertically in front of him on an icy cliff side, its bare rocks so smooth not a snowflake could cling to its surface. Shallow footholds were chiseled into the stone.

"Li Kung, do you know why it snows?"

"The gods are crying."

"No, silly. That's the reason why it rains."

"Then why?"

"Because the gods are scratching their heads, and they have too much dandruff."

He broke into a short laugh. It never snowed like this before. What would she say if she saw this now?

The snow became so dense he thought a white drape was thrown over his eyes. But the wind was losing momentum.

He reached for the first footholds on the vertical ascent and pulled himself. His head was hurting in throbbing pulses, his arms too weak to support his weight. But pain was just an illusion, merely a reflection of his cowardice.

One arm's length at a time, Li Kung climbed the vertical rocks in the dead of night, in the middle of a storm. His eyes were squeezed shut, his lungs swollen and burning. In the distance, he heard the ghosts above him, and it gave him strength.

From the depths of the mountain, deep wailing emerged out of nowhere and roamed the air. The cries grew, turning into a hideous shriek before fading into nothing.

"I bet I could make him take a bath."

Li Kung's eyes widened. Suthachai was his friend—it was his failure. How many times had Shifu One cautioned him not to interfere with the natural course of events? How many times was he warned not to save the world?

The ghost cries reemerged with the wind and became powerful, desperate. Li Kung flinched. The relentless shrieking suggested a demon tearing into its prey, as if someone behind the cliff was being eaten alive.

"Shifu One said everyone must die one day, and we should celebrate death like we celebrate birth. But you better not die before me, Li Kung. I won't be able to bear it."

Li Kung shook his head clear, and with a hoarse cry, hauled himself upward. By the time he reached the peak, the wind was rising and waning at will. He had been climbing forever. Torn with fatigue and pain, the heat of nausea steaming from his face, Li Kung reached for whatever grip he could find, pulled his weight to the top, and, standing tall against the wind, roared into the red heavens. The ghosts answered back, their own hideous cries so loud that Li Kung's voice was drowned. The wind swept powerfully around him. With hair scattered across his face, Li Kung lifted his arms, fists clenched, and screamed.

He thought he saw a tunnel below him. Halfway hidden among a cluster of rocks, the mouth of the tunnel resembled the shape of a demented smile. There was a shallow valley immediately below him, with light evergreen shrubs covered by a thin layer of ice. But his gaze was drawn back to the mouth of the tunnel. It seemed mysterious, evil, dark—it beckoned him. What could be inside this tunnel with the twisted, perverse mouth?

The wind grew again, this time approaching him from behind. He closed his eyes and waited.

The wind slammed him so heavily that he was sent flying off the rock and into the valley. His shoulders brushed against the side of the mountain, just enough to deter his falling momentum before the rest of his body dragged him downward. He slammed against the rocks and slid sideways, bruising and tearing his hands that floundered for a grip. The ghosts trumpeted in triumph, the sound of their cries following him all the way to the bottom.

He landed on thick mud at the mouth of the tunnel,

failing to gather himself before the slippery earth gave under his weight. He slid into the darkness. The stones were wet inside, a film of moss carpeting the surface, and he twisted and groped with all four limbs to no avail. He seemed to slide forever.

He uttered a choked yell when he finally crashed onto a flat surface. It was so dark he couldn't tell whether his eyes were open or closed. He drew the frozen air into his lungs and tried to move his hand, then his legs, but couldn't find the strength. He lay motionless in absolute silence.

· · ·

There were no lanterns at the Blue Lantern Inn. Suthachai stood outside the main entrance, unable to distinguish the Chinese characters on the wooden sign in front of him. He thought he would be looking for blue lanterns.

The words on the sign faded in and out of his vision, sometimes in blurs, often covered by tears or sweat. There was light tapping by his feet again, perhaps it was hot blood dripping on the snow. His blood. The wound had reopened, and he could have been bleeding the whole night. He didn't know how long he had been walking—two days perhaps—nor could he remember how many times he lost consciousness, only to reawaken in the same brutal world he so persistently tried to walk from. Somehow, he had wandered back to the Blue Lantern Inn.

There was no escaping this world. He crumbled to his knees with a defeated sigh. Darkness came over him then. He closed his eyes and waited to die.

She touched him, her voice soft and gentle, and asked him if he was still alive.

"*You have killed me. I am no longer alive.*"

"He's delirious," the voice said again. It was a man's voice. Suthachai lifted his eyes. An innkeeper hovered over him with another man holding a bowl of steaming hot water.

"Did you get the water?"

"Yes, sir."

"Give it to him. His hands are like ice. He may not make it."

"Should we call a doctor?"

The innkeeper shook his head. "Where can we find a doctor at this hour? Let's get him inside first and see if we can stop the bleeding."

"His blood is so dark," the younger man said. He lifted Suthachai's head and held the bowl to his lips. "Isn't he the Mongolian who stayed here a couple of nights ago?"

The innkeeper watched Suthachai finish the water, and then wrapped his arm around the massive shoulders. "Give me a hand. We can't leave him to die out here."

• • •

Utter darkness. Li Kung's heart nagged his rib cage with every pulse. He lifted his arm, painfully, pressing his fingers against his nose, his forehead, pushing hard to confirm there really was flesh on him. A strange stench filled the air—thick air—stifling his lungs with every breath.

So this is death. So lonely, so quiet.

The silence was perfect. For a long time, he couldn't collect himself. Every bone ached. Cuts and bruises were everywhere. He felt pain—all types of pain—eating into his body. He felt old and sick, tired, lost; but he was indifferent to it all.

He wanted to move, but he couldn't find the strength.

Where would he move to anyway? He was in hell, and there was no way out of hell.

He coughed hard. Who knows what spewed from his throat this time?

Li Kung lifted his head, as if he could see through the pitch-blackness, and cocked his ears to listen. Why would there be an echo in hell? Hell was supposed to be an endless span of darkness, with no beginning, no end. There was an echo around him. Maybe this was not hell after all.

He flexed a sore wrist and felt something. A piece of wood next to him?

Li Kung reached for the wood, inched his fingers as if any moment he would touch a sleeping monster.

A torch! It was shaped like a torch!

He sat up, the pain in his body ignored, the excitement injecting strength into his bones. He reached for the green powder in his coat.

He hesitated. What was he prepared to see? What would hell look like?

This was not hell, he thought. He was not that fortunate.

In a moment, a gentle flame danced on the end of the torch. He glanced at the ground in front of him and jolted back.

There were corpses everywhere. Some were shriveled to gray skeletons, many with flesh partly disintegrated, most with clothing still intact. Something about the dried, decaying bodies gnawed at him.

All of them faced the same direction. They were all facing him.

Li Kung's mouth dropped. They all seemed to be crawling, or reaching toward something.

One corpse, apparently a woman, tightly embraced the

body of a man at death. Another couple died holding each other's hand.

They were all trying to leave. They were crawling toward the tunnel he fell in from.

If death in the mundane world led to life in hell, then where would death in hell lead? He was told that at death, a man would be free from his body. He did not feel free. Maybe he was not dead, after all.

He was in a deep cavern, a narrow, endless tunnel, with menacing stalactites hovering over him like thousands of sharp teeth. He felt surrounded by impenetrable darkness despite the small flame, and he could only see a short distance away.

High above his head was the opening he fell in from. It was out of reach. He could see the moss-covered tube, wet with a natural film of slime and reflecting light like polished bronze. There was no way to climb the slippery tube even if he could reach it.

Perhaps there was an exit at the other end of the cavern.

Something shiny caught his eye. It was far away, glittering at him, and he gazed at it for a moment before shifting his eyes to the bodies again. Most of the skeletons were armed, but none of the weapons were drawn. He panned his torch lower to the ground, searching for signs of physical damage, such as sword wounds, cudgel injuries, or any indications of battle. There were none.

There were almost forty bodies in the cavern. At the extreme end was another tunnel, and the same shiny flash that caught his attention now blinked at him, as if beckoning him. He moved closer and noticed a fork at the end of the cavern, forming two dark tunnels pointing into opposite directions.

What am I doing here?

"I'm not doing anything," he said out loud. "I'm just here."

He lowered the torch and stumbled into the right-hand tunnel. Moments later, he was inside a large room. Subtle glittering swarmed his eyes, like millions of dancing fireflies. He tossed green powder onto his torch and watched the brilliant flame grow before gazing into the room again. His mouth dropped.

The room overflowed with gold, gemstones, gold-plated weapons and armor, crowns, diamond-laced necklaces, and coins piled like a mountain. The blinding sparkles overwhelmed him, and he flinched away, closing his eyes. An eerie sense of exhilaration tore through him, briefly, before the nauseous weight in his chest returned.

He would have picked out a necklace for her. He had never given her anything valuable, anything that she had been proud of. He could have bought her clothes made of fine silk, or a gold hairpin so her hair wouldn't fly across her face when she ran. Here, in front of him, was wealth beyond imagination. There was so much gold that he could buy the entire province. He would hire armies of mercenaries to protect him while he lived in utter luxury—he could build a castle on this mountain and be free from the chaos of the Martial Society forever.

He opened his eyes and stared. In the face of wealth and pleasure beyond his wildest dreams, he suddenly felt lonelier than he had ever been. His mentors would laugh at him. He would come home the wealthiest man in the province, but Pun was dead.

A heartbroken sigh escaped his lips. The sight of the treasure entranced him, but there was no one to share it with.

He took a final look at the glittering gold and diamonds, turned, and stumbled back into the tunnel. What lonely hell awaited him if he were to live by himself in luxury?

Li Kung's head throbbed in nagging pulses again. He reached into his coat, fumbled for the emergency herbs he always carried, and swallowed a handful of pills with a painful gulp.

He might as well live. It was not his choice either way.

The fever would be gone soon, and he would feel stronger. He wanted to be tortured, felt the urge to grind coarse sand into the opened wounds on his body so he could laugh in the face of pain. He could tell himself that he was suffering for Pun. Or at least, tell himself that he was not afraid.

How many men would take the lives of others for a fraction of the treasure he just found. Maybe all the skeletons in the cavern were men who somehow died for this treasure.

He was back in the main cavern. There was nothing left to do but try the other tunnel.

The deep passageway, the other tunnel, felt like it would never end, and the flame on his torch was dying. He reached into his coat and felt for the green powder, secretly pleased there was plenty left, though he didn't know for what. He breathed heavily like an old man, hunched over, his feet dragging on the dried floor with every step.

Much later, he found himself in another room. He sprinkled the powder on the end of his torch and rapidly grew the fire.

He kicked something accidentally. He lowered the flame and recognized a clay urn by his feet. It was old, poorly fired, with piles of wooden torches stacked inside. Li Kung breathed quicker then and took a confident step forward with his eyes on the ground. To his right was another object, pottery perhaps, and behind it was an old brick stove half buried under some rocks.

He turned to his left. Crushed under a boulder was an old skeleton, many decades old, wrapped in the coarse clothing of a common villager.

Li Kung stumbled back and onto another skeleton, whose brittle bones caved in under his foot. He gasped and spun around to look. A wider pelvic bone suggested the body of a woman. He brushed away the first layer of soil around her and noticed the bones of a child.

He began to wheeze for air. There was not enough air in this cavern, it seemed. He took a blind step and something else cracked under his weight. He froze, hesitating, not wanting to know what he had crushed. Slowly, he shifted out of position, leaned against the cavern wall, and pointed his torch.

More bones, but smaller ones. He picked up a little skull and stared into the gaping holes that were eye sockets, now brilliantly illuminated by the torch. Children died here, many of them. Their remains lay scattered across the floor.

Li Kung lowered the skull and sat wearily against the wall. The flame began to shrink, and he remained motionless, waiting to be thrown into darkness.

The surface his back pressed against felt strangely irregular. He traced his fingers against the cavern wall, across thin grooves and unnatural lines. He turned around with a start.

There was writing everywhere, deeply carved into the rocks but covered with soil and dust.

"Day four. I am too weak to complete the task. I've licked the moisture off the side of the walls but there is not enough water. I barely have the strength to finish carving this, and I will rest for the night."

Day four? The carvings began to his right.

"Day one. I finally found wood underneath everything, and I made a small fire. Both my legs are broken, and the entire village had been buried. Where did this earthquake come from? If the gods were to destroy our little village, then why was I left to live? I screamed for the entire night, but no one answered. The entire village is dead.

"Day two. My legs are numb. I think there is internal bleeding and I am sure to die. Those more fortunate in our village are already buried in a final resting place. My family, my neighbors, died under the crushing rocks. I am the least fortunate. I was left behind, because the gods wanted me to bury my family before I died.

"Day three. I finally found my neighbor's broken pickax, and I tried to bury my family. I could only finish one grave, and I placed my son in it. If I could only stand, I would be able to dig faster. Why was I left behind with this task, only to have my legs broken so I could never complete it?"

Li Kung stared at the writing for day four. His eyes slowly traveled to a man's skeleton lying against the wall. He lowered the flaming torch and placed it on the ground, curled himself into a ball with his face between his knees, and broke into a long, painful sob.

. . .

The sun was bright—hideously bright. The Flute Demon looked far below her, wondering how the new snow would feel on her bare feet. She twisted her wrist with a flinch, the leather ropes cutting into her flesh. One of the men intentionally drenched the ropes before they strapped her, so the beaming sun could dry the wet leather against her skin.

The Triangle of Reform was a simple structure of three

wooden stakes, spanning two stories tall, and forming a hollow pyramid. Those to be punished were tied by their wrists from the top of the triangle, left to dangle in the air, and whipped. But the key to hanging a person was for all on Redwood Cliff to see, and to humiliate.

She closed her eyes and filtered the noise from her mind. It was too bright, and the reflection from the snow bothered her. Her legs twitched, as if expecting to find support. She never thought she would ever be tied to the Triangle of Reform. She was the beloved daughter of a great leader, a princess of the Martial Society, a respected warrior . . .

Her fake tumor quivered. Tears welled into her eyes. Her father specifically ordered her to leave her disguise on. He would beat his daughter in front of the world, and no one would ever know it. How far would he go to protect his secret?

This day, all on Redwood Cliff gathered and cheered. A giant man ascended the platform, whip in hand.

Fei Fei opened her eyes and stared at the mob in front of her. Just days ago, many of them were under her command. They bowed in respect when she passed. But today, she hung helplessly in the air while they shouted and jeered.

She recalled her father's pale face when she told him she chose not to kill the Mongolian. She wanted to tell him she had never been so happy before, that her only wish was to remain by Suthachai's side, to wait for him to die, so he too could be happy during his remaining days. She wanted to tell her father she had never been more proud of herself, had never been braver.

Master Bin, great leader of the Red Dragon House, never waited for her to speak. He struck so quickly that her arm was pinned against the wall, and a steeled grip was on her throat before she could react. Or was she trained not to react?

The first and only words he said to her were, "Then where were you the past two days? Waiting for him to tell the world about our medicine? You might as well tell Wei Xu yourself!"

She tried to explain. She was his beloved daughter, she would never betray him, she would never bring shame to the family. But he left the room without another glance at her.

Confusion reigned on Redwood Cliff. It was announced that the Flute Demon would be whipped on the Triangle of Reform, and rumors flew like wildfire. The highly favored Flute Demon disobeyed orders? Perhaps she was a traitor, a mercenary who betrayed the Red Dragons for higher pay.

Fei Fei's eyes wandered to the front of the crowd. She looked for her father. Would he at least come to witness his favorite child's whipping?

The whip cracked and tore through her back. Fei Fei heard loud applause in front of her. Then, a hail of snowballs, stones, broken twigs, all struck her at once. She dangled quietly in the frozen air and thought of Suthachai, of the look on his face when she pierced his shoulder and told him it was better for him to die. She thought of how she betrayed the man she loved, and how she sentenced him to eternal torture.

The crowd cheered again, screaming, "Whip the traitor! Whip the traitor!" They threw another volley at her, pelted her like a storm, and she glared at them, so intensely that a few in the front took a step back.

It was clear to her then. The Red Dragon House never really respected her, never really loved her. She fought shoulder to shoulder with them and led them to great victories. But she was still a woman.

The whip cracked across her back again. She felt the

warm blood trickle through her robe and pool around her belt. The crowd roared with approval.

Her eyes roamed across thousands of men, but she couldn't see her father. She wanted to tell him so much, if he would listen. Far away, at a high elevation, stood a figure with long white hair scattered like a lion's mane. She frowned. Tao Hing had returned from his trip and the first thing he came home to see was the Flute Demon being whipped in public.

The crowd continued to cheer.

She twisted against the straps, uttering a soft cry as the whip slashed deep into her back. She could force these ropes to break—they were merely made of leather. But where would she go if she broke free?

She could run to the Blue Lantern Inn. Suthachai would still be there, waiting for her. She stabbed him, but he would be waiting for her—she was certain. She could go to Mongolia with him, and ride against the wind across the never-ending steppe. How much she wanted to be free . . .

The crowd became louder and more obscene. She slowly closed her eyes to shut out the noise and the grisly faces.

She blocked the pain from her mind and thought of the man she loved, the way he made her smile, how he treated her as his equal even without her disguise. She thought of the moment she tasted the black paste, and he shielded her with both arms and held her so she wouldn't fall. A light smile appeared on Fei Fei's lips.

The crowd saw her smile and suddenly calmed. Soft murmurs flew across the cliff, giving birth to new rumors that grew like raging fire.

• • •

Li Kung started, rammed the back of his head against a solid wall, and cried out in pain. Spots of light flashed across his eyes. He had fallen asleep.

Was he alive, fumbling in darkness and clinging to life? Or was he dead, asleep, dreaming of the self perception he couldn't let go of?

It was pitch black. He wheezed for air in short, quick breaths, and for a long time, he couldn't discern where he was. Then he remembered. He had cried himself to sleep, and he was in a dark cavern, with a village buried by an earthquake.

Not completely buried.

He needed light. Any light would give him more comfort than utter darkness. He reached into the pouch of green powder, lifted the cold torch, and paused. Did he really want to see? There was no way out of this cavern. He was certain to die here. If he closed his eyes and just waited, death would come to him, and he would never need to confront the world again.

He shook his head. Shifu One would've been so disappointed if he saw the worthless student he raised. He pulled out his flint stones and reached for the green powder again.

Again, he hesitated, and again, he retracted his hand. The darkness seemed warm, stable. At the very least, if danger stood awaiting him nearby, he would die without ever confronting the horror. But with light, he could see. What if he saw, and he would not be allowed to die? Maybe Pun was there, standing in front of him. Maybe she was angry with him. How could he face her? He gulped, almost afraid that he would be heard, and slowly reached for the green powder again.

"Pun," he called, his voice barely a hoarse whisper. No answer. He struck the flint and ignited the torch.

The fire grew. He leaned forward and stared into the black distance. Nothing. He couldn't wait for his eyes to adjust. He spun to his right, relieved to see nothing, then checked his left and found the same. The cavern became familiar. He began to remember.

The little skull stared at him. Its tiny eye sockets were slightly tilted, directly facing him, beckoning him. He remembered stumbling over this particular skull—it was smaller than the rest—and he had held it before leaving it on the ground. What did the child look like when he was alive? Perhaps he was a chubby boy, with a round face and rosy cheeks and large eyes that watched the world with curiosity and innocence. The little skull pleaded, inviting him closer.

His fingers touched the writings on the wall again. Those were the last words of a man doomed to die in this very cavern, a man both lonely and frightened, yet he had found the courage and heart to bury his loved ones. The writings told of dismay, of suffering, but worst of all, of the slow, agonizing torment of dying alone.

Li Kung stared at the skull on the ground again. The child must have died quickly. It was the man who was left to bury them who was never given a chance, even at death. He must have been afraid.

"I'm also afraid . . . " Li Kung whispered. "I'm also afraid." He rose to his feet with a short sob and began to walk across the cavern floor.

He couldn't help noticing the unused torches, neatly strapped together, left inside the clay urn that he first spotted. Maybe the man left behind in this tragedy thought he would live longer than he actually did, and prepared extra torches so he wouldn't sit in darkness while waiting to die. A cold feeling riveted through him all of a sudden. What if he had to wait for death, alone, in the dark?

Toward the middle of the room, he spotted the broken pickax the man used; green with rust but still intact.

"I have time," he said out loud. His voice echoed. "I have time to finish this job."

He reached for the ax. The ground underneath him was soft enough. He lifted the tool high over his head and brought it down with a scream. The old wooden handle broke in two. He cursed himself. He leaned the torch against a rock, grabbed the metal head of the ax using both hands, and tore his way into the cavern floor.

The hunger struck him then, and he realized he hadn't eaten in days. He had swallowed some snow when he climbed the cliff, but it seemed so long ago, perhaps more than a day had passed since.

For a second, he thought he heard a low rumbling sound behind the cavern walls.

The sound of stones grinding against each other?

Li Kung picked up his torch, spinning around to search for the sound. He was eager for anyone, anything, to coexist with him in the darkness.

There was nothing. For a long time, he stared into all four corners of the pitch black cavern. Perhaps the noise was imagined.

Once again he dropped to his knees, set his torch aside, and began digging.

He heard the low rumbling sound by the cavern walls, this time louder than before. He paused to listen. His torch only illuminated a small circle around him, and beyond that was total darkness. Li Kung threw aside the ax head, grabbed his torch, and bolted toward the noise.

Then he saw it, a piece of the cavern wall behind him moving, opening, yielding an entrance barely wide enough for a large dog to crawl through.

Something, or someone, triggered the wall to open for him. He took a step forward, pointing his torch like a sword, and waited for something to jump out.

"Come out!" he called.

Silence. "My name is Li Kung. I mean no harm! Please, if there's someone here, please come out!"

He inched forward, his breathing short and strained, but he spoke as loud as he could. "If someone is in there, please speak to me . . . " He paused, his throat tightened. "I . . . I don't want to be in here alone. Please speak to me."

He moved closer and slowly extended the torch into the entranceway.

There was another tunnel inside, tall enough to walk through standing erect, yet so narrow that only one person could fit at a time. The tunnel was constructed with fine precision, despite coarse rocks protruding from both sides and stone fragments paving the uneven floor. It was definitely man-made.

Li Kung planted his left hand in the tunnel, his heart pounding, his torch illuminating the floor in front of him. But what if his torch burned up before he could find a way out? He drew back into the room again and returned to the torches in the urn. An unusual feeling of confidence coursed through him. Strange, how things worked out. This tunnel, obviously created by humans, must lead to the outside world.

In a moment, Li Kung climbed through the entrance, straightened his back, and walked down the narrow tunnel. He had five spare torches tucked under his arm, enough to last him all night. Soon, he would be outside, and he would need the extra light to descend the mountain with. He would find food, water, somewhere to lie down for some badly needed rest. And afterward, he would come back to bury the villagers.

There was nothing in the distance. His little flame illuminated only a few paces in front of him, and for a long time, the straight passageway descended steadily.

Perhaps this tunnel was used to transport the treasure in and out of the cavern. Maybe somehow he had triggered a switch that activated the hidden door, and an exit had opened for him.

He felt better then, and more confident now that he was on his way out. The ground became more rugged, the descent steeper. More than once, he stepped on a rock and twisted his ankle, slamming his body against the wall and nearly losing his torch. Hunger nagged him in deep pangs, forcing him to hold his stomach while waiting for the torment to pass.

Then, he froze in his tracks and stared. The road forked in front of him. He thought the tunnel would lead straight to the outside world, but yet, out of nowhere, two identical passageways confronted him.

Which way should he go?

He took a step forward, peering down the passageway to his left, then to his right. He found nothing on the walls. Nothing that resembled a sign, a symbol—not a single character indicating the direction he should take. Perhaps it was never intended for a stranger to walk through these tunnels.

Li Kung decided to go left.

"Wherever this takes me," he said out loud, "it's not my choice either way."

Hearing his own voice brought renewed confidence. The tunnel was wider this time, more rugged. The air was cold, thin, filled with the stench of decay. Li Kung moved quicker, convinced there would be water nearby or the rotting smell couldn't exist.

The tunnel ended as abruptly as before, yielding another fork, this time with three split paths. He stared at the gaping openings and a deep frown covered his face. Where would he go from here?

Then, almost instantly, his face lightened.

"An arrow!" he almost shouted out loud. He ran to the far right tunnel and held his torch close to the wall, where, crudely scratched in a crooked line, was a mark shaped like an arrow. It was barely visible, but it meant the world to him. Someone, anyone, had already left an indication to the way out. All of a sudden he felt less lonely, less afraid. There was no doubt. It was the far right tunnel.

He walked for a long time. The stench became thicker, heavier. Li Kung tucked the spare torches into his coat, pulled out a pouch of herbs and held it against his nose.

There was movement on the floor. He looked down and for a moment stood frozen in shock. His vision blurred, he could not believe his eyes.

There were rats everywhere; so many of them, all fat and enormous beyond belief. Li Kung drew back in fear. With a gasp, he brushed his torch across the ground to drive them back. They were behind him, all around him.

"Damn!" he screamed. The sudden sound of his voice sent the rodents squealing, and he heard chirping and movement far into the tunnel.

The torch was dying. Li Kung drew one of his spares, lit it, and tossed the old one. He bombarded the new flame with green powder, and it roared. The stench was incredible, so intense that he had to breathe through his pouch of herbs.

By the time the flame settled, the rats had left the tunnel. Li Kung hurried forward. He didn't have time to think about the nagging fatigue and hunger. Something was wrong. He felt discouraged all of a sudden. He didn't know why. Perhaps the sight of so many rats meant that humans had not been occupying these tunnels.

He approached another fork, this time split into only two paths again. He hesitated once, just long enough to find an arrow on the wall. He traced the scratch mark with his finger; it pointed down the right tunnel, and with a confident smile, he began moving forward.

Something told him to look carefully. He paused, held his torch along the wall, and studied the opening of the left tunnel.

A different arrow, one with an X on its tail, pointed down the other tunnel. Li Kung felt his heart sink. He had initially followed the first arrow, which he had thought was a certain indicator for the nearest exit, but now there was a new one, and it pointed down a different path.

He felt his stomach burning; he was no longer confident of what to do. But he had to keep moving—there was nothing else he *could* do. He grabbed a loose pebble from the ground and chipped the character "Li" on the wall, then drew an arrow under his name. He stomped the ground to shake off a few rats, and walked forward again.

The tunnel became wider, twisting and turning. He thought it would continue forever.

It didn't take long for the flame on his second torch to falter. He knew then that he would be out of light well before he starved to death. The rats would eat him. He pulled another spare torch from his coat and ignited it, this time without the green powder. He needed to save the powder. He had been foolish enough to indulge in a brilliant light and wasted a torch.

Li Kung hurled the used torch, now a stub of glowing wood, deep into the tunnel. It landed on something, then struck the ground and bounced away. More rats fled. Li Kung waited a second for his new torch to grow before hurrying forward.

It was a pile of clothing chewed to shreds, once a body, now completely devoured by rats. Li Kung pushed aside the strands of clothing, revealing a skull and scattered pieces of bone still somewhat attached to the spine. Most of the spine was in fragments, and the bones were broken down and gnawed open for marrow. The clothing didn't seem that old, yet all resemblance of flesh, once part of the dead body, had been cleanly eaten.

Li Kung turned his face, covered his eyes, and doubled over to vomit. He backed away, his eyes squeezing shut. How did this man get here? How did he die? Maybe he never found his way out and died of starvation. Maybe the rats ate him alive when his last torch was consumed.

A sense of wild fear surged through him.

"No!" he screamed. A faint chorus of rats chirped in response and ran from the human voice. Li Kung took another step back, his eyes on the pile of clothing. This indeed, was the worst punishment: to die alone, in darkness, eaten alive by rats. This was the death that he deserved. His eyebrows were dripping cold sweat. Would Pun want him to go like this?

He gritted his teeth, stepping over the pile of cloth and bones, and began to move forward again.

Much later, Li Kung was faced with another fork in the tunnel. He carved the character "Li" on the wall and drew an arrow before glancing at the far wall.

He dropped his torch in horror. The character "Li" was already on another tunnel wall. His mouth fell open, his face turning ghastly. He had come back to where he had started.

He only had three more torches, and then he would be

plunged into darkness. What should he do when he completely lost light? He would commit suicide. But there was really nothing he could use to kill himself with. He could try dashing his head into a sharp boulder, but that may not kill him, only render him unconscious, and he would awaken to the horror of being eaten alive.

He shook free from the sick thoughts of death and began to walk again. In a moment, he stumbled across another pile—this time of clothing made of thick canvas. The corpse was reduced to a pile of scattered bones. The heavy material seemed intact, except for some rodent chew marks. Otherwise, the canvas had hardly deteriorated. Strange, the rats didn't chew that much of it. Li Kung brought it closer to his face and thought he smelled the light scent of herbs, but shrugged off the thought. A pouch must have opened in his coat. He dropped the clothing with disinterest and proceeded onward.

The tunnel yielded to another triple fork. Li Kung quickly chose one, the center one, scratched his name on the wall and continued onward. There was no time to lose. He could succumb to fatigue any moment, he would lose time resting, and lose some of his torch as well.

He found another body, then another—each of them dressed in coarse canvas. "How many more need to die in here!" he shouted. In front of him was yet another pile, this one in fine silk.

Rats squeaked and ran as he approached. A few scurried away from inside the pile. Li Kung slowed to a walk, the stench overwhelming him. The silk was completely shredded by rats; it covered a partially eaten man, his face in a frozen expression of twisted agony. The body was relatively new—so new the rats hadn't finished him yet.

Li Kung felt nauseous again. He took another glance at the partially eaten man, and cold sweat broke from his neck. The fatigue struck him then, with the hunger, the thirst, the numerous injuries sustained in past days. He collapsed with a murmur. There was no way out. Why did he even bother to try?

. . .

Suthachai fell shuddering to his knees, the heavy saber in his hand dripping with fresh blood. The inn was quiet, almost eerie. There were thirty seasoned swordsmen in his room—all dead.

The warriors of Redwood Cliff had been assigned to a task better suited for junior students. Killing a man dying of poison was beneath them, beneath the skill they prided themselves in. On top of that, they were ordered to attack him together, all thirty of them. Yes, they had heard all about this Mongolian. He was unstoppable in the battle of Redwood Cliff and he was the greatest warrior of the steppe. But it brought mocking laughter to their lips when they saw him curled in bed, hugging his saber like a frightened child.

"The Flute Demon," he said, between gasps for air. "Did she send you to kill me, because she was afraid to do it herself?"

"We don't take orders from the Flute Demon," one of them responded. "We take orders from Master Bin."

"Wei Bin . . . " Suthachai began to laugh. They looked at each other, astounded. The Mongolian was certainly insane, laughing in the face of death.

"Her father is not good enough to kill me . . . "

"Whose father—?"

The heavy saber moved like lightning, cutting down the warrior in mid-sentence. The men drew their weapons, but it was too late.

In seconds, they were all dead. No one had time to run. No one had time to scream.

Outside, the weather was equally violent. Large pellets of ice came down and hammered the roof like endless drumbeats. He had slashed open the windowpanes. Then, trembling in wild spasms, Suthachai threw himself out the window, screaming all the way down from the second floor.

He scrambled in the snow, lifted his face to the heavens, and screamed.

Blood began to flow from his nostrils.

He had heard of the whipping on Redwood Cliff.

When would she come to see him?

. . .

Fei Fei's bed was enclosed in fine silk. Layer upon layer of translucent material hung from the ceiling, so that at every three steps there was a rippling wall of soft pink, making it impossible to see her bed from anywhere in the room. Not that anyone would ever venture into her personal chambers. Staring at the princess in public would mean losing one's eyes. Staring at the princess in private would mean instant death.

She grew up in this room. Inside these silk curtains, she would glue on her fake tumor every day, attach her crooked nose and webbed skin. Once behind the hideous mask, she would be a respected warrior.

The sun was high in the heavens. Fei Fei crawled out of bed and flexed the wounds on her back. She had suffered more injuries and more traumas in the past week than she had ever experienced in her life. She was trained to endure pain, to set aside pride when victory was at risk. She was taught to face her battles calmly, scorning the traditional woman who lived only to provide comfort for a man. Yet, as she slept off her injuries, she dreamed of him. She dreamed of the one man she would die to protect, to live and provide comfort for.

Fei Fei reached under her bed for the familiar rosewood chest. Inside was the infamous tumor, the twisted upper lip, the oil that made her cheeks waxen and grotesque.

A wound on her back reopened when she pulled the heavy chest, and she flinched in pain.

They jeered at her, threw things at her, applauded when she was disgraced on the Triangle of Reform. The same men normally followed her like dogs. She could barely believe her eyes when they gathered to humiliate her.

The lamp by her bed was recently replenished, filled with plenty of oil. She poured everything into the chest, threw in a flame and watched it ignite.

She enjoyed being ugly.

In a moment, most of her disguise was in cinders. She closed the chest with a violent slam and shoved it under the bed. The Flute Demon died under the whip. There would be no one to take her place.

The princess of the Red Dragon House threw on her feminine clothes, drew back her hair, lined her eyelashes with a deep blue pigment, coated her full lips with a vibrant red, and stormed out of her sacred chambers.

The two guards stationed outside, forgetting their orders, stared with mouths gaping open.

Beauty that could destroy entire kingdoms, Suthachai once said. Let them stare. She smiled a cool, mysterious smile that could have brought death to many.

"Look at me," she said. The two guards instantly lowered their eyes. She recognized one of them. He stood in front of the crowd when she was being whipped, his lips spewing the vilest insults.

"Look at me," she said again. "You're guards of Redwood Cliff. You should at least look at your enemy before you die."

The two men started in alarm, but it was too late. Fei Fei shot forward, drew a sword, and cleanly decapitated one, then the other. She walked away without a word. Both headless bodies crumbled into the snow.

Redwood Cliff was inside a cloud. She thought she had stepped into a dream, vaguely treading on a familiar road, the suffocating sea of white so dense she could barely see her own feet. It was a straight path to the Grand Stairway, despite the heavy clouds, and in a matter of minutes, she would be on her way down. Once on the narrow stairs, there would be no one who could stop her.

Her long hair flew across her small, pouting lips, her lithe figure moving nimbly. With her disguise in ashes, she suddenly felt free, alive, uninhibited. The men she once commanded had joined in a chorus to humiliate her. She no longer needed to hide behind her disguise—she was no longer a respected warrior of the Red Dragon House.

She tried to look at the structures of Redwood Cliff, the only home she knew. What if she would never set foot on her beloved home again? What would her father do when he discovered that she ran off to protect the Mongolian, who knew the very details of his secret? How would she face a battle against her own men?

The Martial Society would know her as a traitor, and those once close to her would be turned against her. She would have nowhere to go to after Suthachai died of poison. There was nothing but self-destruction ahead.

With a deep sigh, Fei Fei began descending the Grand Stairway.

· · ·

Li Kung had one more torch left. When that died, he would be alone, in utter darkness, surrounded by hungry rats. What kept the rodents away was fear of the dancing flame. But he knew they could sense fear. They must have seen this before. A pathetic human lost in the tunnels; tired, weak, and out of torches. They came upon a feast every time this happened. Why would they lose patience now?

Li Kung leaned against the tunnel wall and stared at the flame. Directly above him was an arrow with the characters "Li Kung" carved under it. He couldn't remember when he scratched those words, but after another attempt through long, winding tunnels, he returned to where he was earlier in the night. Hope was still with him then.

Would it matter if he lit his final torch and stared at the dark tunnels for a little while longer? Maybe he would be satisfied if once, just once, he could encounter a dead end in the tunnels. He would be able to backtrack and scratch the words "dead end" on the wall. Now, after so many forks, so many "Li Kungs" etched on the wall, he could no longer remember which tunnel brought him back to where he started.

He had seen too many bodies to count. Why did so many of the remains, randomly scattered across the tunnel floors, wear the same type of canvas? Maybe they all came in together. But wouldn't they stay together, especially when faced with death?

A circle of rats gathered around him, waiting for his flame to go. He drew his final spare torch, ignited it, and leveled both flames in front of him. The rats began to run side to side, no longer afraid of the dying human, despite his flame.

In less than an hour, this last torch would die, and the rats would be victorious. Li Kung hoped to die in a more heroic manner, but this certainly was why he was left behind in the living world. To be tortured, to face his end with humiliation and fear.

A cold smile erupted on his face. He swayed between the brink of laughing and crying. The rats inched closer again.

"What are you waiting for?"

The rats scurried back. Li Kung sat up. "You know your way around the tunnels and I don't. You win . . . "

He stopped. The rats knew the way! Rats knew their way out of everything!

Strength shot into his veins then. His bones, his every sinew of muscle, suddenly became alive. He never realized, never saw so clearly, that what he really wanted was just to live. An image of Suthachai grew before his eyes. He gritted his teeth, his fist tightly clenched on the torch until his knuckles turned white. He rose to his feet in cold rage. He would live, so Pun wouldn't have died for nothing.

With a roar that sent the rats fleeing in all directions, Li Kung the whimpering boy charged forward.

There was murder in his eyes. The older torch had died. He reeled back and threw the burnt stick of wood behind him. The flame on the new torch whipped backwards, almost searing his face. His twisted lips curled into a scornful smile. Slightly before him was a pile of canvas—one of many he encountered—and without slowing his pace, Li Kung scooped down and grabbed the coarse fabric. There was little time to lose. He shook off the old bones caught in the creases, spotted another pile of canvas, and, tucking the first bunch under one arm, snatched the next acquisition off the ground with one fluid motion.

Very quickly, he was back to where he started. He glanced once at the marking "Li Kung" before charging down another passageway.

His lungs strained for air, his ribs flashed with pain. The fatigue was about to overwhelm him, and he knew that when it did, he would never find the same momentum again. He couldn't stop. With a deep cry, Li Kung scooped another heap of canvas and squeezed it under his arm. He lifted his face, the cords bulging on his thin neck, and he screamed at the top of his lungs.

Ahead was the next fork in the tunnels. He stripped a piece of canvas from under his arm, placed the torch underneath it, igniting it. The growing flame jerked. When his hand could no longer withstand the heat, Li Kung hurled the flaming canvas into the middle of the intersection. He jumped on it, stomping it out. A haze of stinging smoke arose. Li Kung took a step back. It was more smoke than he ever imagined. In the distance, he heard the rats screeching. They were running from the smoke.

He ignited more canvas and charged down another tunnel. Again, he stomped out the fire to discharge the smoke. Li Kung watched the rats scurrying off. He picked up his pace then, following the rats to the next intersection where three passageways stood before him. He could smell it already. Smoke was surging from one of the passages. He lit another pile of canvas and whipped it against the wall to extinguish it.

So much smoke. He could hardly breathe. He followed the rats down the left tunnel, careful to note that some scurried into small openings that they had burrowed in the walls. But they always reemerged from another hole, into the main passageways, when the smoke began to trap them.

He approached another intersection, and clearly, the rats were scurrying down the middle. Both the left and right tunnels were already saturated with smoke. He tossed a flaming ball of canvas, followed the rats, and passed another intersection. One of these tunnels would eventually lead to their source of water. Li Kung smiled. More rats joined out of nowhere. They took a sharp turn and scampered down a smaller tunnel to the right.

The tunnel tapered into a narrow, snaking passageway, and soon, he had to walk sideways. He struggled to keep up with the frightened rodents.

Out of nowhere, a small copper jar, old and brittle, stood in his way. Li Kung bent down sideways, picked it up with two fingers and twisted the rusted lid. A piece of sheepskin, tightly rolled, and a smaller piece of cloth was tucked inside.

His rodent guides were still running. He drew the sheepskin from the jar and held it against the light.

It was a map. Li Kung couldn't believe his eyes. The map was drawn with great detail; each line, shape, and character inscription still impeccably clear, despite its age. In the center of the map was a large rectangle, with the characters "Main Chasm," large and bold, written on it. Side passageways, drawn in curved lines leading to other rooms, covered the rest of the map. On the bottom of the map was a short arrow with the inscription "Tunnel Entrance," and another area titled, "Treasure Room of Snow Wolf."

Snow Wolf! Li Kung's eyes devoured the map, searching for her name again. He saw an array of little rooms surrounding the Main Chasm and a few tunnels that were not labeled—and that was all.

Rampant thoughts surged through his mind; images of a great heroine facing hundreds of bandits alone, of a leader who brought the common people together to fight famine and disease, of a legend that kept honor and justice alive. He thought of the stories he heard since he came to the north, from the blind storyteller in He Ku, from Little Butterfly, from Old Gu.

A wave of smoke struck him. His eyes burned, forcing him to squeeze them shut. He felt the last stream of squeaking rats brush past him, and he knew he had to follow quickly or be lost forever. He threw his eyes open, snatched the small piece of cloth at the bottom of the jar, tossed the copper container, and ran as hard he could. The tunnel began to widen, twisting and turning. More than once, he failed to see a turn, scraped himself against harsh rock, and opened up old wounds on his body. But he didn't care. Wild thoughts roamed through his mind. He envisioned Snow Wolf, alive, at the end of the tunnel. He would meet her. He would ask her to come out of seclusion, so once again she would settle the chaos in the world.

There was a distant sound of running water. Li Kung shouted out in exhilaration. He was close. He saw indicators for running water on the map, and the unmistakable whisper of hurried streams never sounded better. With the map and the cloth in one hand and the torch in the other, Li Kung charged through the snake-like turns of the narrow passageway. He felt alive, worthy even. There was hope for him to do something for this world; perhaps he could bring back the hero long lost. Suffering may end, integrity and honor would reestablish itself in the Martial Society, and his own losses would have been worthwhile, would it not?

All of a sudden he broke through into a chamber where blaring white sunlight slashed down in heavy beams, blinding him, causing him to fall into a heap. The opening appeared out of nowhere.

The ground was soft. He lay still for a moment, eager to see where he was, but the sunlight was intense and he couldn't open his eyes. He curled his body into a ball. The soothing smell of fresh water urged him to rest quietly.

Much later, he opened his eyes and looked around.

There really was running water. A thin waterfall that dropped in from the heavens thrashed the bare rocks on the side of the cavern wall. It struck a little pool of water like millions of dancing needles, creating a filmy mist of vapor. The streaking sunlight, like stretched veils of fine silk, penetrated from an opening high above, illuminating the entire chamber with a dreary mist. The subtle whispers of the waterfall told him that he was tired, and he should sleep.

Li Kung shook the fatigue from his head and supported himself on one elbow. The cavern was deep. The rats disappeared, strangely, and no other animal seemed to inhabit this place where light and water flowed in abundance. Not even a fruit bat.

He was inside a chasm where a steep drop from the surface somewhere on the side of the mountain must have prevented other animals from entering. Yet, weeds and moss grew everywhere.

He almost forgot the map in his hand. Li Kung fumbled with the folded sheepskin. He was inside the Main Chasm. In the large rectangular chamber, across the narrow stream of water, a small line of words leaped out at him.

"Tomb of Snow Wolf."

He climbed to his knees and sat back. Snow Wolf's Tomb . . .

Maybe she was not alive after all. Maybe he really was alone in the inner depths of this mountain.

The mist seemed to clear before his very eyes, perhaps because he finally grew accustomed to the light, or because he finally knew what to look for. A short distance away was a massive tombstone. He couldn't see the engravings on the tablet, but he knew what it was. After fifty years, the final resting site of Snow Wolf was revisited.

Her tomb, barren of any embellishments, simple in architecture, and almost lonely in appearance, stood only a few steps away. He twitched, the agony of hunger, of old injuries, of pure fatigue and disappointment striking him at once. No, he was not going to meet her. She had been dead for fifty years.

Not even feeling pride at being the first to find her tomb, Li Kung stood frozen and stared.

He had come across wealth beyond belief, had survived a maze of tunnels so many had died in, and now, he discovered the burial ground of Snow Wolf. Somehow, he couldn't bring himself to feel his accomplishments. They weren't accomplishments at all.

Li Kung lowered his head, a deep, perplexed frown on his face. He eyed the tomb and wanted to cry.

She really was dead.

His eyes fell on the crumbled map in his hands, then at the small piece of the cloth still held between his fingers.

He had neglected the little piece of cloth. He quickly unfolded it, and read under his breath:

Snow Wolf never intended for her wealth to fall into the hands of others, yet, the existence of this map was overlooked when she finally reached immortality. Now, also faced with inevitable death in this dreaded maze, we, her apprentices, hereby ask that this sheepskin be buried behind her tomb, if it were ever found. The amassed treasure must not fall into evil hands. Let no other person lay claim to it, should those with dark intentions steal the wealth and become powerful overnight.

Become powerful overnight . . . Li Kung's face twisted in a bitter smile. He was too worthless to ever become powerful—even with so much gold. He gazed at the map, at the hidden door on his far left, which led to the Hexagon Room. The Treasure Room of Snow Wolf. So even more valuable items were hidden in that room. He already turned his back to one room full of diamond and gold. Why would he bother with another?

Snow Wolf was right, in her eternal wisdom. If he buried the map now, no one would ever know about it, and mankind would never kill each other for it.

He stepped forward, one foot in front of the other, and approached her tomb. The sense of doom hovered. He had, for many years, believed that he was worthy of something, meant for something. He secretly disputed Shifu One's lectures, told himself that he was capable of changing the world, like Snow Wolf once did so many years ago.

Li Kung clutched the map in his fist. It felt unimportant to him. He was about to bury a map that no one would ever find, just to ensure that no one would ever find it.

Her tablet was tall and narrow, and it stood on a heavy, carved rock. Li Kung slowed, noticed that behind her tablet was a small area covered with soil.

He read her chiseled name and date of death on the tablet. A surge of mixed emotions clouded his eyes. He felt a lump in his throat. He wanted to pray to her and ask her for strength. He wanted to close his eyes and blot out the image of her tomb, hoping still that she was alive somewhere, and that she would come forth to help him, to help the world. But most of all, he wanted to cry.

He dropped to his knees and crawled to the back of her headstone. If it was her wish to have the map buried there, then so be it. He dug his fingers into the moist earth, and began to claw the soil.

There was a long line of writing behind her tomb. On the very top were the characters: *"Hence I foresee the events of the world after my death."*

Underneath was a long poem.

A blind guide seeks direction
The dormant engravings foretold
The dreamer's potion discovered
Converging thunderheads opposed

Amid the barbaric horsemen
The Jade Dragon surfaced North
The light of the firefly resembles
The towering glow of the sun

Two soaring dragons know no regrets
With filial piety as vanguard
Both deaf dragons were not forewarned
They ascend the white wolf's lair

Death and power but a dance
In a romance of murder and ruin
Revelations quelled in silence
As eggs bombarded the stone

A hero born from chaos
Courage nurtured by misfortune
Genius fed by desperation
Can ambition spring from fear?

Disorder, monstrosity, disaster
Thus daughters butcher their parents
Hence, parents murder their sons

Faceless heroes, pathetic kings
Ignorant of collapsing mountains
Weapons sharpened, shields positioned
The fattened pigs await slaughter

With courage, there is silence
The concealed knife unforeseen
In futile defiance of destiny
Retribution continues, unexpected

Ten thousand myriad beings
Bleed to retain control
Yet birth among the living
Death inevitably precedes

In the face of death and the dread of dying
The heavens were forced to clear
The redemption brought a neutral calm
The legend of Snow Wolf brings eternal fear

How long he gazed at the writing, or how many times
he read the poem, he could no longer remember. The time
of day ceased to be a concern for him. By the time Li Kung
began digging again, the cavern was no longer as bright, perhaps because it was overcast outside, or more likely, the sun
was setting. Soon, he would be in darkness again. How many
more times did he have to dig the earth in the same week,
first to bury Pun, then to bury the villagers, now to bury a

map? It didn't matter. Each time, he felt obligated. Either way it was not his choice.

He shook his head in absurd amusement, tossing the dirt farther away from him, deeply entrenching his fingers for one final scoop before lowering the map into the hole. His fingers struck metal. He froze, uncertain of what to do. He peered into the little ditch. It was certainly metal, though rusted into a dull tan. He swept away the surrounding soil for a closer look. It was heavy, no larger than a gift box, very similar to the metal jar he found in the tunnels.

He didn't know what to think then. Inside the box was a long letter written on canvas. There were three books at the bottom of the box.

He held the letter with both hands and sat back to read.

Destiny has brought you to this region, and chaos has driven you to brave the haunted mountain. Your desire to know, to explore, has brought you down the tunnel at the peak of my mountain. But unlike the treasure seekers, who died from the poison coated on the gold, you displayed contempt for the material wealth and sought for something higher than basic human greed. In an act of kindness even in the face of doom, you decided to bury the skeletons of dead villagers, subsequently triggering the mechanisms I have prepared for you. Thus, with the help of the torches I left behind, you were permitted to enter the maze.

You displayed superior intelligence by mastering the maze before the torches were exhausted, or before you died of fatigue and starvation. Yes, I supplied you with a rat population to guide you through the maze. But it was you who found the courage and possessed the wit that pulled you through the face of a dark, lonely death. You paid careful attention to details, which allowed you to find the treasure map even in the confusion of running through the tunnels, and you noticed the short message that instructed you to bury the map. Again, you proved your lack of greed and the inherent wisdom that brought you here when you decided that it was more dangerous to permit such wealth to resurface in the world. Today, you have proven yourself worthy, and henceforth, you are my chosen warrior.

Li Kung gasped. He could not believe his eyes. He thought back for a quick second and remembered the bodies in the first cavern that he fell into, the jeweled sword, the short tunnel that led to the gold. They were all treasure seekers, and apparently, touched the treasures and died of poison. That was why none of them had their swords drawn, and they were trying to leave the cavern at once, to seek help outside.

He thought of the dead villagers, now clearly not villagers at all, but merely bodies that Snow Wolf arranged with a story on the wall, and the unusual population of rats that he never pondered over. The contents of this letter could not be truer. Even the excessive smoke from the burning canvas was more smoke than he had ever seen. His mouth dropped open in amazement. He read on:

The map in your hand is useless, for the only treasures available are the ones poisoned in the front room. I have left three books for you, plus two urns, each buried on either side of my headstone. The larger one contains an ancient formula of herbs, soaked in alcohol and certainly at its most potent by the time you find this. You are to drink a small quantity every night, and over the course of weeks, you will see your physical abilities enhanced. The other urn contains the antidote for the poison I coated on the gold. Submerge the treasures inside this solution and the poison will be neutralized. You are to take this wealth that I confiscated from the Sun Cult, and use it to fight the evil in this world.

Finally, the three books I left behind for you are writings that I have prepared for many years. You must study each of them carefully, so you can attain the knowledge that I have intended for you. You will carry out your duties as a supreme warrior in the Martial Society.

A narrow tunnel behind the waterfall will lead you into an enclosed valley on the outside world. There, you will find an abundance of food and water, where you will be able to study in safety. The cliffs that surround the valley are impossible to climb, unless you master the martial arts in my books.

Li Kung stared at the signature. "*Lady Wu, styled Snow Wolf.*"

. . .

Lord Xu's one-armed servant, known as Uncle Tan, touched his burning wick to a long row of torches. Most of the torches illuminating the Grand Hall were lit, but half of the wall near the entrance remained untouched as Uncle Tan worked slowly. He was weak, hunched over, toiling without a word of complaint.

"The guests are about to arrive!" a voice boomed behind Uncle Tan's ear. The servant started at the sudden noise before realizing it was the young master.

"Why aren't the torches ready yet?" the young master asked again.

Lord Xu stepped into the room, the gold dagger in his topknot glistening against the light. "Uncle Tan can take as long as he wants. The guests can wait!"

Jian withdrew. "Yes, father."

"Uncle Tan only has one hand," Lord Xu said. "You have both your hands but I don't see you doing anything useful with your life."

Stump emerged in the front doorway, standing rigid with chest held high, and announced, "Master Song of the Sword Forging House!"

A middle-aged man, coarsely dressed with two followers, stepped into the Grand Hall and bowed.

Stump shouted, "Master Gao of the Northern Mantis House!"

Then immediately, "Master Chen of the Tuo Shan House! Master Liang of the White Tiger House!"

One after the other, leaders of the Martial Society were announced. Lord Xu stood on his feet, his hands clasped together, greeting each party with a bow. After formalities were exchanged, Lord Xu stood in the front of the room and said nothing. Someone was missing, someone crucial. Then Stump shouted, "Liu Yun of the Iron Palm School!"

A murmur flew across the room. Liu Yun walked in; a long spear brandished by his side, the white headband of mourning strapped under his hairline. Lord Xu took his hand and led him to a seat in the front.

"Master Xu," Liu Yun said with a bow.

"No need for formalities," Lord Xu said, like a gentle grandfather. "How do you feel? Have your wounds healed?"

"Yes, sir. I'm ready for battle."

Lord Xu stepped to the front and waited a second for each person to settle before clasping his hands together. "We're here today because a great injustice has befallen the Martial Society. I'm ashamed to stand in front of you here and talk about this, but I must. I've invited young Liu Yun here to formally apologize to him. I've let his father down. I was too late to assist the Iron Palm School when they called upon me for help, and as a result of my mistake, disaster has befallen upon them."

The audience glanced once at Liu Yun before returning their attention to Lord Xu, who continued, "They were slaughtered in cold blood, and I'm sure you all know that the Red Dragons are responsible for this."

He paused, carefully watching every face. "I'm sure you suspect. As the power of Wei Bin's ambitious House grows, we'll gather here more frequently to lament the dead."

He took a deep breath. "Fellow leaders of the Martial Society. We are warriors, each with a special responsibility, a commitment. Our commitments were established when we began our studies of the martial arts. And in these unspoken vows, we promised to fight the evil of the land and maintain balance in the world. We promised to bring peace to the common people."

"My twin has taken venomous steps to overthrow this balance—first with the slaughter of his guests on Redwood Cliff . . ." He paused to allow his words to sink in. "At his own mother's funeral, even—then, without offering any explanation, he exterminated an entire school of the Martial Society. He destroyed a school established for generations, one that has earned respect and benevolence among us. Why, if not to slowly eliminate those who have the power to keep his ambitions in check? Why else would he kill so many people who never sought trouble with him?"

He stopped again, and there was silence across the room.

Master Song, his long beard grazing his chest, stood up to address the room. "Master Bin's actions have perplexed us for some time. That's why months ago, we were gathered here in this same place to discuss the coalition that we must create." He looked at Master Gao of the Northern Mantis School, who promptly stood up to speak.

"Yes, we've thought over the situation carefully," Master Gao began. "Whatever his plans are, we are the weaker schools, and we have no means of stopping him. The only way to bring balance back to the Martial Society would be to work together."

"It's time to form the coalition," Master Song instantly piped in. "It's time to form the coalition," Master Song repeated, louder this time. "We need to unite and supervise ourselves under laws that we all agree upon. We need to join together when evil arises. Right now, the Martial Society is a handful of scattered sand, blown apart by a slight gust of wind. But if we all cement together as a union, and oversee the conduct of each member as a single unit, the world will quickly be at peace."

"And I, for one, believe that Lord Xu is the natural leader of this new coalition," Master Gao said, his voice projecting across the room.

There was a short murmur across the Grand Hall.

"I oppose forming a coalition right now," Lord Xu suddenly said, to the surprise of every man in the audience. "Organizing a good union takes time, and I suspect that time is not on our side. We need to reduce the immediate threats before us. But I agree, we must all work together. That's why, today, I asked you to visit my humble quarters, so I can propose a simple plan against the Red Dragons."

"Destroy the Red Dragons?" someone asked in the back.

"Certainly not," Lord Xu said with a smile. "There are many fine warriors on Redwood Cliff, many righteous men of integrity. We are to invade Redwood Cliff and liberate these innocent men from the evil clutches of Wei Bin!"

Master Gao and Master Song stood up to cheer. Their students followed suit. Leaders of other schools eyed each other, and then rose to their feet for an ovation. Very quickly, the entire Grand Hall thundered with applause.

Lord Xu smiled, immersed in the moment. Suddenly, someone in the back shouted, "Wait!"

The room fell silent. Master Chen of the Tuo Shan House stepped forward. "How do you intend to invade Redwood Cliff? It's a natural fortress, impossible to penetrate."

"Even if the imperial government were to send ten thousand crack troops," another added. "They wouldn't be able to penetrate a thousand Red Dragons defending Redwood Cliff."

"But that's not true," Lord Xu said. "Not if the very elite of the Red Dragons—the Gentle Swordsmen and the Red Headbands—are away from the cliff. Between our schools, we have enough men and enough skilled warriors to run over Redwood Cliff three times! Now, I do have a humble plan."

"Please, let us hear your wisdom," Master Gao pitched in.

"Taking over the Red Dragons," Lord Xu began with a calm glance at his audience, "and reuniting the Dragon House has been my lifelong wish. And although I know that you would all aid me in reclaiming what is rightfully mine, I would never be able to accept such honor. How would I be able to command the respect of my men if I couldn't fight my own battles? How would my ancestors grant me leadership of a united Dragon House if I rely on the strengths of my allies? The Martial Society would laugh at me, and I would be ashamed to show my face in public again."

Master Chen glanced around the room. "We were discussing an invasion of Redwood Cliff. Didn't you ask us to come here—"

"Not I!" Lord Xu appeared startled. "You're not here to help me. I myself came here today to help another."

"Then who are we here to help?"

Lord Xu turned to Liu Yun, and pointed. "We didn't come to the aid of the Liu family, and as a result, the entire Iron Palm School was exterminated. Only one heavily injured son is left behind as witness to Master Bin's cruelty. How can we call ourselves the heroes of the land if we cower away from this act of evil? How do we lead the Martial Society if we permit such atrocious acts to go unpunished? That's why I'm here! That's why I will send my men into battle—so that the youths of tomorrow will join the Martial Society knowing that the leaders are upright men, and not cowards. So that those who respect us as masters, who look to us for guidance, who study the values we teach, will not be disappointed!"

The room was silent. A light smile flickered across Lord Xu's face before he forced the solemn look back into his eyes. He continued, "Today, I propose a plan for Liu Yun, and with my utmost respect to his late father, I am asking him to lead the assault on the Red Dragons. He has agreed not to approach this with murder in mind, but with the intent of liberating the fine warriors of Redwood Cliff, so they will no longer be forced to serve under evil! Now, my plan is a simple one."

Lord Xu walked to the middle of the room and looked at each person for a moment before beginning, "The Red Dragons are on a natural fortress, it's true. But being higher up means they are vulnerable to fire. We can launch fireballs straight up the Grand Stairway while we ascend, and the Red Dragon guards will be forced to retreat. As we move up, we sweep away the balls of burning hay, and we continue to bombard the Red Dragons with fire until we reach the surface. Then we will attack together. Now, the key to the plan, of course, is that Wei Bin, the Gentle Swordsmen, and the Red Headbands are not on Redwood Cliff. Here is what I intend to do. I will ask my brother to come forth and negotiate a truce—considered a formal communication between our two Houses. The world will know I intend to make peace with him. The Martial Society, everyone, will urge him to comply. He'll be left with no choice. He has to come forth, because he's not ready to stare down the entire Martial Society." Lord Xu chuckled to himself. "But, my brother is a suspicious man. He'll see that the meeting place can be ambushed, so he will come carefully. He'll bring his Gentle Swordsmen and Red Headbands."

"That's when we attack Redwood Cliff?" Chen asked.

"Yes!" Lord Xu said with a smile. "And we'll make arrangements to delay him, so by the time he returns, Redwood Cliff will already be occupied. Then, you will be holding his fortress, and he will have nowhere to go. I'll bring my men and corner him at the base of his own cliff. He'll surrender. He cannot face two fronts at once."

"Can we enlist the help of Black Shadow?" Master Chen asked. "With his help . . . "

Lord Xu shook his head. "Black Shadow comes and goes as he pleases. I have no way of finding him. But we don't need him. Together, we're already ten times more powerful than the Red Dragons!" He spun around and walked back to the front of the room. The guests edged back to their seats. Lord Xu held up his palms. "I have pledged what little resources I have to helping Liu Yun avenge his family, and to protect other small Houses from being annihilated by Master Bin. Will all of you join me?" He watched the faces in front of him, as they turned to each other, and, left with no choice, nodded.

"Will all of you join me!" he called again.

• • •

Li Kung's eyes blurred. The wind died, and the icy air began to settle onto the barren rocks. But his fire was strong, and he was comfortable. Soon, he would have to return to the cavern to sleep, or the cold may kill him. But while firewood was abundant and the crackling flame danced, he preferred to stay in the open air.

The valley was completely surrounded by walls of bare cliffs—impossible to climb—as Snow Wolf wrote in her letter. She had prepared this space for him to train. There was a large population of rabbits, roaming unchecked in the valley, for him to use as food. The little animals, free from predators for so many generations, no longer knew how to flee from danger. He didn't even need to make a weapon to hunt with. Each day, he ate in abundance, and drank the herbal concoction that Snow Wolf left behind. His wounds healed, and by the second day, he was able to begin training.

Among the three books excavated behind her headstone, the one instructing him in martial arts was the thinnest one. From cover to cover, the book described only one technique, called the Flame Cutter.

There was no time to wonder why. The thickest of the three books had been consuming all his time, and each day, he would fling away the heavy volume in frustration, slap himself across the head again and again, only to recover the book and study late into the night.

Again, he opened to the first page and began to read:

There is no greater desire in the Martial Society than to acquire a superior fighting skill, so that he or she can become invincible in battle. Yet, the strongest fighter is no more than a good henchman, while the strategists are the true leaders. One who understands the way of strategy never goes into battle, and is therefore invincible in battle; never needs physical strength, and is therefore immeasurably strong; never cornered in a situation where he runs out of time, and is therefore infinitely quick. A warrior able in strategy understands the past and the present, and therefore maintains control of the future.

Li Kung sat back. The words she used were simple. Why couldn't he understand?

The two key elements of strategy lie in deceit, and preparation.

Life is inefficient if one does not think of death. Pleasure is ineffective unless one thinks of disaster. Such is the way of preparation.

War is but a brawl of brutes without the subtle changes between attack and retreat. Varying the use of attack and retreat: retreating for the purpose of attacking, attacking for the purpose of retreating, attacking to develop continuous attacks, retreating to lay grounds for further retreats—all give rise to infinite possibilities and variations. By using this system of change to the point where the enemy cannot fathom one's intentions, one has employed the way of deceit.

Li Kung buried his head between his knees. He was a doctor, a scholar, an educated man. In the face of Snow Wolf's writings, he felt like a child once again.

He finally set the book aside, reached for the third volume, and began to read:

I have closely watched the numerology of the heavens, and I have pondered the outcome of the future after my death. Upon monitoring the constellations for many nights, I pick up my brush to foretell the events of coming years.

The Dragon House, with its enormous wealth and tens of thousands in members, will remain the dominant leader of the Martial Society for some time. The family tradition of training their sons to be warriors will ensure that the establishment will not be lost by worthless younger generations. Yet, the two brothers destined to succeed the organization are equal in talent and ambition, each shrewd and cunning in his own way, but both intolerant of each other. For one to easily dispose of the other would be an impossible event. Thus, the Dragon House will be divided equally among the brothers. As the House separates, so will the struggle for power begin. With the death of Lin Cha, death and destruction will thrive without hindrance.

The gods will signal the time for unity. The symbol for the leadership, the missing jade dragon, will resurface in Mongolia in the hands of a common nomad in no less than forty years, and a long struggle to possess the jade will ensue. Chaos will reign across the land, blood will flow like rivers, and the outlook for peace in the Martial Society will be bleak. The struggle between the divided Dragon Houses will seep into the lives of the common citizens, and famine will strike once again.

Li Kung nearly dropped the book. How could this be possible? Almost fifty years ago, Snow Wolf knew about the battle on Redwood Cliff. She knew that Suthachai had the jade, that it would be discovered and reclaimed by the Dragon House in no less than forty years after her death—closer to fifty years to be exact. Maybe she really was a goddess, able to divine the future. He lowered his eyes again and continued to read:

Yet, a new evil will be born, and the brother in possession of Redwood Cliff will harness it. A secret alchemy with unusual effects will surface, one designed not to take a man's life, but his soul. The user of this alchemy will gradually face the destruction of his mind, and he will be incapable of shaking his dependency on the poison.

The leader of the split Dragon House on Redwood Cliff will initially develop this alchemy to control the warriors of the Martial Society. Yet, as his power expands and his ambitions grow, the poison will be implemented in the civilian population, and mankind will face a new plague. Families will be separated, children will die of hunger, lives will be lost, and Redwood Cliff will reap the power and wealth from this excursion.

If measures are not taken to stop the expansion of this alchemy, then chaos will flood the world. If the villains of the Dragon Houses are not destroyed, then innocent civilians across the land will fall victim to the greed of a single man. Then, the superior warrior that I painstakingly hope to create, many years after my death, for the purpose of preventing this catastrophe, will have failed me, and all will be lost.

Li Kung sucked in the cold air, his trembling hands barely able to hold the thin book. She knew about the poison that his mentors came to investigate. She prepared to fight it so many years after her death. And she was addressing him. She devised incredible measures to choose him, to train him, for the purpose of fighting this new evil that was destined to surface.

He didn't know what to think then, or how to feel. He combed the words again to make sure he didn't miss anything. She found him, knowing he would live up to the task, because she chose a man who was righteous, who cared, who bothered to bury the innocent dead even in the face of his own doom. He felt fortunate, suddenly alive, despite the fear of what was ahead. Snow Wolf chose him for an impossible task, and he was the one who passed her tests.

If the villains of the Dragon Houses were not destroyed . . .

What if he destroyed their formula, so the poison could not be created?

He shook his head. She wanted the twins destroyed for a reason. The villains of the Dragon Houses, as she wrote. The evil would eventually resurface unless both Houses were uprooted, perhaps not as the same poison, but as something equal in ambition and ruthlessness.

He sat back and tilted the book to the campfire. The words jumped out at him.

Eventually, the poison will destroy the common people of the Northern regions, but still unsatisfied, the empire will be challenged, the nation weakened, and the barbarians of the North will take this opportunity to invade China.

Could her prediction be true? Li Kung's eyes widened in shock. Could it be possible that a civilization as massive as China meet its end from this secret alchemy? Li Kung's breathing became quick and short, his heart was pounding. Snow Wolf divined her predictions from the constellations. She was accurate with the reemergence of the jade, the division of the Dragon Houses, and the wars they fought against each other. She predicted the appearance of Master Bin's poison. How could she be wrong?

It was up to him to stop this. He was chosen. He could not fail her.

He threw aside the book, grabbed the manual for the Flame Cutter and leaped to his feet. There was no time. The task in front of him meant the survival of his world. He needed to leave this valley as soon as possible.

. . .

Suthachai opened his eyes and stared at the crumbled ceiling, the battered bedpost both chipped and fractured, the holes in the wall. They were all a result of his violent shifts from anger to self-pity, and from regret to scorn. He tossed the thick glove from his hand and touched his own forehead, unsure of what the cold skin and the tenderness really meant. Was he about to die? He looked forward to it. He waited each day, lying in the Blue Lantern Inn, while the innkeeper cringed each time he was summoned. Suthachai ate and drank what he could to stay alive. He couldn't take the coward's path and abandon life. Each day that he lived and suffered, he told himself that when the time came he would go into the next world as a warrior. He fought his best.

The innkeeper truly regretted carrying him in from the snow, and bringing him back to life with food and hot water. Since then, thirty men from the Red Dragons had bullied their way into the inn and frightened off his customers. Much later, when he found them all dead in the Mongolian's room, he had to clean the blood, transport the bodies back to Redwood Cliff, and explain to neighbors why there was so much bloodshed in his inn.

And each day, Suthachai stared at the door of his room. The innkeeper once dared to ask whom he was waiting for, but receiving no reply, he quickly hauled away the washbasin beside the Mongolian's bed. It was full of dark blood. He had seen Suthachai during one of his attacks, had witnessed the pale face of a dying man smash the walls in a deranged frenzy. So much blood was coughed from his body that the innkeeper often wondered how much more blood was in him. Every night, the innkeeper would pray for Suthachai to die quickly, both for his own sake and for the good of the inn.

But the Mongolian's life lingered on. Every day that he stared at the door, he seemed to grow weaker. He often lost consciousness in the middle of the day, with blood spooling from his nostrils, and the innkeeper who went in to check on him thought he really was dead. Yet, Suthachai refused to go, and he would eventually awaken to stare at his door once more.

Suthachai had never felt more fragile before. He no longer remembered how many weeks it had been since he left Mongolia, nor did he recall how many weeks the Elder expected him to live. But it would be soon now—he was losing hope, though he continued to stare at the door. It would be soon.

Somehow, he dozed off that night.

The door creaked open, sometime in the middle of the night, just enough to waken him. He remained motionless, partially opening his eyes while his hand closed around his weapon, and he waited. The person outside hesitated for what seemed to be half the night, before completely opening the door.

She stood there, with a yellow lantern in her hand, dressed in a woman's robe, with her long hair carefully braided and pinned together. He had never seen her so beautiful before. She had powdered her cheeks with a light blush, her full lips were coated with a deep red. She stepped into the room gracefully, no longer wearing the boots of a warrior. Her embroidered cloth shoes gently tread the floor.

He thought he smelled her scent, and he knew she had bathed in rose petals before she came.

Suthachai closed his eyes and waited, pretending to be asleep. He sensed her approaching, heard the sound of her taking something from her pocket, felt her soft hand brush a silk handkerchief across his face, to wipe beads of sweat that he could not control.

She leaned over and kissed him. Her sweet scent enveloped him, and he could not resist. He had waited every minute of every day for her, even though he was about to die; he only wanted to see her one last time. She finally came back, whether to kill him or to care for him, it didn't matter. He only wanted to see her one last time.

He opened his eyes and stared; he was stunned by her beauty, yet he calmly took in the face he knew so well. She watched him and opened her mouth to say something, but he lifted his finger and held it to her lips.

"Don't say it," he whispered.

She froze for a second and tried to say something again. A tear rolled down her cheek, which he touched with his finger. She leaned forward and kissed him, as if asking him to forgive her, her warm tears flowing then, and he understood. He wanted to tell her that he did forgive her, that nothing mattered now that she had come back, but he could not say it. He knew that she too, understood.

He lifted his other hand to touch her earlobe, his heart throbbing, his lungs drawing in the scent of her hair, her sweet breath, as she bent forward and whispered something in his ear. He didn't hear her and inquired into her eyes. She smiled and brought her lips to his ear again.

"I love you."

His heart thumped painfully. He opened his mouth and tried to say something, to tell her how he felt about her, how he waited for her every day. But she placed a finger on his lips, like he did to her, and said, "I know. Don't say it."

She sunk into his embrace, wrapped her arms tightly around his neck, pressed her body into his, and squeezed her eyes shut, and for a moment, the pain, the desperation, the hopelessness were forgotten.

. . .

It was daybreak when Suthachai opened his eyes. She was sleeping peacefully beside him. How beautiful she was when she slept. He supported himself on one elbow and gently glided his fingers across her soft skin until his arm was completely around her waist. She sighed softly, a light smile illuminating her face, a smile so heavenly that Suthachai felt his heart pound strongly in his chest once more. What did he do to deserve a creature so beautiful?

He leaned over and kissed her parted lips, and she pouted them in response. She was still sleeping, and he wondered what dreams she was having that made her smile so peacefully.

He rested his head across her belly, pressed his cheek against skin like fine silk, and listened to her quiet breathing. She placed a hand on his head and lightly scratched him. He turned his face to breathe in her scent and kissed her. She giggled.

He closed his eyes and dozed off. It was late in the afternoon when he heard her voice.

"What were you dreaming about?" she asked.

He opened his eyes. "Dreaming?"

"The silly smile on your face. You were dreaming."

He climbed back to the pillow, their skin softly gliding against each other. He reached around her and snuggled against the side of her neck. "I don't know."

There was a long pause. He kissed the cool skin on the

base of her throat. "The morning just went by. The sun is high in the heavens already."

"I know."

"In Mongolia, I would be feeding my horses at this time. The sheep and the cattle we allow to graze by themselves. But my horses are special. I feed them the best."

She smiled and murmured something. He closed his eyes, resting his face in her hair. "Then, later in the afternoon, when we know the animals are full and ready to be rounded up, we chase them into a circle and make them stand together, so we would not need so many men to watch them. That is when I have time to ride with my brothers—at least until the sun sets, we would not need to come back and tend to the animals."

"Where would you ride to?"

"The steppe is endless. There is nowhere to ride to, so we can ride anywhere. Sometimes, we play shooting games, but most of the time, we race each other. My brothers are all good riders, and they can always shoot perfectly, no matter how fast they are riding. That is why we always end up competing—we try to see who can shoot down the other man's arrows, instead of who can hit the center of the target."

Fei Fei reached over to stroke the side of his face. "Do you always win?"

"I never win. I am not good with the bow and arrow. That is why when there is a big hunt, I sometimes jump off my horse and fight the beasts face to face. I am better with that."

"I've heard about that."

"Then, when the sun set, we would stay on top of a hill to watch the animals, and we would cook strips of meat on top of a big fire without a pot or any water. We would drink wine instead of tea, and at least half of us would get drunk.

We would sleep peacefully under the stars. There are so many stars in the skies back home. More stars than in China. And the moon is brighter too. I think the moon is happier when it travels over the steppe, so it shines brighter."

"I haven't watched the stars for so long now," she said. "Each morning, I spend time putting on my disguise. Then I go outside and I train the senior students. I've rarely left my room without the disguise. Now I don't know why I needed it. I used to think that I fight better in disguise—at least most men lost confidence in battle when they saw my ugly face." She laughed. "Maybe it was my confidence. I needed to hide behind a mask."

There was brief silence. "Then, once a month," she continued, "I would go south and escort the gold coins back to Redwood Cliff—mostly the money we collect from selling salt in other provinces. When we march with the Red Dragon flag high above our heads, no one harasses us. But sometimes bandits do attack, and we kill them." A proud smile emerged on her face, just for a brief second, before it faded with the thought. "Yes, we killed every one of them. We often sought out their lair so we could destroy the entire group, and we burned their homes and killed their women."

"Even after they ran away, you continued to attack their camp?"

"Yes."

"Why?"

She paused.

"Why?" he asked again.

"To make a statement," she finally blurted, her voice slightly higher. "To tell the rest of the Martial Society that our wealth must not be touched, or the consequences would be so severe, that ... that ... " She couldn't finish. Suthachai placed a finger over her lips and kissed the soft skin on the side of her neck. She relaxed.

"Your world is so complicated," he said. "It is so much easier to raise sheep."

"But life is so primitive on the steppe," she said. "Something so simple as finding water is complicated. Or even to stay warm in winter."

"There is always water if you know where to find it. And the sheepskin can keep us warm when we run out of dried manure for fire."

"Here, in China, we have a written language. We have art, we have a sophisticated system of trade—we use money instead of skins from dead animals, we have a high form of cuisine, poetry, literature . . . The women ride in wooden carriages instead of bare horseback. Every day we look forward to more than tending sheep and cattle . . . "

"Do you look forward to killing, or being killed?"

"You've killed in Mongolia," she said, her voice softer then. "And you can also be killed."

Suthachai took her hand. "We kill other men. Sure, we kill when we have to. But we are never afraid of our brothers or our neighbors—no one in our clan needs to run from their own father. We cannot steal each other's cattle, because we share our meat. We never hide little gold coins from each other because we do not have any. We protect each other when there is danger, and I do not refer to danger from other men, but danger from the cold, or the wind, or the animals dying. We may worry about our precious animals—in case horse robbers come to steal from us—but they come as rarely as sand storms, and each time, we are well prepared."

He paused. "Your clan has so much wealth," he finally continued, his voice a low whisper. "But that only means more people would kill you for it. Your people build large houses and dress in fine silk, so other people who have less would hate them for it. I do not understand. Why would your women want to be in a carriage when they could ride against the horse's mane and allow the wind to blow through their hair?"

Fei Fei remained silent. Suthachai opened his mouth to say something else, but the words would not come. Fei Fei turned to him and kissed him on the forehead.

"Tell me," she whispered.

He hesitated for a second. "What if we really can be together? What if I do not die, and somehow, all our troubles go away?"

Fei Fei was speechless. Suthachai gazed into her eyes and understood. She would ride with him, as he had always wanted, not as a formidable warrior, but as his woman. But he was dying, and soon, she would be left alone.

Tears welled into her eyes.

"Everyone has to die," he said. "When the time comes to die, we must part, whether it is tomorrow or forty years later. If we already know how it will end, then why do we not treasure our time before it ends, even if it is only another day, or another month?"

"You want me to go to Mongolia with you?"

Suthachai reached around and held her. He lifted himself to look into her eyes. "Yes!" he whispered. "The moon shines brighter across the plains. And more stars want to come out at night. It is because there are less people watching them, so they are not afraid to come out."

• • •

A row of dried branches stood in a perfectly straight line, planted vertically in the ground, each exactly one step apart and spanning a distance of twenty steps. Twenty torturous steps. One by one, Li Kung lit them on fire for the fiftieth time—or was it really sixty?—he had completely lost count. Nevertheless, his shoes were torn and burnt to shreds, and his body ached from the heavy stress.

The Flame Cutter. He originally thought Snow Wolf left behind a sword technique of finesse, where a small flame would be cut by a sword in a grand display of precision and control. But little did he know, the flames were to be extinguished by his feet while he ran across burning sticks of wood. The speed he had to generate in order to swipe the flame, yet avoid breaking the flimsy branches, was beyond his wildest dreams.

It took him days to run across heavy sticks of wood protruding from the ground. When he finally retained his balance, he had to use smaller and more fragile sticks.

The theory, as outlined in Snow Wolf's writings, was simple. If his feet remained flexible, he could run on any surface. If he generated enough speed, the heat would not have time to burn him. If every ounce of energy went into the forward momentum, then there would be no pressure on the wooden sticks, and none of them would topple.

He reached into the massive urn hauled from Snow Wolf's tomb and took a long sip of the ancient herbal concoction. The alcohol struck him then, and a faint dizziness simmered over his brow. He stood still for a second and stared at the row of flaming branches, eager to continue, yet uncertain. How much more exertion could his body take?

But each day he drank Snow Wolf's herbs, he became stronger, faster. His tendons grew like iron, his muscles became dense and elastic. Yet, it was never intended for him to accomplish the first stage of the Flame Cutter in less than a month. Each day, the thought of Master Bin's poison drove him to stand when he was too weak to sit, run when he was too weak to walk. At moments when he collapsed against the snow, his feet burnt and charred from running across the flame, or when his head throbbed with fatigue and even the rabbits seemed to laugh at his failure, Li Kung thought of Suthachai. He thought of the moment when the heavy saber slashed across Pun's body, when the Mongolian pretended not to recognize the girl who came to help him and coldly walked away. Li Kung would climb to his feet then, replant the broken branches, and light them on fire.

The Flame Cutter. He needed to cut the flame with his running speed.

· · ·

"And the location for this meeting?" Master Bin asked. He poured light green tea into a jade cup. The messenger, standing somewhat bowed in the center of the room, fumbled with the scroll in his hand. "The Chestnut Pavilion, Master Bin."

Dong and Cricket were each seated on either side of the room, completely silent, waiting patiently for their father to dismiss the messenger.

"I will notify Wei Xu of my decision," Master Bin said with a smile. "You may go."

Tao Hing stormed into the room and nearly ran into the messenger. The old strategist brushed him aside, sweat covering his brow, and asked, "Has the princess been found?"

Master Bin laughed and shook his head. "Tao Hing, you're more worried than I am. No, that messenger was from my brother. No new information on Fei Fei."

Tao Hing was about to protest, but out of the corner of his eye, he noticed the seat next to Dong was empty. The Flute Demon didn't come to the meeting.

"You may be seated," Master Bin said.

Tao Hing acknowledged, but paused long enough to say, "Master Bin, you're not even worried? Your daughter has been missing for days."

"I'm aware of that," Master Bin replied, impatient.

"The two guards by her door were beheaded, and you're not afraid for her life? Do we know who captured her yet?"

Master Bin shook his head. "Fei Fei left on her own accord. Whoever killed my guards, she went with willingly. I've spoiled this daughter. She'll come back when she pleases."

He implied that his daughter ran off with a forbidden lover. Tao Hing shook his head, unconvinced.

"The messenger came from the Green Dragons," Master Bin said. "They want a treaty. They want peace. They want it done on neutral territory, such as the Chestnut Pavilion."

"Chestnut Pavilion!" Dong shouted. "Why would we want to make peace with them? They've killed our men, started so much bloodshed in front of our ancestral tombs, and now they want peace? Is this some sort of joke? I request permission to go down there with a legion of warriors and kill every one of them!"

"Quiet, Dong," Master Bin ordered. He glanced at the empty chair in front of him, the chair that the Flute Demon used to sit in. With a frown, he addressed his youngest son. "Cricket, do you think we need to make peace with them?"

Cricket paused for a second, and he too, glanced at the empty chair beside him. "Make peace with Uncle Xu?"

Master Bin's smile widened. "Tell us what you really think. By the way, Tao Hing," he said, suddenly turning to the old strategist, with the corner of his eye still on Cricket. "I'm sure you've heard. The Flute Demon died last night from her injuries. So, leave it in the journals that she was executed for disobeying orders."

Tao Hing frowned, but nodded. "I will, Master Bin."

"Chestnut Pavilion," Cricket began, his childish face stiff with anxiety. "It's deep in a valley, with the denser foliage and higher elevations on their side of the land. It would be easier for them to set an ambush than for us to set one, because their scouts are everywhere in that part of the forest. If we go, we could be facing danger."

Master Bin nodded with a smile. "My brother already released rumors that he wants peace. We need to send someone, anyone."

"I'll go," Dong said. "I'll go prepared with heavy shields and two groups of archers in the flanks. We don't need to worry about ambush."

Master Bin glanced at him coldly before looking away. "Tao Hing, what are your views on this?"

"This is a classic example of 'tricking the tiger to leave the mountain, in order to attack its lair,'" Tao Hing said. "Wei Xu knows that we'll suspect ambush, though we have no choice but to go. The Martial Society expects us to. He knows we don't want the Martial Society sympathetic to the Green Dragons. So he expects us to bring our Gentle Swordsmen and Red Headbands—our very best. He can't attack us at the meeting—there's too much risk in fighting our best warriors. That's why he'll attack elsewhere. He'll seize the opportunity to attack Redwood Cliff."

"What nonsense!" Dong said. "Redwood Cliff is a fortress. How could a few Green Dragons penetrate?"

"It's possible," Tao Hing said. "We're not as well protected as we'd like to believe. Being on a high elevation has its advantages. At the same time, we're vulnerable against smoke and fire."

Master Bin nodded. "It sounds exactly like what my

brother would do. What a dirty little trick, using fire to attack Redwood Cliff. What do you suggest, Tao Hing?"

"It's winter. They won't be able to set a large enough fire to choke us with smoke; they can only burn their way up the Grand Stairway. But once past the stairway, they still need to storm the surface of the cliff. If our elite fighters are waiting for them, right here at home, they will never win."

"Precisely what I had in mind," Master Bin said with a smile. "Dong! Organize a small group of expendable junior students and send them to the Chestnut Pavilion next week. I'll stay on Redwood Cliff, right here at home, and wait for my dear twin. You are to prepare one hundred archers and ambush the Grand Stairway when they invade."

"Yes, father."

"Cricket!" Master Bin continued. "The Flute Demon is gone, and the Butcher will remain by my side during this invasion. It's time for you to fight a crucial battle by yourself. Take two hundred men and hold off your uncle, and inflict as many casualties as you can before they get to the surface of Redwood Cliff. Once on the surface, I will personally supervise their capture. You are to consult with Tao Hing on how to do this."

Cricket bowed. "Yes, father."

• • •

The way of the Flame Cutter. Unpredictable shifts in varying directions, subtle angles, accelerating momentum, impossible speed. Snow Wolf would never have foreseen that the weakling she chose to inherit her art reached a speed unheard of in decades—all in a short three weeks.

Li Kung calmly folded the thin manual and tucked it

into his deepest inner pockets. The other two books were already well hidden on his body.

That night, he ran up the side of the mountain and stared into the outside world. It seemed so long ago since he last stepped into civilization. He was so different then.

He stared at the lights in the distance, at the city of He Ku. Near the center of the city was the Blue Lantern Inn. If Suthachai was still alive, he could still be in that inn. He had nowhere else to go.

At daybreak, Li Kung would leave the valley, return to the home of his three mentors, and gather equipment and provisions. He was not strong enough to hurt Suthachai—he knew that well—but he was fast enough at long range. He needed something to inflict damage with, something that he could use to strike from great distances. Maybe he could use fire.

The air was sweet, refreshing. In the background, a familiar sound emerged and faded with the wind. The weeping of the mountain ghosts. Li Kung closed his eyes, listened carefully, calmly distinguished the direction of the sound, and waited. Soon, the wailing grew out of nowhere again.

He no longer withdrew at the first sounds of danger. He was no longer weak. Faced with a task that meant the existence of his civilization, a magnitude he was afraid to comprehend, he told himself each day that he needed to be strong, that he must not be afraid. His body had become much more powerful, and his studies brought new life to his confidence.

With a twist of the body, pivoting off legs forged like steel, Li Kung bolted toward the direction of the cries. His feet barely scanned the rocky snow. His body leaned slightly forward, his abdomen sucked in, and his pointed toes tapped the front of each surface as if a flame grew from the ice. In a flash, he was at the foot of the mountainside. Drawing his energy, compressing in his abdomen harder, he sprang upward and forward with a quick bound, and, using the incredible thrust force that he generated, began to run up the vertical rocks. As the initial momentum faded, he gathered himself, pounced like a cat on a foothold, and rebuilt enough force to run upward again.

The wind lifted and clawed at his face. The cries of the ghosts became louder. In a matter of seconds, he was so high up that a slip of the foot or a meager loss of focus would mean a long, screaming drop to the bottom. But for the user of the Flame Cutter, there was no such thing as a stupid mistake. His sense of weight and balance had been sharpened to the point where every minute change on the surface was felt and understood. With three more massive bounds, he leaped to the top of the peak and stood motionless, waiting for the ghosts to call him once more. He had to find out this night. He had to know who, or what, was emitting the horrible cries.

The wailing arose again. This time, he was certain that it came from the same direction, somewhere on the wall of the mountain. He ran across the peak and slowed in front of a sharp, vertical drop. He inched closer to the edge and cocked his ears to listen. The cries were loudest somewhere below him.

Li Kung dropped to his knees, slid against his belly, and peered over the edge of the cliff. The wall of the mountain was completely vertical, impossible to descend, and even more unthinkable to climb from the bottom up.

But something told him that the source of the wailing was somehow accessible. The cliff was too perfect to not hide something in.

He slid farther over the edge, leaned his entire body over

the endless vertical drop, and then saw it. Reflected against the silver moonlight were small, subtle footholds, chiseled on the side of the wall. Each foothold was so far apart that an ordinary man could never jump from one to the other. But not for someone using the Flame Cutter.

Li Kung calculated the momentum he would need to return to the top, noted that it would take two steps on the vertical rocks between footholds. It was a lunge that he could accomplish. He threw his body over the cliff, hanging only by his fingertips, and, quickly making contact with the smooth rocks, slid straight down to the first footholds. The cries of the mountain ghosts roared.

He saw a hollowed wind tunnel on the side of the cliff, in a narrow gap between two slabs of stone where high winds continuously streamed through. Li Kung stepped off his last foothold and edged into the opening. The force of the air currents almost threw him into the wind tunnel, while the haunted cries became deafening. He couldn't light a flame against the roaring wind.

Large wooden structures almost twice his height stood before him. He could barely see them, but he noticed the thick shapes filling the entire tunnel. There were different-sized holes in them.

Wind horns, Li Kung thought with a smile. Permanent instruments that created ghostly noises. They kept the ordinary traveler away. He groped around for etchings of some sort, perhaps Snow Wolf's signature, or any indication that she was responsible for this. In a moment, he found it. Carved behind one of the wooden structures, on the side that the wind would not erode, were several lines of writing. He leaped over the instrument and stood safely away from the wind before igniting a small bundle of twigs for light. It was a poem.

Afraid to gawk at the glaring sun,
Scorning its radiance, beneath my sword.
Darkness, darkness, stop beckoning me,
Darkness, darkness, if my blade can find,
The path to conquer the falling sun.

There was something about the etched writing, perhaps the fluid script, that he had seen before.

The stone tablet under the lake. Li Kung breathed in alarm. The handwriting was the same.

But it couldn't be. The stone tablet led to so much slaughter, so many wars. Snow Wolf left behind a legacy of peace and prosperity. She could not be the goddess who sent the stone tablet into the lake.

Li Kung violently shook his head. Immediately underneath the poem, in small, weak etchings, as if ashamed of her own name, was the signature:

Lady Wu, styled Snow Wolf.

• • •

Fei Fei's return was never expected on Redwood Cliff. Rumors traveled far and wide concerning her fate. The guards outside her door were beheaded, and she was captured, perhaps a victim of Green Dragon vengeance. Some believed the Flute Demon took her. But then came the announcement that the Flute Demon died of her injuries. Since then, all on Redwood Cliff was convinced. Black Shadow infiltrated their *zhuang* and captured Master Bin's daughter.

Fei Fei passed the guards by the Grand Stairway, a double-edged sword tucked in her belt, her eyes cold. The guards turned to each other, speechless. She was dressed in the elegant robes of a Chinese lady, and she was more beautiful than ever. Yet, the long, heavy sword against her hip was unmistakable. No one understood why.

As Fei Fei, she never publicly entered the training halls. The violence was deemed unsuitable for a lady. But nothing was too violent for the Flute Demon. Each day, when she stepped in to supervise the Red Headbands' training, the guards posted at the front door would bow with due respect.

This day, she stormed past the startled guards, straight to the metal doors, stomped through it with a single kick, and walked into the midst of hundreds of warriors.

Fei Fei passed by a Red Headband. She drew her sword like lightning and pinned the blade into his armpit. "How many times did I tell you not to raise your arm when sidestepping? Your armpits are exposed."

The warrior stared, his mouth wide open. The entire courtyard instantly silenced. She sheathed the blade, and without another glance, moved toward Master Bin's private quarters. The path cleared in front of her so quickly that she was almost amused.

He asked her to go to Mongolia with him. He didn't have many days left, but he told her that, if a single breath remained in him, he would like to be with her, and he would like to be free.

Fei Fei approached the heavy doors. She could almost sense her father waiting behind them, a fickle smile on his face as he prepared to torment her with words, with guilt, with the concept of duty. She paused.

"When are you coming back?" she seemed to hear Suthachai say. His voice was loud and eager.

"Tonight," she said. *"We'll leave for Mongolia tonight. I'll meet the Elder, I'll meet Jocholai and all the men you ride with, and . . . "*

"Why can't we leave now?"

"We can't, Suthachai. The people in this land . . . How can I be free if I know my father will imprison them with the black paste? Wait for me, Suthachai. I need to do this first. Wait for me . . . "

With a sigh, Fei Fei pushed. Master Bin stood in the middle of the room, a smile on his face. He stood with the awesomeness of a great general, his hands lightly held behind his back, his chest upright like an impenetrable shield. He had been expecting her.

"Is the Mongolian dead?" Master Bin asked, almost casually.

"Only the Flute Demon."

"I'm aware of that." He smiled.

"I came to tell you a story, father."

Master Bin gestured toward the little table in the corner of the room. "A little wine?"

She shook her head.

"You prefer to stand by the door?"

"Yes."

"Well, my child, are you standing by the door because it's the closest exit? Or are you foolish enough to stand by an entrance used by my personal swordsmen?"

"Your personal swordsmen are no match for me."

"I see. You have no intention of being captured and punished this time."

"I came to tell you a story, father."

Master Bin laughed out loud. "You're strong, just like your mother. Go on, tell me your story. With your back to the door."

"I came to tell you the story of how your cousin died."

Master Bin's smile faded. "My cousin? What are you talking about?"

"Your cousin Su Ling. She was eighteen when she died.

She used to sing to you and Uncle Xu, because grandmother never had time to care for you. Do you remember?"

Master Bin's face grew red, and he unconsciously bit his lip. "Who are you to speak of my childhood?" he said.

"I'm merely telling a story, father. A story told to me long ago."

Master Bin calmed, his rigid face relaxed, in control. "I notice you've burned your disguise. You're going to carry on as Fei Fei?"

"I'd like to tell you a story. Afterward, I'll leave."

Master Bin tensed, startled. "And where will you go after you leave, my child?"

"It depends on how you react to my story."

He forced a smile and sat back, his eyes fastened to hers.

"Su Ling was your older cousin, father," she began. "She was gentle, beautiful, soft at heart but firm in resolve. She cared for her family, for her twin cousins, and sang to them, and told them stories. You and Uncle Xu—her twin cousins."

"I know who you're referring to."

"Do you know how she died, father?"

"Enlighten me, my child."

"It was almost fifty years ago. There was famine everywhere, the cold and the blizzards were devastating. So many people died from hunger, but even more froze to death. No one stood forward from our House to help the common people. No one really cared."

Master Bin opened his mouth to say something but Fei Fei quickly raised her voice. "Not grandmother. Grandmother never cared about the people. Everyone knew that, though no one dared say anything. Grandmother took credit for fighting the famine after Snow Wolf died, but she never did a thing to help the people."

"Where did you hear that?"

"It's just a story," Fei Fei said with a smile. "Good stories have no origin. They may not be true."

Master Bin sat back and pressed his fingers together. "Go on," he said.

"Su Ling took the supplies she had access to and traveled to the village that suffered most. She went to Pan Tong Village, you know, the village you exterminated a few weeks ago."

"I'm aware of that."

"Su Ling had no one with her," Fei Fei said, slightly louder this time. "She gathered the villagers behind fortified walls, taught them how to stay warm while conserving firewood. She gave them food, extra blankets and coats that she carried by herself from Redwood Cliff. Most of Pan Tong Village could have lived for another fifty years, at least until you decided to kill them."

Master Bin eyed her with a sneer. "Are you lecturing me, Fei Fei?"

"But Su Ling didn't have the opportunity to save the entire village. As a result, half the population perished."

"Is that the story you came to tell me, Fei Fei? About how Su Ling sacrificed herself to save the villagers and ended up contracting disease?"

"No father. She died from the Soaring Dragon poison. She was murdered by grandmother."

Master Bin slammed the armrest of his chair and stood up. "What are you talking about?"

"Old Snake was but a twelve-year-old boy then," Fei Fei said, her voice monotonous and calm. "His master just devised the Soaring Dragon Candles. Do you remember? Old Snake and his master were grandmother's favorites. That night, there were rumors that my granduncle Fei Long was mortally injured in a duel with the Sun Cult. Snow Wolf came back to defend Redwood Cliff. Old Snake was summoned in the middle of the night, and he was told to bring the new candles to Su Ling's room in Pan Tong Village. He was told to act with secrecy. It was an assignment issued by grandmother herself. Old Snake placed the candles within Su Ling's reach and hid outside to watch. He watched her burn the candles to her father's dead spirit. She died instantly."

"What are you talking about, Fei Fei?" Master Bin's voice lowered. "Where did you hear this?"

"Back then, no one recognized the killing capabilities of these candles, so no one really knew how Su Ling died," Fei Fei said. "Only Old Snake knew, because he stayed outside to watch. He was also sent to search her body for the jade dragon."

"So Old Snake is responsible for telling these stories of blasphemy . . . "

"I am responsible for telling this story," Fei Fei said, her voice suddenly raised above his. "I have many more stories to tell, to many other people. We had one superior weapon and our family used it to kill each other. For power? For control? Now we have another superior poison. Who will die next, father? Are you really going to use it to destroy Uncle Xu, or am I going to be next? Do you see those closest to you becoming a threat to your power? Are you going to use this black paste to control them too? Your sons? Tao Hing? How about Old Snake? He's been loyal to you all his life. He may have the ability to neutralize your black paste, so why don't you find an excuse and have him killed too? Don't tell me you haven't thought of it, father!"

Fei Fei paused, and watched for a change in her father's face. Master Bin maintained a light smile, his eyes alert but not focused, his face lightly blushed with anger. He exerted his remarkable ability to remain calm, and once again, resembled a man taking a leisurely stroll in the woods.

Taking a deep breath, Fei Fei forced the muscles on her face to relax. Her father was impenetrable, impossible to waver. With a light smile, she turned to open the door. "I came to tell you a story, and now I've told it. Goodbye, father."

"Fei Fei," Master Bin called after her.

Fei Fei partially turned and faced him with her side.

"The truth is, my child. Su Ling died of an illness she contracted in the village. Her father Fei Long died fighting the Sun Cult, and his wife Snow Wolf died destroying the Sun Cult to avenge him. That's how the family chronicles recorded it, so that's how it really happened. Years later, our family chronicles might record that you were captured by Black Shadow, and were tortured, violated, then killed by Uncle Xu himself. This then led to my relentless pursuit for revenge, and finally, I reunited the Dragon House. Or, it could be written that the Flute Demon did not die. She was secretly assigned to recover Fei Fei, which of course she did, and in retaliation for kidnapping my daughter, I sought vengeance against Wei Xu and ultimately reunited the Dragon House. With the Flute Demon fighting by my side, of course."

Fei Fei felt her heart sink to her stomach. She struggled against the fear that began to envelop her. "That's not how it really happened," she said. "The truth is, Fei Fei toured the Martial Society to tell stories, like how Su Ling told stories to her twin cousins many decades ago. The Martial Society then suspected the evil alchemy being formed on Redwood Cliff, and united together to prevent it from materializing. In sheer anger, Master Bin killed his beloved daughter in public, for the second time."

She turned and stormed out, slamming the heavy

wooden doors. In alarm, Master Bin leaped forward and tore the doors open. But she was nowhere in sight. He called for his guards, ordered them to strike the bells on every roof, and to hoist the yellow flag.

Fei Fei ran as hard as she could. It was only a matter of time. Her father would realize where she was going. The bells had been sounded, and she saw the yellow flag. Soon, hundreds of warriors would surround the Grand Stairway to prevent her from leaving Redwood Cliff—so she could not tour the Martial Society and tell stories. She ducked into the bushes and headed for the Pine Forest, a brief smile on her face. This time, her father overlooked her ruse.

The black paste was made in an underground room, accessible behind a dead tree, through a narrow tunnel between the rocks. Old Snake recognized the toxic elements in the soil that killed the tree, and he found the underground facilities. The old poison-user never told anyone, but he told Fei Fei. He even showed her where the sheepskin was hidden.

Soon, her father would realize she was not headed for the Grand Stairway. Hopefully, it would be enough time for her to destroy the equipment used to produce the black paste, and to escape with the sheepskin in hand. Her father must have memorized the formula by now. But the alchemy would be worthless if a counteragent was created elsewhere, and with the sheepskin, she could find someone to devise an antidote. At the very least, her father would be afraid that an antidote exists, and he would refrain from producing large quantities.

She thought of Suthachai, of his tall figure slowly trudging through He Ku, buying provisions for their trip. She was to leave for Mongolia at nightfall. What if her father, when he realized her intentions, did not send his best men to stop her in the Pine Forest? What if he left them to guard the Grand Stairway? How would she fight through the Butcher and the Gentle Swordsmen?

Her head churned, and anxiety crept through her body. She promised Suthachai. She had to descend the cliff by sunset.

. . .

The Butcher stood with his back to the dead oak tree, protecting the entrance of the underground laboratory. Both swords were sheathed and tucked behind him; he was alone. While the rest of Redwood Cliff broke into alarm and sealed off the Grand Stairway, the Butcher stood guarding Master Bin's secret facilities.

Moments later, the intruder arrived, and he reached for his swords. Then he froze. The dark, crooked smile on his face faded, and his hands dropped to his sides.

"Fei Fei," he said under his breath. Then loudly, "There's been an intruder on Redwood Cliff, and the yellow flag has been raised. I'll escort you to safety and . . . "

Fei Fei drew her sword, threw her head back, and laughed.

"Flute Demon," he said. "The Flute Demon died of her injuries . . . "

"She did," Fei Fei said. She stared down her father's star warrior. Behind his towering figure, behind the two deadly swords, was the entrance to Master Bin's secret facilities.

"My father will reward you for killing his beloved daughter," she said.

The Butcher hesitated, a glimpse of uncertainty on his face. Fei Fei lunged forward and slashed at his throat.

She approached like lightning. The Butcher jerked his body back and endured the stroke diagonally across his chest before pulling his left-hand sword.

Fei Fei threw herself into the entrance of the underground room and bolted straight for the secret compartment Old Snake had shown her. The sheepskin was there, as expected. She buried it deep in her robe.

All around her were shelves packed with porcelain jars. Clay pots filled with liquids lined the floor; furnaces and urns were scattered across the room. She heard the Butcher's footsteps. She lowered her sword, grabbed two jars in each hand and hurled them at his face.

The Butcher ran down the narrow stairs, only to leap back and away from the flying weapons. Two porcelain jars crashed harmlessly against the wall, and crushed herbs exploded onto the ground. He took another step back.

Moments later, Fei Fei emptied an entire shelf of jars. She threw herself forward, naked blade flashing, but the Butcher lived up to his name, and for a moment, neither side could overwhelm the other. Sparks flew as bare steel rained on each other, colliding sometimes with deafening vibrations but often with the dull sound of scraping metal.

Fei Fei had fought too many battles in the past weeks; she had too many injuries. Her old wounds began to reopen. She knew the initial cut on the Butcher's chest was not significant in a long, drawn-out battle. When the element of surprise wore off, when her advantage of speed, location, and decisiveness disappeared, the Butcher would emerge as the superior fighter.

The largest urn in the room sat in the middle, reaching her waist in height. She leaped forward with a shout and pelted it with a flying kick. A curtain of liquid streamed across the room, for a second seeming to suspend itself in midair, and then dropped all at once in an explosion of fluids.

Alcohol! She smiled to herself. Somehow, she knew the paste was mixed in alcohol. She jabbed at the Butcher with her blade, pretending to commit herself, enticing him to plant his feet and sustain the impact that never came, then suddenly drew back to the wall. She grabbed a nearby torch, ignited it, and held it in front of her with a smile. The Butcher paused.

In seconds, the underground room was reduced to a thick pool of wet herbs, soaked in muddied liquid. Countless fragments of broken porcelain and clay floated everywhere. The smell of alcohol permeated the room.

Fei Fei took a moment to catch her breath.

She had already taken the sheepskin. If she burned everything in the room, her father would never know that she controlled his formula. He would merely rebuild. The Butcher would most likely survive the fire, regardless.

With a sigh, Fei Fei backed toward the narrow stairs. She needed a plan, but her mind was numb, tired. She had been so eager to see the room in flames, burned to a charred cake of black permanently infused in the cement floor, so her father could never use this room again. But it was more important now for her to leave the cliff with the sheepskin.

Fei Fei wondered whether she had time to reach the surface. Then she remembered. She came to Redwood Cliff with a plan, one designed specifically for the Butcher. She almost forgot, and recalling it brought a smile to her face.

All his life, the Butcher had been afraid of Old Snake.

She leaped halfway up the stairs, produced a small pouch from her robes, shook it open, and threw it out in front of her. Black powder scattered from the bag and floated down the steps. She threw her head back and laughed.

"Why do you think Old Snake treats me like a daughter? Do you really believe he has no apprentice?"

She turned to leave. The Butcher stalled, his eyes frozen, the powder on the stairs forming a new barrier between them.

Fei Fei knew that, at the very least, he would wait for the black powder to settle before attempting to pursue. She pulled out of the tunnel, a smile on her face. The powder was merely coal residue taken from the kitchen furnace at the Blue Lantern Inn.

There were growing shouts in the distance. Master Bin had realized her true intentions. Her father's elite warriors were approaching her, and she breathed with relief. The Grand Stairway would be poorly guarded. She quickly planted the decoys that she had prepared and ran for the back hills. She would reach the Grand Stairway unhindered.

· · ·

Phoenix Eye Peak was warmer than normal. The light winds, normally shrill and biting, lovingly caressed the side of his face. But Li Kung's eyes were frozen on the generous land in front of him, while each mechanical step hardly grazed the dense snow below his feet. He was leaving his training grounds behind, leaving the safety and seclusion of Snow Wolf's tunnels to the past. He was now her chosen warrior.

Suthachai was still alive. He was certain of it. Fate could not possibly be so cruel as to kill off his mortal enemy before he accomplished the skills he needed for revenge. He would kill the Mongolian himself. He looked forward to it, every moment of every night, when he tossed and turned in his sleep, when he opened his eyes to the morning sun. Before doing Snow Wolf's work, before shouldering the burden of destroying the Dragon Houses, before worrying about the common people being poisoned and crippled, he would seek revenge for Pun's murder.

A calm smile emerged on his lips.